VAMPIRE-TECH

Bryan Romer

VAMPIRE-TECH

Chapter One

The Mark V Direct Neural Interface Avionics (DNIA) experimental aircraft banked and then dived at supersonic speed, cutting through the air like the edge of a blade. The world spun dizzyingly around the cockpit and the shifting G-forces pushed and twisted at the body of test pilot Tara Harker, and her advanced G-suit crushed her body like an affectionate anaconda.

Unlike the pilot of an ordinary aircraft, she had the advantage of not needing to manually operate a joystick or throttle. Increasing thrust, she pulled up and went into a combat Immelman, but by using the advanced thrust vectoring abilities and the flexible wings of her aircraft, she skidded across the sky as the plane turned on its horizontal axis rather than coming to an almost-stall like in the famed Hammerhead manoeuvre. At the same time her fingers tapped at the dome shaped control pads under her hands, simultaneously designating targets 130 degrees apart for two of her wing mounted missiles. Without any visible motion of her body she launched both weapons, which dropped free of the wings before their motors ignited, sending them shooting off in almost opposite directions. Using a visual targeting system that tracked the movement of her eyeballs she locked the stubby ceramic composite barrel of the retractable, turret-mounted 20 mm railgun on a third target and fired off a two-second burst. Moments later, two of the drones exploded and the third shattered into smoking fragments which tumbled from the sky like metal confetti. Allowing herself a tiny smile of satisfaction, Tara levelled off and throttled back to below supersonic speed. Her intercom crackled.

"Great show Tara. The combat tracking system integration seems to be working perfectly." Viktor Tiranul, her co-pilot, gave her a thumbs up, which he knew she would see in her simulated three hundred and sixty degree vision strip which was part of her virtual Head Up Display (HUD). The production aircraft would be a single seater, but the prototype she was flying had a back-seat with ordinary fly-by-wire controls which could take over in the event of a failure of the main controls (or the pilot). The chase plane waggled its wings and Vincent gave it a thumbs up.

Tara toggled her microphone. "Dragon Base, Dragon One over." Dragon Base acknowledged and Tara advised that she was coming in for a landing. The airfield advised that the runway was clear for landing and her own radar showed that the airspace was empty except for the chase plane. She tagged the runway on her navigation screen and activated the auto-landing system. She felt the front and port side wheels deploy and lock and then frowned when she did not "feel" the third set of wheels deploy. She checked the visual indicator on the control panel again and it still showed green, but she could not detect a complete undercarriage lock down through the neural control system.

"Chase One, Dragon One, over."

"Right here, Dragon one, over," replied the pilot of the chase plane, a converted MIG 21 which they had bought for just over twenty thousand dollars. Although old, it had the speed and acceleration to keep up with the experimental plane - much of the time anyway.

"Give me visual confirmation that my undercarriage is fully deployed, over."

Chase One acknowledged the request and moved to fly just below and behind Dragon One. After a moment, Chase One confirmed that the undercarriage was down.

"What's the matter Tara?" Viktor asked.

"Nothing. Just thought I saw a flicker in the undercarriage lights," she said, unwilling to admit to 'feeling' a problem with the aircraft. She had to be very careful not to allow her imagination or her own senses to contaminate the actual feedback from the aircraft itself. "Preparing to land." Dragon One's autopilot brought it into proper approach position relative to the runway, and the aircraft smoothly followed the glide path to touchdown. But just as the rubber of the rear wheels made contact, Tara "felt" the wheel column lock give way. In a fraction of a second the aircraft's wing was going to drop and strike the tarmac, and the plane would cartwheel to destruction.

A normal pilot and aircraft would have been doomed. By the time the pilot could have detected the sudden tilt, mentally determined the cause and pushed the throttle forward, it would have been far too late. But Tara had sensed the failure of the undercarriage and started to react before the wing had even begun to tilt. The engines were spooling up to emergency power and thrust was being diverted to the VTOL system before her hands could even twitch. The vertical thrust was just barely sufficient to keep the aircraft level as it built up speed again and began to lift. The auto VSTOL program activated and took over from Tara's manual balancing of the thrust vectoring and Dragon One climbed back into the sky. Tara slumped in her seat, shaking from the jolt of adrenaline that had flooded her body while the plane went into an automatic holding pattern above the airfield.

"What the hell happened?" shouted Viktor now that they were flying safely. His instruments still showed the undercarriage as fully functional and Tara's recovery had been so fast that he did not realise how close they had just come to death. Dragon Base was asking the same question, if in a more professional tone.

"Dragon One, this is Jason. Why did you abort, over?"

Tara considered her answer for a second and decided that telling everyone that she had 'felt' a malfunction in the undercarriage through the neural interface could wait until she was on the ground. She retracted the undercarriage and redeployed it several times but it malfunction each time. "Viktor, I'm performing and emergency manual deployment of the undercarriage."

"I don't understand. Undercarriage shows green. I repeat, undercarriage is green."

"Trust me Viktor. I'll explain after we've landed."

"OK, it's your arse that Jason will kick,"

"Thanks a lot."

"You're welcome."

Tara twisted the large red knob. This was a totally mechanical system designed to be used in the event of a complete electrical failure. "Activating manual undercarriage deployment now," she said, both for Viktor and the cockpit recorder. She pushed the knob inward and seconds later there was a loud thump as compressed air cartridges locked the undercarriage down. The wheels could now only be retracted after the technicians had manually unlocked the struts and replaced the air cartridges on the ground. "Dragon Base, Dragon One. Coming in again."

"Roger Dragon One. Activating crash rescue. Good luck."

As the aircraft banked to reposition for landing, Tara could see the red flashing lights on the Airfield Crash Tender as it charged out of the Fire Station and onto the runway, followed by a water tender and the Fire Chief's pickup. Down on the ground the sirens would be blaring and all non-essential crew would be running for shelter.

Tara decided to perform a vertical landing in order to minimise the stress on the undercarriage. The automated landing system rapidly decelerated the plane to a hover above the airfield, throwing Tara and Viktor forwards against their harnesses with the powerful thrust of the engines directed fully downwards. The aircraft was balanced and levelled by the on-board computers and then it dropped like a rock. At the last second, when it appeared that the aircraft would crash into the ground, the immensely powerful engines blasted and slowed the drop to a steady, perfect touchdown. Unlike the old Harriers and the F-35 Lightning II of the previous generation, the Mark V DNIA handled more like an aircraft from a classic science fiction film. Using a combination of thrust vectoring, wing warping and an advance diverted thrust Response Control System or RCS, the experimental aircraft was even more manoeuvrable than a rotary winged aircraft due to its advance Artificial Intelligence system and neural interface with the pilot.

The ground crew rushed up to the aircraft with a specially formed ladder, which mated perfectly with the side of the aircraft. They clambered up onto the fuselage and helped Tara and Viktor unplug themselves and get out of the cockpit. On the ground, the fire safety and engineering crew buzzed around the undercarriage.

Viktor had just reached the ground behind Tara when they both heard exclamations from the ground crew. Stooping over, she walked over to the crew and said, "What's the matter?" Even though she had a good idea what had gone wrong, she waited for the engineer holding the tablet PC that performed the ground maintenance systems analysis to give his report.

The engineer looked at Tara and said, "A small section of the starboard locking bolt has sheared off near the tip. The bolt still deploys and the sensors would have shown a green light, but under the pressure of a normal landing it would have failed and the entire assembly would have collapsed. It was a freak failure of the metal in the bolt, a million to one chance. If you had not activated the mechanical carriage lock the plane might have flipped on landing. You were extremely lucky."

She ignored Viktor's stare and just said, "Yes, I

suppose I was."

***

At the debrief, Tara described the feeling that she had experienced prior to the landing and the reasons for her decisions.

Dr Jason Whittle, the designer of the DNIA aircraft and Dr Rowland Harker, Tara's father and inventor of the nano-biological interface, studied Tara with both concern and excitement.

Dr Harker said, "If the engineers and the bio-feedback records verify it, this could be the most significant breakthrough that we've made since the start of the project."

Dr Whittle nodded and said, "I agree. But we need to isolate the electro-mechanical channels that are interacting with the bio-feedback system to give Tara the sensory images. At the moment, it's almost sheer chance that it works."

Tara frowned and said, "Perhaps not. The human mind is amazingly adaptable. It may be that so long as the aircraft's sensors provide sufficiently accurate readings, my mind is able to adapt and interpret patterns in the variations of signal strength and frequency that are not even noted or utilised by the instruments."

Rubbing his chin, her father said, "I see what you mean. The altimeter takes the data from the air pressure gauge, the downward looking radar and the laser range finder and reports the altitude. But the same readings also carry information about tiny vibrations in the fuselage and variations in the power systems, conductivity and temperature of the aircraft. The nano-interface feeds this to Tara's brain, which uses this kind of data from all the instruments and forms a mental picture of the aircraft. Any change, such as a dent in the skin, a loss of pressure, a rise in bearing temperature, will send ripples through the entire aircraft and subtly alter that mental image. By constantly comparing the old image with the new, her mind can sense changes or flaws that no instrument could possibly detect."

Viktor half rose from his seat and said, "What are you talking about? The nano-interface is supposed to allow the pilot to control the aircraft using his thoughts, shortening the command-feedback-reaction loop and making the pilot faster and more efficient. I've never seen anything in the technical summaries that mention what you're talking about. Why have I been kept in the dark?"

Tara noted his use of "he" in referring to the Mark V DNIA prototype's pilot, but decided not to make an issue of it, although her pen punched a hole through the notepaper.

Dr Harker waved his hands apologetically at Viktor. "I'm sorry Viktor, but we had good reasons for keeping the extent of the nano implant secret."

Viktor did not appear to be mollified by Dr Harker's apology and folded his arms across his chest. "Well, what are these good reasons?" he asked.

Harker glanced at his associate and Dr Whittle nodded.

"Go ahead Rowland. We can trust him," Whittle said.

Harker sighed and said, "I've been working on expanding the function of the nano-interface system from a simple hands free flight control to an actual integration of the pilot's brain and nervous system with the aircraft, incorporating a two-way feedback and response loop.

"And what the hell does that mean?" Viktor growled.

Tara leaned forward on her elbows and said, "It means that theoretically, I should be able to feel and control the aircraft as if it was part of my own body."

Viktor's eyes widened as he said, "So that was what this morning was all about."

Tara nodded. "As we were coming in for a landing, I felt a weakness in the undercarriage that the instruments didn't detect."

Viktor grinned. "That's incredible. I haven't heard of anyone who is doing anything even near to that, not even the big boys like Lockheed Martin. So when do I get to try it?"

Dr Harker's face darkened. He said, "I'm afraid that we haven't gotten to that stage just yet, Viktor."

Viktor started to get angry again. "You still don't trust me, is that it?"

Dr Whittle held up his hand to forestall Viktor's outburst. "Not at all Viktor. However, there are still obstacles that we need to overcome before we can expand field trials to another pilot."

Viktor refused to be placated. He pointed at Dr Harker and said, "That's bullshit. You were confident enough to use it on your own daughter."

Tara shook her head and softly said, "Viktor, once my father had gotten past virtual and animal trials, I was one of three initial trial human subjects. Father had objected, but I insisted that if we were sure enough to try it on human volunteers, then I should be willing to be one of them." Viktor looked as if he was about to interrupt with another angry outburst, but Tara rose in her chair and leaned towards him. "Viktor, of the three test subjects, I'm the only survivor."

Viktor's face whitened in shock. "The other two pilots died?"

For a moment, Dr Harker's face showed the incredible guilt that he felt. "Almost immediately. For some reason that I still haven't been able to determine, they simply went into shock and all their autonomic systems failed simultaneously. So you can see why we aren't planning on having any more human trials at the moment."

Viktor was immediately apologetic. "I'm sorry Dr Harker. I just assumed that you didn't trust me and I...."

Dr Harker tiredly shook his head and said, "No, I quite understand. But you can see that this is not something we want openly discussed."

Tara touched her father's arm and said, "But now we know it works. Better than we had ever dreamed. We know that it can be safe. I'm proof of that. We're nearly there, father."

Harker straightened and nodded. "You're right. We owe it to those two brave men to make it work."

Dr Whittle rubbed his hands together and said, "Right then. I'll work out a new set of tests based on this new information and the readouts from today's flight. Then we'll re-schedule the flights."

Viktor stood up and walked over to Whittle. "I'll help you with the readouts."

Tara gave her father a hug and said, "Come on handsome. Let's go back to my place and I'll cook you dinner."

***

It had been a long day and everyone had gone to bed soon after dinner except Dr Whittle and Viktor, who had stayed up to work on the testing schedule. It was nearly midnight when the engineering genius had yawned and declared that he was headed for his recharging station. Viktor finished his cold coffee, and walked back to his accommodation unit, giving the security patrol a wave in passing. Once inside his air conditioned container, he sat down on the edge of his bed and stared blankly at the wall, the fingers of his right hand tapping restlessly on his knee. Nearly half an hour later, his fingers stopped moving and he reached under his bed to pull out a locked storage box. He unfastened the padlock using the key that hung around his neck. He glanced at the windows and door, and then flipped the lid of the box open and extracted a satellite telephone. He dialled a number from memory and waited.

The ring tone stopped and a man's voice said, "Speak."

Viktor cleared his throat and said, "The shipment is ready for delivery. But now it's in two packages. One needs special handling. And I want more."

"How much?" said the voice.

"Fifteen million – Euros," Viktor said.

"Too much."

"The specs have changed. We have full two-way interaction."

There was a hiss of surprise at the other end. "Are you sure?"

Viktor grinned. "Absolutely. I saw it in action today, and I sat in on the planning for new test protocols."

"Fifteen million. Agreed. But you better be right."

Viktor punched the air in triumph, but his voice remained steady. "The second package is critical and unique. There are no duplicates."

"Excellent. The recovery team will be on standby. Don't screw it up."

Victor said, "No worries. I'm in full control."

***

Two days later, Tara and her father stood on the tarmac looking at the glistening aircraft that held all their hopes and dreams. "Well, today we'll find out what she can really do."

Dr Harker put his arm around his daughter's waist. "Be careful up there Tara, and I don't just mean with your flying. We still aren't sure why the nano-interface only works with you so far, and it could simply fail at

14

any time under stress. If you feel anything strange at all, you abort immediately and we'll have the ambulance waiting for you on the ground."

"I will, father. Don't worry. Everything will be fine. I can feel it right here," Tara said, patting herself on the tummy. She kissed him on the cheek, accepted the flight helmet from him and turned to walk across the tarmac towards the DNIA. The aircraft's self-repairing anti-drag finish gleamed with golden highlights in the morning sun. The service crew were dragging away their equipment, leaving only the Crew Chief waiting for her in the chilly open air. As always, the smell of aviation fuel, various lubricants and heated metal blended oddly with the scents of nature that surrounded the field. Since the NDIA was the only aircraft on the field it was quiet enough for the crunching of gravel under her boots to sound unnaturally loud, modified only by the distant sound of some wise guy in the hanger playing the Top Gun theme. Tara grinned and had to resist the urge to strut to the sound of Steve Steven's guitar solo. Victor was already waiting by the plane and she nodded when he waved at her.

He patted the smooth metal curve of the plane's fuselage. "The chief says she's ready and raring to go."

"*He's* ready. I like to think of the NDIA as a 'he'. I don't need mood swings and PMS in something that's linked to my mind," Tara said as she fitted the custom helmet onto her head.

Viktor chuckled and donned his own helmet, not knowing how literally the test pilot had meant what she said.

Tara walked slowly around the sleek craft, her trained eyes scanning every rivet, cable, and port. Unlike most modern "stealthed" military aircraft, the NDIA's fuselage did not possess the odd angular planes needed to break up its radar signature since it was designed to test and demonstrate something entirely different —

extreme manoeuvrability and responsiveness to control at a level vastly beyond anything ever previously achieved. The ultimate goal was to enable to pilot, Tara, to fly as if the aircraft was a living extension of her body in the same way that research into mechanical/electronic exoskeletons aim to magnify the performance of the human body on the ground. What Tara had not told anyone, even her father, was that she suspected the integration between her mind and the NDIA's systems were on the verge of being much deeper than anyone had suspected. It was as if the user of an advanced prosthetic arm had begun to feel on a visceral level not only tactile sensations but the position and angle of every part of the artificial limb.

When she was satisfied she climbed up the boarding ladder towards the cockpit. Viktor was already on board and busy in the back seat checking his instruments, and when her head came level with the cockpit, the infra-red connection in her helmet came to life and she could feel the tiny signals from Victor's instruments even as the rest of the experimental aircraft came to life in her consciousness. Each time she connected with this latest version of the system, her brain and the implanted nano-interface seemed to pick up more feedback from the aircraft sensors and instruments.

Around the back of the seat in front of him Viktor watched Tara settle herself into position as the automated safety harness locked itself around her while her suit linked itself to the umbilical from the cockpit. The pre-flight checklist appeared on her internal HUD and she mentally ticked each item off as she ran through it. The completed checklist would be stored in the NDIA's black box.

"All green back here," Viktor said, his voice clear and natural over the high-definition audio system and intelligent noise cancellation.

Tara did not have to manually select the radio channel, simply her intention was sufficient. "Tower, Dragon One requesting clearance for take-off."

"Dragon One, you are cleared for take-off."

Although her hands were on the digital controls that were part of the arm-rests, she initiated take-off simply by willing it. In a manner she couldn't describe in words she felt the engines spooling up, while the rest of the aircraft preparing for flight felt like the tensing of a runner's muscles at the starting block.

Viktor nervously checked the Velcro fastening on the thigh pocket of his flight suit and the accessibility of the small .22 calibre pistol inside. He had deliberately chosen the small calibre weapon to avoid serious damage to the aircraft or to Tara herself in the event he was forced to actually use it.

Takeoff in STOL (Short Take Off and Landing) mode felt like springing into the air, and it made Tara gleefully light headed as she and the aircraft climbed into the sky at a steep, nearly vertical angle accompanied by the god-like thunder of the engines. As they levelled out, a course indicator appeared in her HUD like a translucent red ribbon stretching through the sky with a diamond shaped carat marking the first waypoint.

On his MFD (Multi Function Display) screen, Viktor studied the overhead view of the planned course and the moving aircraft symbol that moved smoothly along it, and his eyes were irresistibly drawn to the mountainous plateau that showed up clearly on the scrolling map. It was a large patch of even colour surrounded by the mottled greens and browns of the craggy terrain that surrounded it. A marker blinked on the course ribbon just before it neared the plateau, a marker he knew did not appear on Tara's HUD.

Tara was relaxed, letting the data and feedback from the aircraft flow into her mind. The first circuit of today's planned flight was to confirm instrument and performance base lines and to ensure that everything, including the neural interface, appeared to be fully functional. Only after that was established would the tests begin. She realised that after the previous incident, the nano-interface in her brain seemed to have developed a greater integration with her senses. Whether this was due to her brain adapting to the system or the system itself changing and adapting she would have to leave to her father and his team. All she knew was that she could feel the air-friction induced heat on the NDIA's skin as if it were sunlight warming her own skin. The sensations steadily expanded as they flew, and soon she could even feel the mass of herself and Viktor inside the cockpit from the subtle shifting of their bodies combined with the multi-spectrum video cameras built into the cockpit. Similar optical sensors buried in the skin of the aircraft gave her a spherical view around the entire aircraft. Although her human senses couldn't make sense of a spherical viewpoint, she had developed a kind of "peripheral vision" for movement outside of her normal angle of vision. If she sensed unusual movement she could simply will her viewpoint to swivel around so that she could see it. This morning she realised that by concentrating, she could even look into the cockpit. Looking at herself was disorientating, but she could study the rest of the cockpit, including Viktor, by simply willing it.

"Coming up on Waypoint Alpha," Viktor announced. He had deliberately placed the next waypoint above the plateau, and he felt his hand and arm involuntarily tensing.

"Are you all right Viktor? You sound a little funny," Tara asked in concern. They would have to cancel the test flight if he was ill. The violent aerobatics planned would not suit an already upset stomach. They were almost at the second waypoint and it would be a good time to turn back even if it would be a disappointment.

"No, I'm fine," Viktor replied even as his gloved hand brought the pistol out of his pocket.

The tension in her navigator's voice was unmistakable and Tara frowned. Without consciously willing it, an inset screen appeared in the upper-right corner of her field of vision, allowing her to see Viktor without taking her gaze away from the front. At first everything looked all right, and then she focused on his hand. "Viktor, what's that you have in your…" She froze when she realised that her navigator had a gun pointed at her back. But Tara had a test pilot's nerves and reflexes, and she realised that the small calibre pistol was unlikely to penetrate the bulk of the navigation instruments as well as the back of her ejector seat, which meant that he would have to raise it up and around the head-rest of her seat in order to get a shot at her head or neck.

Annoyed that the pilot had spotted his gun before he was ready he said, "I have a gun, Tara. And it's pointed at your back. I'm taking the plane. You're going to land us on the approaching plateau."

"And if I don't?"

"I'll shoot you and land the plane myself."

"On that plateau? Be sensible, you won't be able to perform a vertical landing using the rear backup controls or a neural link."

"Well if I can't then I'll shoot you and eject, so you'd better be a good girl and land this thing."

"And then you'll shoot me anyway," she said tersely.

"Don't be stupid. You're part of the package. But if I have to, I'll deliver just your head. It won't be as good, but I'm sure my employers can reverse engineer your father's work from your brain."

They were nearly above the plateau and Tara searched furiously for a way out of her predicament. She had no desire to be vivisected in some research lab, nor did she want to die. A James Bond style ejector seat move would require ejecting the canopy first, which would give him time to shoot her before their seats were blasted from the cockpit. Then she realised that she didn't need anything so drastic as a rocket propelled chair. She focused on the position of the aircraft in relation to the rapidly approaching plateau. "You can go to hell!" she shouted and simultaneously issued a series of mental commands.

The catches on Viktor's safety harness silently disengaged just as he shoved his hand and the slim automatic pistol between Tara's head-rest and the canopy. He screamed in shock when Tara threw the aircraft into a tight outside loop and the extreme g-forces flung him at the canopy as if he had been shot out of a circus canon. His helmet protected his head from being smashed when it crashed into the canopy followed by his shoulders and upper back, but the impact and rapidly shifting g-forces stunned him more efficiently than a Taser. Unfortunately, it also caused his fingers to involuntarily contract and pull the trigger of his pistol.

Tara's helmet protected her from the blast of noise from the gun going off right next to her ear, but the bullet punched through her suit and went almost straight down behind her collar-bone and into her lung. Despite the shock and pain of her wound, Tara knew that she had to land the plane before she blacked out. When the NDIA pulled out of the loop she targeted the plateau and engaged the semi-automated landing system, praying that it would work properly this time and not auger them into the mountainous terrain. She could feel the blood pumping out of the tiny wound, and moving her right arm was agony and she couldn't feel her fingers. Any normal aircraft, even a VTOL craft such as the V-22 Osprey, would have been doomed, but so long as she could remain conscious they had a chance. She was having trouble breathing, but the oxygen system automatically compensated by increasing the air pressure and oxygen mixture in her mask. She felt something slide over her thigh and glancing down she saw it was a small chrome plated pistol. A glance at the rear cockpit monitor showed Viktor slumped bonelessly in his seat, tangled in the loose straps of his harness.

The aircraft swooped down towards the flat barren looking surface of the plateau and Tara felt the engines and wings easing into vertical mode. The thrust blasted downwards, slowing the plane's fall in preparation for landing and the undercarriage came down and locked with a thump. She could see the ground beneath the fuselage through the skin cameras with an overlay of slowly shrinking concentric rings indicating the precise height of the undercarriage above ground. She was nearly there. Just a few moments more and she could relax and apply whatever first aid she could manage. She had already activated the emergency beacon and frantic queries were coming in over the radio but for the moment she had blocked them off, unable to spare the concentration or breath to deal with any kind of conversation.

The wheels were just a metre above the ground when she saw the surface of the plateau immediately below the plane crumble and collapse under the ferocious pounding of the jet engines. The unfairness of it all made Tara want to slam her fist against the arm-rest, but instead she did the only thing she could, which was to trigger the zero-zero low level ejection and a time delayed emergency engine shut down. Explosive bolts blew the canopy up and free of the fuselage, and small rockets ignited, designed to lift the occupants high enough for parachutes to safely lower them to ground. But by this time the ground had completely collapsed, and without Tara's guidance the engines were unable to compensate. The aircraft toppled, with the nose going down first, followed a moment later by the tail. She knew there had to have been a huge roar of falling rock and earth, but it was drowned out by the sound of the engines. The aircraft was completely underground and almost vertical when the ejection rockets finally fired at full thrust and the engines shut down. For a second she thought that she was going to die, crushed like an insect against the cave wall by the power of the rockets and the mass of the ejection seat. Then she realised that the cavern was a huge yawing dark space, several hundred metres across and about fifty meters deep, at least as far as she could see. The parachute deployed and the seat fell away, slowing her horizontal as well as vertical flight. Because the aircraft was not actually on the ground, she actually had much further to fall than normal in a zero-zero ejection.

In the darkness the impact of touchdown came as a complete surprise and agony flared bright in her chest and shoulder. Worse still, Tara had landed on a slope and immediately began to slide. The parachute caught on some unseen projection and she choked and coughed up blood when the harness jerked her to an abrupt halt. She had an emergency LED torch in her trouser pocket, but her right arm was completely useless and she couldn't reach it. There was a faint amount of light coming from the hole that her landing had created and it seemed as if there was level ground not too far below. She hoped fervently that it wasn't water as she slapped the quick release catch in the middle of her chest. The slope was slippery and she immediately began to helplessly slide and tumble, and she would have screamed in pain if she had been able to draw enough breath to do so. She was unconscious by the time she hit bottom.

***

Viktor had been thrown several metres further than Tara and had drifted even farther because his parachute had not become entangled like hers. His body still hung limply from the parachute harness as he fell. The sides of the cave were almost vertical where he was and he fell straight to the bottom and bonelessly struck the strangely smooth and curved surface before sliding along the curve and toppling into a jagged hole, disappearing from sight.

***

The NDIA slid down the near vertical ramp of earth and rock, its undercarriage crumpling and snapping as the plane slid all the way down to the bottom of the cavern, crumpling the nose and radar dome as it struck. Inside the cockpit the bright red light of the emergency beacon continued to flash while it blasted out its electronic call for help. However the frantic personnel back at the airfield were not the only recipients of the beacon's signal, and slowly, dimly, something began to flicker and glow at the bottom of the cavern.

A colony of bats darted and fluttered across the huge dark emptiness, their high pitched squeaks protesting the invasion of their home, and then silence settled over the ancient cavern once more.

Chapter Two

The first thing that Viktor noticed when he regained consciousness was the lack of pain. The only reason he could think of to explain this gratifying condition was that he had somehow been taken to a hospital. But the hard and uncomfortable surface beneath him argued against this and a sniff of the damp musty air further supported the conclusion, so he decided to open his eyes. The first thing he saw were the lines of his parachute, leading up towards the shroud which seemed to be tangled in something, but it was too dark to see. He frowned. There shouldn't have been any light at all. Slowly, carefully, he turned his head. What he saw made him start violently and scramble away on elbows and feet, dragging the lines with him until he was stopped by something solid and heavy. Now that he was at a safer distance, he realised that the thing which had been hovering by his side was mechanical and not biological. It was also the source of the soft glowing light.

His self-possession returned when the object or device did not follow or act in any way that might be interpreted as threatening. He raised his hand and slowly moved it in front of himself and his pulse accelerated again when he saw a small, seemingly corresponding movement on the device. Then he stiffened, and the fear returned in full force. There was something clinging to the back of his hand. Thoughts of poisonous spiders and centipedes made him freeze with his hand still raised in front of him like an archetypal Native American offering a greeting. His skin crawling, he narrowed his eyes in the semi-gloom and tried to discern what the thing on his hand was. After a minute of staring until his eyes burned, the thing had still not moved, and by very slowly angling his hand so that more of the light from the still unidentified thing that squatted there looking at him, he was able to make out that the object adhering to the back of his hand was too regular and angular in shape to be biological. Very cautiously he brought his trembling hand closer to his face and realised that the thing was roughly in the shape of a Celtic cross. It had four arms at right angles to each other with a disc shape beneath, centred on where the arms joined. There were semi-circular indentations at the corner of each junction, and the arms themselves were covered with a complicated tracery of lines.

Still taking care not to make any abrupt moves, Viktor pushed himself into a sitting position and then wriggled his fingers. When there was no pain or response from the cross-like object, he dared to reach out a finger to touch it. Nothing. He tapped harder. Still nothing. He gripped one of the arms and gently tried to move it sideways, but it clung obstinately to his skin. Since it didn't seem to be hurting him and he had no desire to tear off a piece of skin, he decided to leave it in place for the moment and turned his attention to the patiently waiting machine or robot. He freed himself from the parachute harness, and on hands and knees he very slowly crawled towards the device. It was roughly oval in shape, with four smooth ridges on its back linked to a shallow indentation in its middle. After a moment he realised that the shapes also formed the outline of a Celtic cross. Its entire upper surface glowed dimly. Tiny movements of what looked like clusters of lenses at the end facing him indicated that it was still aware of and watching him. He stopped crawling when he was within reach of it and that was when he saw the shielded opening in its casing that was the same size and shape as the object that was stuck to his hand. Sudden inspiration struck him, and his mind connected his inexplicable good health, the object on his hand, and the device. Was it possible that the glowing thing was some sort of advanced first aid kit? If so, who on Earth could build such a thing?

Just then, the cross on Viktor's hand emitted a high pitched series of squeals and a dim flash of light, and then abruptly detached itself and fell onto the floor with a dull clonk. The back of his hand was unmarked and undamaged, other than a slight reddening and indentation of the skin. He stared closer at his hand and frowned. Was his hand and wrist hairier than normal? Dismissing the thought, he picked up the fallen object and examined its underside. Holding it closer to the unmoving machine, he used its glow to study the script printed on the underside of the arms. Each arm bore words from a distinctly different script, but more importantly, none of them were of any language that he had ever seen. Combined with the odd machine and the wreckage of the huge craft or structure in which he presently stood, there seemed to be only one conclusion. Excitement filled him, overcoming the shock and disappointment of losing the NDIA and Tara. His employers would be unhappy, but if he was right, what he had in his hands was worth far more. In fact, his discovery was priceless.

It took him nearly half an hour to work out how to move the glowing device because simply pushing or pulling it produced no results at all. It was as if it was bolted to the floor. But finally he found a small cross-like unit seated in a depression at the join of the ridges of the machine's back. A gentle tug pulled it free, and when he moved away, the device lifted approximately half a meter off the ground and followed. Pressing the control unit against his suit made it firmly stick there, while a second push made it let go. There was a packing case wedged against a rib of the wrecked craft with more of them piled in the shadows, and at the cost of a broken nail he found the correct way to open the smooth plastic-like box. The sight of several hundred of the cross-like devices that had fallen off his hand made him gasp. He re-sealed the box and made his way towards the jaggedly torn side of the vessel. The NDIA's emergency beacon would draw a rescue team to the cavern and he had to be gone before they arrived and discovered the wreckage of the plane and, hopefully, Tara's corpse. He would have preferred to confirm her demise, one way or another, but it was too dark and the cavern too huge for him to risk it. It was more important to be gone.

The collapse caused by the NDIA's landing had created a steep ramp of rocks and gravel and he was able to find it and climb out of the cave, guided by the glow of the sky through the hole in the roof of the cave. To his delight the machine was able to ascend the slope with no difficulty, following him like a faithful dog as he pushed the smooth plastic crate ahead of him. Once on the surface he took a deep breath of the fresh air, hoisted the crate onto his shoulder, and began to run. He had studied the plateau endlessly and knew precisely where to find a path that would take him downwards and into cover where he could hide from the rescuers and call his employer for a pick up. He glanced over his shoulder at the floating machine and grinned even as he scratched at the back of his neck.

***

Tara was dreaming – or at least it felt like a dream. A particularly vivid and really strange dream. She was flying an aircraft again – no, it wasn't an aircraft, it was some kind of silly science-fiction spaceship, although the controls and instruments looked a lot more realistic than was usual on TV. But more disturbing was the fact that she was naked except for the sleek covering of hair all over her body, not to mention the wing webs that stretched between her arms and her torso. Her hands only had four claw-tipped fingers, all mutually opposing. She knew something was wrong, but she couldn't say exactly what. All she knew was that there was something important in the ship, something she had to deliver – and something, someone was trying to stop her. All this anxiety made her fangs itch and she sucked reflexively as if for comfort. Her head twisted to one side at the sound of a high pitched "scree – scree – scree" coming from the instruments as well as something inside her head, similar to the NDIA's interface, but different.

Looking out of the cockpit she saw the familiar blue green and white globe of Earth, which was approaching at an impossible speed. The ship began to vibrate as it hit the edge of the atmosphere. Somehow she knew that her ship was capable of trans-atmospheric and true atmospheric flight, so the threat of burning up wasn't what frightened her. The tremendous, teeth rattling blow that struck the ship confirmed that there was truly something to be afraid of. A screen appeared in her vision, much like the NDIA's visual camera feeds and she gasped when she saw the jagged, smoke-trailing hole in the side of "her" ship and the tumbling stream of cargo falling out into the thin air. The ship was losing power fast and the ground was approaching even faster. Looking out of the cockpit, to her amazement she recognized the plateau where her aircraft had recently crashed, although the pattern of vegetation looked different.

Then she was back in her own body. She remembered the bullet wound and braced herself for the return of the terrible pain and the suffocating damage to her lung. When the pain failed to appear she frowned. Perhaps she was still hallucinating? Then she moved her leg and winced. She had clearly sprained something and she doubted if hallucinations could hurt that much. Reaching up to her shoulder with her hand she stiffened in shock when she felt the bullet hole in her flight suit. If she had really been shot, then …

To her shock and surprise, the mental query activated her bio-monitor display, which should have been impossible since she wasn't connected to the aircraft. A green 3D outline of a human female body – her body – appeared, seemingly floating in mid-air. The familiar readouts, blood pressure, pulse, temperature, were in there accustomed places. Normally, the NDIA would just take the readings from her suit sensors and display the level of pressure being exerted by the suit on various parts of her body as well as any suit failures. But now there were additional indicators, things she had never seen before and weren't even supposed to be possible. A patch of red on the leg of the display matched the pain she was feeling as well as indicators in various other places where she was slowly becoming aware of aches and pains. She looked at the top of her shoulder on the display and shuddered when a blue moving indicator appeared and penetrated the body, plunging down from the shoulder and into the lung. The display zoomed in, showing details of the damage, with matching status readings as her body went into shock. Then as she watched, the savage injuries began to undo themselves in the display. At first she thought it was simply the gunshot played in reverse, but there was a definite purpose and order to the reversal. First the pleural cavity re-sealed itself, severed arteries joined and healed, the damage to the lung faded, and finally the muscles and skin re-formed over as the animation ended. Impossible as it seemed, she had somehow been healed. Then her fingertips felt something hard and dense caught in the folds of her suit. After a moment she managed to push it out of the tear in the shoulder. She stared dumbfounded at the small calibre bullet she held between thumb and fingers.

Tara realised that she was inside the same cockpit she had seen in her dream, draped awkwardly and uncomfortably sideways over the oddly shaped pilot's seat. Looking up, she saw that a section of the very solid looking cockpit canopy had been lifted. She remembered sliding down the sloping cave floor, and she must have somehow slid into the opening and on down onto the strangely clean looking seat. With a certain amount of undignified kicking and squirming she managed to bring herself to a sitting position. That's when she noticed the thing stuck to the back of her hand. Unlike Viktor she had the aid of the strangely informative bio-monitor display of her HUD. When she focused on the cross shaped thing stuck to her hand, it immediately flashed the bright red cross symbol that normally meant that she should seek medical attention because one or more of her vital signs was dangerously out of line. Testing, she looked away. The flashing cross disappeared. When she looked back the display flashed once more. It could mean the thing was killing her, but given the inexplicable healing of what had been most likely a fatal gunshot wound, she was more inclined to believe that it indicated some sort of medical device. Looking at the uncomfortably high and short arm rest she saw a recess with the same shape as the thing on her hand and a flexible arm next to it that might have been an applicator. She jumped in fright when the thing on her hand suddenly squealed and fell off onto her lap, but she quickly recovered and picked it up and stuffed it into a pocket.

She suddenly realised that she shouldn't be able to see at all in the darkness of the cave. When she consciously made the effort to see her surroundings, things grew even brighter. It seemed that she had acquired some form of night vision in addition to accelerated healing. Then she remembered Viktor. If he was still alive he might be looking for her in order to finish what he had started. The NDIA was damaged but not totally destroyed, and if whoever had bought him off recovered it and captured her, Viktor would still have achieved his objective. She had to get out of the cave and evade capture until help arrived. She would have loved to spend more time slowly searching the amazing vessel – she couldn't bring herself to call it a UFO – but it would be all too easy for Viktor or his friends to camp out around the hole created by her crashed aeroplane and catch her like a mole sticking its head out of its burrow when she tried to leave.

Testing her leg again, she found that the pain and soreness had greatly diminished, and a check of the strangely upgraded medical display showed that it agreed with her. When she climbed out of the seat she saw that there was a doorway behind her leading into the rest of the ship, but she had to suppress her burning curiosity in the interests of self-preservation. Standing on the seat she was able to step up onto the edge of the cockpit and by using the edge of the canopy which appeared to had slid up and forward, and the step out onto the rock of the cave wall. The side that she had come down was too smooth and steep, so she was forced to attempt the opposite side. It was only after she had climbed out onto the damp rock that she realised there was a yawning crevasse just metres in front of the alien ship's nose, and clinging to the steep slope she broke into a cold sweat. If it had not been for the night vision with which she had suddenly been blessed, she could have simply stepped off the edge and fallen into what looked like a bottomless pit. Things like this always look so exciting in the films, but right now it was just terrifying. The unpleasant sliminess of the rock became a lethal threat. If she slipped half way up she could very likely miss the cockpit and fall to her death. As it was, she was looking up at a difficult climb leading out of the trench in which the alien ship was wedged. "Well, just standing here isn't going to get me out of this hole," she said aloud. Taking a deep breath she began to climb.

Tara had never done any rock climbing, and she found it hard, her arms and legs quivering with strain as she plastered herself against the face of the cave wall.

She grimaced in disgust when her fingers and face pressed in clumps of what she realised was bat guano. Half way up the handholds became fewer and shallower, and some of the rock crumbled under the pressure of her fingers and toes, and panic began to clutch at her heart. She resisted the urge to whimper and grimly struggled on, stretching her arm out for the next shallow crevice. Then the rock under her foot cracked and fell away. She cried out in fright, finding herself dangling from her desperately gripping fingers. Her other foot slipped from its precarious toe hold and she knew that her fingers were not strong enough to hold her weight. Throwing a glance over her shoulder she saw that she had drifted sideways and was dangling over the black emptiness. Gritting her teeth she pulled with all the strength of her arms even as she felt her fingers slipping.

Unsummoned, her HUD flashed to life.

"EMERGENCY DETECTED. ACTIVATE BIO-OVERRIDE? YES/NO."

Since it seemed likely that she would be dead in seconds anyway, she mentally moved the cursor to the "YES" and clicked on it.

"WARNING - EFFECTS MAY BE IRREVERSABLE. PROCEED? YES/NO."

Despite the ominous tone she once again clicked on the "YES". She continued to slip and her fingers began to straighten under the load. She felt a flash of disappointment. Perhaps she was simply hallucinating after all. Then the pain hit her. It felt as if she was being torn apart from the inside out. She would have screamed like a banshee except that she had lost all voluntary control of her muscles. Fire streamed along her nerves and her heartbeat pounded in her ears and temples like a kettledrum. Things shifted inside her and it felt like tendons all over her body were being torn and twisted. The agony was incredible, impossible. The torture seemed to go on for hours, days, but then with just as little warning it was gone.

"BIO-OVERRIDE COMPLETED. CAUTION IS ADVISED."

Caution? What was she supposed to be cautious about? Stupid options that caused unbearable pain? Then she realised that she wasn't slipping any more. She was still hanging from her fingers, but she barely felt any strain at all. In fact … with hardly any effort she began to climb the slippery surface with the surety of a spider climbing a wall. Visions of comic book heroes streamed luridly through her mind, but a quick check confirmed that her fingertips were not sticky and none of her orifices displayed any desire to exude web. But her fingertips clicked against the rock when she shifted her grip and she gingerly raised her index finger and leaned her head closer. She didn't know whether to be pleased or horrified when she saw the claw-like hardening of her fingertip. She gripped harder, and she was startled when her fingertips actually dug into the rock. "Oh my." Flexing her shoulders she pulled and simultaneously scrabbled around with her feet. Moments later she was crawling up the slippery slope as if it was the most natural thing in the world. When she finally reached the top and her fingers went over the ledge, she pulled hard, hoping to get her upper body up onto safety. Instead, the thrust of her arms and shoulders threw her up into the air and into a half-somersault. She had always been bad at gymnastics, but she found that she now had an incredible awareness of her body and its position as it flew and tumbled through the air. She landed in a half-squat, arms outspread, and totally amazed at her own hitherto unsuspected gymnastic ability. Out of the trench and the bulk of the alien ship, it was easy to see the glow of sunlight coming from the breach in the ceiling of the cavern and reflected off the polished skin of the surprisingly intact NDIA. Unfortunately, it and the rocky ramp leading to the surface was on the other side of the trench. She could see a way across, a natural bridge, but it meant a long walk in the semi-darkness, with the constant threat of Viktor springing out at her at any point. Even if she was stronger than she used to be, that would not protect her from having her skull bashed in by a rock. But simply hiding would only give Viktor's allies time to arrive and not just capture her, but ambush the unsuspecting rescue party from the airfield, including her father. No, she had to risk a confrontation with Viktor and get out to the surface. She was half-way around the cave before she remembered the pistol and she cursed under her breath. There was no way that she would risk the climb back down to the cockpit and then back up again. For one thing, she had no guarantee that her strange new abilities would last. It could be the alien equivalent of a shot of adrenaline or amphetamine which could wear off at any time.

Parts of the bridge turned out to be less than half a metre wide and the gloom beneath it so dark that even her improved eyesight had been unable to see the bottom. Crossing it had been the most terrifying thing she had done so far, with the possibility that the rock might crumble beneath each new step that she took, plunging her to her death. She sank to her hands and knees in relief when she finally reached the other side, and it was in that position that she saw Viktor scrambling up the slope past the NDIA towards the surface. Her eyes narrowed and she frowned in puzzlement when she saw that he was pushing something ahead of him and that there was another something that was emitting a bright glow following him up the crumbled rock. She sprang to her feet, and freed of the threat of an attack by Viktor she began to jog towards the exit. With every step the light grew brighter and without realising it she accelerated until she was running faster than an Olympic athlete, slowing down only when she reached the base of the scree covered slope and the painfully bright sky that shone through the hole above her. Although unlikely, it was possible that Viktor was waiting for her on the surface, so she slowed to a stealthy creep. With her arms stretched out to her sides she glided silently up the slope until she was just below the opening. Cautiously sticking her head out would be to invite an impromptu game of "whack-a-mole" if Viktor was waiting, so instead she braced herself and threw her body forward, aiming for a quick sprint, drop, and roll. To her dismay, she realised too late that she was still underestimating her new found capabilities. She shot out of the aircraft-sized hole as if she was still seated in her ejection seat, and with a balance and skill even a gymnast couldn't match, flipped and landed on her feet, transitioning to an all out run without missing a step. Somehow she had also managed to capture a photographic image of her immediate surroundings during her brief flight and she knew exactly the path she needed to take in order to reach cover and get off of the plateau in the shortest possible time. In addition, there was no sign of anyone on the flat treeless expanse of the plateau, which meant that Viktor was also making his way off of the heights and she would have to be careful not to bump into him.

While she ran, Tara realised that she was lucky that the plateau was not in the Alpine zone of the Făgăraş Mountains, which were freezing cold most of the year round. Being early summer, the weather was relatively mild for this part of Romania. There was not a huge amount of cover, with rocky stretches covered with juniper interspersed with clusters of mountain pine, but it looked sufficient to hide her from Viktor until help came.

Scrambling down the slope she spotted an indentation sheltered by a cluster of pine. She had just settled into it when a terrifying roar and howl shattered the silence and made her jump. It sounded like a monumentally pissed off wolf, and from the volume, a particularly huge one.

***

Viktor frowned. He paused, staring back uphill. It seemed to him that just for a second he had seen a figure outlined against the skyline, but a blink of an eye later it was gone. He shook his head. Even uninjured, Tara could not possibly have moved that fast. Besides, he had a more serious problem on his mind. He itched all over, he ached as if he was suffering from the grandfather of all fevers, and his vision was flickering and fading in an out in a most unusual manner. It was possible that the alien stimulant was finally wearing off and he was feeling the symptoms of concussion, but his head didn't hurt and rather than feeling ill, he was feeling stronger and more energetic than ever. But still, something was definitely wrong. His body felt ... strange. His fingers trembled and his knuckles ached as if he had arthritis. The alien device and other items that he had collected fell from his grip and then he dropped to his knees. He heard a ripping sound, and realised that it was coming from the back of his tough protective flight suit. His face hurt, especially his jaw, and he couldn't form words when he tried to speak. The pain expanded and grew to an unbearable level as consciousness began to fade, and in the midst of his delirium he heard someone ... something ... roar.

***

A shiver ran down Tara's spine upon hearing the sound. More alarmingly, the "Hostile Active Target

36

Acquisition Radar" warning began to flash in her HUD, which was impossible, since there was no aircraft around her to detect. It was particularly alarming because the last time the nano implant had malfunctioned, the user had died. Just as the icon had begun to fade the roar came again and the warning icon returned, sliding around her field of vision to point in the direction from which the sound had come. Somehow, she just knew that what she was hearing was something terrifyingly dangerous and that she had to run away, to escape. Her first thought was to climb, but the slim, almost stunted looking trees offered little concealment or safety. She could run, but it would take her away from the route back up to the plateau and eventual rescue. Or would it? The cliff face was nearly vertical, but it offered more crevices, foot and handholds than the inside of the cave. However the penalty for failure was falling to an almost certain death. For several minutes she crouched there, torn by indecision. After all the threat might be no more than an amorous wolf, and she could imagine her father and the crew laughing when she told her story.

The sound of a heavy body crashing through the pines and more roaring, followed immediately by a "Missile Lock On" warning in her HUD pointing in the direction of those sounds eliminated any doubts or fear of humiliation in Tara's mind. She sprang to her feet, ran towards the cliff, and literally threw herself up and at the rock face. The rock face came towards her at alarming speed, and then she found herself clinging to the near vertical surface three metres above the ground. Behind and below her she heard the scrabbling of clawed feet and more snapping of heavy branches rapidly approaching. Without any time for doubt she began to climb, and gasped in amazement when she scuttled up the cliff face like a wall climbing gecko, except that her hands and feet didn't stick to the rock. "At least that rules out radioactive spiders," she muttered to herself as she continued her impossible ascent.

A rock crashed against the cliff a metre away from her head, showering her face with sand and rock splinters. Tara looked down, something she had been avoiding until now, and quickly wished she hadn't. "No way!" she gasped at the sight of the fucking werewolf in a torn flight suit beneath her. "Viktor, is that you?"

The thing … it certainly looked like a cinema werewolf … growled angrily, tried to climb, and after that failed leapt frighteningly high, clawing at her and only missing by what looked like several centimetres.

"Shit!" Driven by panic Tara scrambled up the cliff almost as if it was level ground and threw herself over the top and back onto the plateau. Still on all fours she spun around and peered down over the edge, only to see the werewolf thing stalking back towards the path that lead up to the plateau. Tara looked around in desperation. If it, he, made it back up, she had the choice of being chased around the flat arena-like space or she could play hide and seek with it back in the cavern. She was faster and stronger than she had ever been, but she still didn't fancy her chances against the claws and obvious strength of the werewolf. She was tempted to tell herself that this was all a delusion and that she was actually still sitting in the cockpit with a cracked skull, but she was pretty sure she could tell the difference. But … werewolves? She sank down into a squat and pressed the heels of her palms against her eyes.

A new, very faint sound intruded on the idyllic mountain scene. It was too regular to be the werewolf, but when she looked up there was nothing in sight to account for it. Then she realised that it was the sound of a distant helicopter. An uncomfortable pressure against her breast made her frown, and then she remembered her emergency beacon. Without the satellite facilities available to governments the range of the beacon was limited, as was its battery life. Plus there was the fact that Viktor's allies would be monitoring the same frequency. When she concentrated, the sound became clearer. Her head turned from side to side like a quizzical dog and impossibly, she detected fine details of the sounds produced by the helicopter's rotors and engine and she frowned harder. Somehow it sounded familiar. A deep throated roar from across the plateau made her mind up for her and she pulled the beacon from her breast pocket, activating it with a press and slide of the single red button. Now it was a race between the chopper and the new, hirsute version of that murderous bastard Viktor.

In the end, the SAR aircraft and the monster came into view at nearly the same time. Tara leapt to her feet at the sight of the familiar reconditioned Russian Mi-17 painted in custom colours with a big red cross on its side and began to run. A glance over her shoulder revealed the unwelcome sight of the werewolf coming up onto the surface of the plateau. She waved her hands frantically when Viktor dropped onto all fours and bounded towards her, covering the distance at a horrifying rate.

"What the hell is that thing behind you?" her father's voice blasted from the Mi-17's PA system.

Tara didn't bother shouting back and simply ran towards the spot where the chopper was coming in for a landing. Her adrenaline fuelled rush revealed an even greater capacity for speed, and she covered the distance in a blur of motion. At the same time, someone on the chopper must have decided that Viktor looked too much like a threat and a pistol shot cracked, muffled by the open air and the thumping of the helicopter rotors.

The Mi-17 was still two metres off the ground, its twin turbines thundering, when Tara reached it. Rather than waiting she sprang upwards, her arms outstretched and fingers clawed. The Mi-17 did not have landing skids like a Jet Ranger or Huey, so there was no possibility of cinematically grabbing and dangling from a skid. The only available handhold on the smooth curved fuselage was the ledge of the open door. Her fingers slammed against it like the prongs of a pair of grappling hooks, her grip actually digging furrows in the metal while the rest of her body dangled precariously beneath the aircraft, her flight suit flapping madly in the rotor wash. An urgent flashing of her HUD made her twist her neck around owl-like to look over her shoulder and her eyes widened in alarm.

The thing that Tara assumed was Viktor was charging straight towards them at high speed, his elongated jaws gaping, revealing a terrifying set of fangs. The SAR crewman with the pistol fired again, three shots snapping out in quick succession. Tara saw the bullets hit and she heard the crewman's gasp when the charging horror ignored them as if the bullets were nothing more than insects hitting a windscreen. And then it sprang, pushing off the ground with its hind legs and shooting into the air like a fighter being launched by the catapult of an aircraft carrier. Claws extended, it slammed heavily into the door of the helicopter which had been slid back along the fuselage in its open position, making the aircraft sway and rock in the air even as the pilot tried to lift up and away from the ground. The claws on the werewolf's hands and feet punched through the metal as if it was aluminium foil, giving it a firm grip. It turned its head and snarled exultantly at Tara.

"Get out of the way so I can get in," Tara screamed at the crewman, who was leaning out of the door and bravely trying to get another shot at the furry horror clinging to the exterior of the helicopter.

The werewolf lashed out just as the crewman fired. The bullet had just as little effect as before despite the point blank range and hitting the creature right in the middle of its chest. However its claws proved to be just as effective against human flesh as they were against metal.

The crewman screamed in horror and agony when the werewolf's claws ripped open his belly and he toppled out of the helicopter, only to dangle beneath the aircraft from his harness that was connected to the rescue winch.

With the crewman out of the way, the werewolf turned his attention back to Tara. Gripping the edge of the open door with its blood soaked claws, it bared its fangs in a savage grin and released the grip of its other hand in order to edge closer and within reach of Tara. Once she was dealt with, it would climb into the helicopter to get at the rest of its occupants.

Tara knew that unless she did something, she would be dead in seconds, and her father not long after that. The Mi-17 was moving forward at speed now and she was being battered by both horizontal and vertical torrents of wind, pushing her body towards the back of the aircraft. A desperate idea came to her, and she acted without taking the time to think about whether it was even possible. Drawing both feet towards her body, she used the new found strength of her arms and shoulders, assisted by the pounding pressure of the wind, to swivel her body into a horizontal position as if she was flying through the air, shifting her grip to the side of the doorway as she moved. Then with a convulsive effort and a shout of terrified rage, she straightened her body and arms, snapping her legs out like a hydraulic ram. She felt the metal of the doorway twisting under her hands, and the soles of her boots smashed into the side of the werewolf's chest with crushing force. She felt its ribs flex and snap under the soles of her feet. There was a deafening screech of rending metal, and the entire door broke off of its sliding mount. It tumbled away and down, with the werewolf still clinging to it. A howl of rage rang in her ears as the monster faded from sight.

Hands gripped her body and Tara gasped with

relief when she was drawn into the fuselage.

"Tara! Thank god you're all right," Rowland Harker cried.

Tara pointed out of the door and at the quivering line that stretched from the winch. "The crewman! He might be still alive."

"My god! I'd forgotten..." Harker gasped and lurched across to slap the red mushroom shaped rewind button. The powerful winch whined as it drew the vibrating cable in and he slapped the middle stop button when the crewman's limp and slowly spinning body appeared in the doorway. He cried out in shock at the sight of the man's intestines hanging from the gaping wound in his belly. Up to now, he had thought that the crewman had simply fallen, knocked out of the aircraft by the werewolf's blow. "Help me get him inside, quickly!"

The pilot brought the helicopter to a hover again, while everyone else struggled to pull the limp and bloodied form in against the downdraught.

"My god, he's still alive!" the EMT cried, his gloved hands busy working to stuff the victim's innards back into place assisted by Rowland, who was a biologist as well as a nano-engineer.

"What about Viktor?" the pilot asked over the intercom.

Tara, who had donned a headset said, "That thing that attacked us *was* Viktor!"

"Get us back to base as fast as you can," Rowland said grimly to the pilot. "And radio base to prepare a second team to secure the wreckage. You'll take them aboard and shuttle them back here as soon as we land. Tell them they need to be armed. Shotguns and rifles."

The security team were experienced ex-special forces men supplied by a contractor, but Tara had doubts about their ability to handle whatever Viktor had become, assuming he was still alive. Somehow she knew that the fall wouldn't kill him, although it might disable him long enough for them to recover the plane. They would also need a special team to recover the other thing in the cavern, but she would need to discuss that with her father first.

Chapter Three

Rowland stared at the sample of Tara's blood displayed on one large LED screen and the readings from the biological monitors attached to Tara's naked body on the other. "I can't believe you're even alive."

"Thanks a lot," Tara said, staring in awful fascination at the impossible readings. "I know I've lost some weight, but I don't think I look that bad. In fact, one of the guys said that he would – "

"I don't need to hear that, thank you very much. You're still my daughter – and you know very well that's not what I'm talking about," he said.

"Well it's hard to be worried when I feel so damned good. In fact I've never felt so good. Can I get dressed now or should I tell the on-line girlie magazines to start bidding? I'm told the printed ones are just about dead. On the other hand, Playboy is still paying quite well – "

"Tara! Please be serious just for a moment."

"I am being serious. Look, I'm fine, the nano-interface system is reporting one-hundred percent operational and, you can't do anything about the changes anyway. Besides, that poor crewman – What's his name anyway? – is the one who needs your concern."

Her father nodded tiredly. "It's a miracle, but it looks like he'll live; and his name's Andrei. You're stable now, but what worries me is that there are signs that your body is still changing. Who knows if the next change will not be harmful or even fatal. Look, right here. It shows that something is happening to your teeth and jaws. It's subtle but there are definite changes going on," he said pointing at a particular set of figures and graphs.

Tara pulled the monitor leads off of her body and slipped on a white lab coat. "You don't have to tell me, I can feel it. But I don't think the changes are random. Whatever is in me is – I hate to use the word –

intelligent."

Her father looked shocked. "You think it's alive? Some kind of parasite or symbiont?"

She felt her jaw with her fingertips. "No, not like that. More limited and specialised – like a very advanced SCADA or fly-by-wire system. It monitors my intentions and the feedback from my body and makes changes as necessary. It's definitely interacting with my nano-interface implants and the HUD display."

"And what about the nightmares?" Rowland asked, his concern and frustration clear upon his face.

She pulled the lab coat tighter around her. "That's the thing. I don't think they're nightmares or dreams at all."

"What then. Visions?" he said, eyebrow raised sceptically.

The idea made her laugh. "No. Don't worry, I'm not going to suddenly claim to be possessed."

"That's a relief. I have enough problems without dealing with the ghost of King Tut."

Tara hesitated. She knew her father wasn't going to like her idea any more than he did the phantom of a long dead Egyptian pharaoh. She took a deep breath. "I think they're memories. Recorded memories." She saw him about to protest and held up her hand. "Hear me out. Remember I fell, half dead, into the cockpit of some kind of highly advanced aircraft or spaceship. When I woke up, I had been ... fixed, by something that had attached itself to the back of my hand. Now just imagine for a moment that you were designing such a ship. What do all modern high-performance aircraft have in their cockpits apart from flight controls?"

Her father's eyes narrowed in thought. He was a brilliant research engineer whose ability to think far, far out of the box had made him an outcast and he knew his daughter had inherited those traits. Slowly he said, "Life support, and ... a black box! I think I see where you're going."

Tara nodded eagerly. "My dreams have been exactly the same each time, although they're getting clearer and more precise. I'm always in the cockpit and flying the ship. I'm very high up, high enough to see the curvature of the Earth, and it is the Earth, and not some alien planet. I feel concerned, worried. Not about the ship, but something else. A threat. And I feel … driven. I have to do something. My ship … no, the cargo in the ship is important. Then the instruments start to make noise and flash and there's some kind of impact or explosion … and then the dream ends."

Rowland nodded. "That would make sense. Instead of a sound or even video recording, the cockpit systems actually record the pilot's memories. It would not only heal the pilot's injuries but restore an accurate memory of the moments before the crash – to the pilot or to the crash investigators if the pilot is killed."

"That's what I'm guessing," Tara said. "But there's something more."

"Oh?" Rowland said suspiciously.

"I told you the dreams are getting clearer. Well the one I had last night told me something new."

"Which was?" he prompted, tapping his foot impatiently.

"The pilot wasn't human."

"What!"

"He, I'm pretty sure it was a he and that they had two sexes just like us, was bipedal, but looked more like a cross between a man and a … bat."

Rowland slumped into a chair. "Oh my god. That's even worse. We've got to get that thing out of you. It could kill you if it decides you don't look sufficiently like a bat and tries to fix it."

"No, I don't think so. I believe that it already knows it's in the wrong kind of body. If I had been anyone else, it might have done serious harm. In fact, I'll wager that's what happened to Viktor. But the … whatever it is … found a way to interact, communicate, with my body."

Her father pushed himself upright. "Your nano-interface implants!" He swivelled his chair around and tapped rapidly on the keyboard of the medical display console. "Your bio-monitor contains hard coded parameters for all your critical functions, pulse, blood-pressure, oxygen levels, and all the biochemical and hormonal ranges. My god, the alien medikit must be incredibly sophisticated, with what almost amounts to an AI, an artificial intelligence."

"I know what AI means, daddy. Medikit? Really?" she countered teasingly.

"Hey, I played Doom and X-Com. I wasn't always a stuffy old fart, you know," he sniffed. "It seemed appropriate. One touch and you get an instant health level boost."

She nodded thoughtfully. "You're right. And if you're the wrong species, an instant make-over as well."

"From the empty packing crates in the alien ship's hold and the used um, medikit you recovered, it appears that it was a freighter delivering medical supplies. Damn that Viktor. He must have survived the fall and led whoever he was working for back to the ship. They had almost cleaned it out before our people arrived and drove them off. Fortunately they weren't equipped for a fight and our people were loaded for bear, or werewolf."

"He must have changed back into a human, then. He didn't seem to be communicating very well in his hirsute form." Tara shuddered, remembering the fangs and claws reaching for her.

"You said the medikit warned you that the changes it made to you were irreversible. Have you had any other messages since you got back? Perhaps you can get it to reverse the process."

"I think irreversible meant just that. But I haven't

changed into a giant bat or anything, so the er, medikit is able to control the changes in my case. It only seems to respond to physical damage or surges of adrenaline, and its smart enough to only give me what I need."

"What about your teeth and jaws then? I don't suppose you've had an irresistible craving for raw meat or industrial strength chewing gum lately that might have triggered a response from the medikit?"

"Perhaps some of the changes were linked. And it is operating in an alien environment under emergency conditions. I'm lucky I'm not already dead."

"Well at least your teeth show no signs of falling out. In fact, several cavities seem to have disappeared."

Tara yawned and stretched. "I'm shagged. Unless you want to stick more needles into my bum I'm off to bed."

"There'll be someone sitting in the hallway all night, so just shout if you feel anything."

She paused in the doorway and turned back to look at her father. "They better be armed. Just in case." Her father's expression told her that he had already considered that eventuality.

"Fortunately, the security team have some Tasers," he said, trying unsuccessfully to sound comforting.

***

Tara snapped from dream state into alertness with shocking suddenness. She had turned off all the lights because her eyes had been feeling uncomfortably sensitive, so the room was in complete darkness. Then she heard the sound again, the sound of oiled metal sliding and clicking against metal. She stealthily reached out for the light switch, but her frantically searching fingers were unable to find it. The fear and panic of the dream had carried over into her waking state and she felt an irresistible need to see what was in the room.

Something clicked in her mind, and she felt her throat tighten and her chest strain as if she were trying to make a sound, but nothing appeared come out of her mouth. The world abruptly turned green, her HUD activated, and her vision seemed to ripple as if she was under water, but despite the imperfections, she could actually see! She realised that the ripples were happening in time to the involuntary contractions of her chest, and then it hit her. Sonar. She was "seeing" using pulses of ultrasonic sound.

Turning her head, she managed to find the light switch and gasped in relief when the room lit up. The sonar display immediately disappeared, along with the HUD itself. She sat on the edge of her bed, stunned by this latest revelation, until her lips curled in a grin. She had sonar! It was like living in a superhero origin comic. Then she remembered the metallic sound that had alarmed her in the first place. Looking around she didn't see anything in the room that seemed a likely culprit. She got up and went to the door. It was only when she opened it that she remembered what her father had said about a guard.

The uniformed guard looked up from his magazine. "Good evening, Miss Harker. Is everything all right?" She noted that he was wearing a Taser clipped to his belt.

"Good evening. Did you hear anything unusual just now? Some kind of metallic sound."

He frowned. "No, I didn't … um, wait. I did unload and work the slide of my pistol just now. It's been sticking a bit lately. But how did you – "

She smiled and shook her head. "Probably just some trick of acoustics. You know how sounds can sometimes travel."

"Er, yes miss. I suppose so," the guard said doubtfully. "Have a good night."

"Goodnight," she said, closing the door again. She

reached up under her hair to feel her ears and sighed with relief when she found that they hadn't become pointy. "The last thing I need right now are Vulcan ears," she muttered to herself. "Did you hear that? I said no pointy ears," she said to the thing inside of her. "Or fur. Definitely no fur. I hate shaving my legs."

***

The fall had broken half the bones in Viktor's body, probably ruptured organs, and had hurt like hell — and that didn't include the three broken ribs and internal damage that bitch Tara had given him when she had kicked him off of the helicopter. He had never known that she was that athletic. Perhaps he should have tried harder to get her into bed, he thought with a grin. A rib grated, twisted and popped back into place, and he winced in pain. His memories of what happened after he took a tumble half-way down the slope from the top of the plateau were hazy, tinged with red and memories of a furious blinding rage and the irresistible urge to hunt and kill. What was clear was that the healing device had done a lot more than fix his wounds. There was no way that his old self would have survived the fall or healed so incredibly quickly. He sat up, the pain in his ribs and internal organs already fading into memory. He had to recover the alien artefacts and get back to the plateau and meet his employer's representatives. They would be unhappy about the aircraft, but he was confident that he now possessed something better. Much better.

***

"It appears to be broken," the slim bespectacled man said, shaking his head disapprovingly.

"You can still get most of the important technology. It was a good landing and a slow fall into the

50

cavern," Viktor protested. The man looked like an accountant or nerdy IT guy, but Viktor knew better than to underestimate him. Felix Hoch was one of his employer's field operatives and he didn't keep his job by being soft.

"What good is it without the pilot? You weren't able to capture an unarmed girl who trusted you?" The scorn in Hoch's voice was scathing.

"Something happened after we crashed. That's what I wanted to tell you about. Just listen to me for a moment."

"Our time is limited. Harker's recovery team will be coming soon. Be brief." Hoch glanced over at the hole where is own salvage team were setting up to extract what they could from the wreckage.

Viktor described the events after the crash as plainly and logically as he could. "What I have here is proof of what I just told you," he finished, pointing at the alien device and box of cruciform medical units.

Hoch was flanked by two rough looking men who had an unmistakeable military air about them. He glanced at the one to his right and then back at Viktor. "You failed to deliver, after taking the Corporation's money, and you allowed a witness to escape. I'm afraid you've become a liability Mr Tiranul, and I'm obliged to do something about it." He turned his back on Viktor and said to the two mercenaries, "I'm going back to the helicopter to make a report. You two clean up here and make sure the technicians get everything. Goodbye Mr Tiranul."

"No, wait Mr Hoch. I'm telling you the truth. What I have here is worth a fortune!" Viktor shouted at Hoch's retreating back.

"Don't waste your breath," said one of the mercenaries in a British accent, raising the muzzle of his HK MP5 submachine gun.

"You handle the pilot. I'll go and check on the

salvage crew," the other mercenary, a Russian, said nodding in the direction of the crash site.

The British merc smiled at Viktor. "Hold still and I'll make it painless. Try to run and I'll take out your knees first." To his surprise, Viktor extended his arms out to his sides and smiled back. "Go ahead. But I'm telling you that you're making a mistake."

"Don't think so, mate," the mercenary grunted and raised his weapon to his shoulder.

The Russian paused in his stride when a burst of three shots cracked flatly in the open air behind him, training and instinct making him want to drop and seek cover. Forcing himself not to look back and make himself look stupid, he continued walking. But a shout of alarm and a second, longer burst of automatic fire made him spin around and raise his own weapon. "Yóbanny v rot!" he exclaimed at the sight that met his eyes. Some kind of big hairy creature was ripping a leg off of the other merc, totally ignoring the combat dagger that the Englishman was repeatedly driving into its body. From the damage he could see, the Englishman was already dead so he fired from where he stood, emptying the magazine and hitting both the monster and his fellow merc.

The gunfire had alerted Hoch as well. When he saw what was happening he turned to the pilot. "Get this fucking thing off the ground right now!"

The pilot was another combat veteran and knew when the shit had hit the fan. Without another word he twisted the throttle and hit the starter button. "Where are we going?" he asked over the intercom.

"Nowhere. Just take us up a hundred metres and hover, but be prepared to move out if we start taking fire," Hoch replied, staring out of the side door. "Hmm, it seems I owe Mr Tiranul an apology."

"What?"

"I'm not talking to you," Hoch said absently to the

pilot as he watched the events on the ground in fascination. Viktor, the monster, had finished ripping the first guard apart and was headed for the Russian. Hoch could see the muzzle flashes as the man reloaded and fired another magazine at the charging beast. It was obvious to Hoch and to the Russian that attempting to flee would be futile given the speed at which the monster was moving, and the guard had obviously chosen to fight to the death. He was still firing when Viktor crashed into him. Hoch watched in fascination as the Russian was torn apart with such violence that his blood painted a sunburst on the sand and grass around where he and his killer stood.

The monster roared defiantly at the helicopter hovering above it, but retained sufficient logical thought to understand that the noisy machine was too far away for even it to reach. It looked around and when it didn't spot any visible threats, it squatted down and started to eat.

Hoch was intrigued by the fact that the monster, Viktor, didn't go after the technicians in the cavern below.

"What should we do now?" the horrified pilot asked, trying not to vomit.

"Keep us within sight of that thing. I suspect something interesting is going to happen soon." Hoch said calmly and continued to watch as the aircraft slowly circled the plateau. After twelve minutes had passed, he narrowed his eyes and pressed his nose to the polycarbonate of the window. "Get closer. Something's happening."

The pilot brought the helicopter back to a hover and edged down and closer to the splash of darkening blood and the thing that squatted within it.

"Ah! I was hoping this was the case," Hoch said. "Put us down."

"But sir, what about the – "

"Do as I say or I'll have you left here and you can walk home. If I have to, I can fly this thing myself." This wasn't true, but the threat was quite real. Hoch didn't tolerate incompetence or disobedience. He hated unprofessionalism. When the pale faced pilot finally landed the helicopter, Hoch saw that Viktor was fully human in appearance once more, albeit naked and liberally spattered in blood. He jumped out of the aircraft, bending over beneath the spinning rotors, and strode casually towards the waiting test pilot. He made sure to stay out of the line of fire of the crewman operating the Dillon Aero Gatling gun mounted on a pintle in the helicopter behind him. He wasn't sure that even that weapon could kill whatever Viktor had become, but he was confident it would disable Viktor long enough for an escape should the test pilot turn violent. He stopped as soon as he was within shouting distance. "If you can restrain yourself from tearing me apart, we can talk."

Viktor rubbed at the blood staining his hands and arms. "I'm completely lucid and human at the moment. It's your men – and you – who were responsible for their own deaths."

Hoch waved his hand dismissively. "A misunderstanding. It seems you did find something of value after all. I'm sure that our mutual employer will be suitably grateful for your efforts."

This change in attitude made Victor laugh. "I'm sure he will. By the way, as I was trying to tell you before, there are more of these boxes in the hold of the alien ship down there."

"Alien ship?" Hoch said with raised eyebrows. He shrugged. "If you say so. It's a pity that we won't have the time to examine it in detail before Harker's people arrive."

"The ship's a wreck, and from what I could see, all the usable technology has been destroyed, whether by the crash or deliberately I couldn't tell in the dark and without instruments." Viktor ripped the remaining shreds of his flight suit from his body, and ignoring his own nakedness he said, "If you will tell your man to safe the Gatling gun, I'll go down and help the technicians. I don't want to be here when Harker's security team arrives. I have no illusions that I'm immortal." He was about to walk away when Hock raised his hand.

"Wait. You're sure that Tara Harker survived the crash?"

"Yes. I told you, that bitch kicked me off of the helicopter or I would have got her and her father."

"You said you had previously shot her in the chest?" Hoch said slowly, as if speaking to someone particularly dim witted.

"Yes, yes, I told you that – oh!"

"Oh, indeed. It would appear that Miss Harker also encountered one of these miraculous healing devices, and apparently with none of the um, side effects," Hoch said, nodding at the blood and scraps of flesh that littered the ground around Viktor. "She too may have taken souvenirs of her visit to your alien vessel. Plus she still possesses the nano-interface technology."

Viktor grinned. "Then we should pay Tara and her father a visit. With the security team busy out here, it will be just the father and daughter, Whittle, and a bunch of technicians."

Hoch nodded. "We still have two guards, and the Gatling gun. The four of us should be enough to deal with them. I shall leave you to deal with Miss Harker in the event she has developed any new abilities. The fact that she ran from you indicates that she is not inclined to sudden hair growth, and it would be very useful if we can discover why. Perhaps it is gender linked," he speculated.

Chapter Four

The flashing of her HUD woke her up. According to the internal clock it was just before four a.m. Then she noticed the IFF "Hostile Aircraft" indicator was flashing. A moment later she realised that she could hear the faint drone of an approaching helicopter. After all that had happened, she was not inclined to take chances, so she sprang out of bed, slipped on her socks and boots and dashed to the door. To her relief the guard was still there. "Go and wake my father. Tell him there's a hostile helicopter approaching."

"But…" The guard stared at her suspiciously, wondering if he should reach for his Taser.

"Stop wasting time and get my father," she snapped.

The guard decided that compliance was his best course of action and ran off towards Rowland Harker's bedroom.

Tara ran to the front of the building which served as air tower, offices, and accommodations for the team. She stepped out of the front door and scanned the horizon with her new night vision. There! A speck of movement, no larger than a flying gnat in the black sky caught her attention. Her vision seemed to focus and zoom in on the mote. It was definitely a helicopter. She hesitated and bit her lip. It could be anybody. Military, forestry service, even a civilian traveller. How could she be sure it was a danger? As if in response to her mental query, a new icon appeared in her HUD. She frowned. What on Earth did that shape mean? It was not part of the standard symbol set, and yet it looked … then she saw it. It was Viktor, or a cartoon version of what Viktor had become. Somehow she could detect others who had been treated with the alien "medikit". She wondered if Viktor could detect her.

Rowland came up behind her and put his hand on

her shoulder. "Tara, the guard said you were acting strangely and something about a helicopter."

"Viktor's coming. I can see the helicopter, and my HUD tells me Viktor's on it." She turned to grab her father's shoulders. "You've got to believe me. If I'm right, he's coming for me and your work, and he won't leave witnesses. If I'm wrong you can blame it on me and a delayed reaction to the crash."

He nodded. "All right." He pulled the transceiver from his belt. "Security, this is Harker. You are authorised to draw assault weapons from the arms locker. Assemble in front of the main building and prepare to receive hostile helicopter. Do not fire unless I give the order or you are fired upon."

"Father, we only have three guards left. Viktor knows that the security team would have gone to the plateau along with the recovery people. He wouldn't be coming if he wasn't prepared to take us on. We have to be prepared to abandon the facility."

Rowland hesitated for a moment, and then said, "All right. I'll gather my files. If we have to we can retreat into the woods. It's a good thing Whittle has already left for London. They'll never find us without dogs." Then he remembered Viktor's transformation. "Oh shit," he whispered.

Tara's guard came up with two gun belts with holstered pistols and spare ammunition, as well as two Daewoo USAS-12 automatic shotguns. He had a HK G3 rifle slung over his shoulder. By now all of them could hear the rotors of the approaching helicopter, and he nodded to Tara as he handed a gun belt to her. "We don't have any more rifles, but the shotguns might help against that… against Viktor. He tossed a canvas bag on the ground. "More shot shells. Good luck." With that he ran off to join the other two guards.

Her father had gone into the building so Tara strapped on the gun belt and then slung the shotgun and bag of ammunition on her shoulders. There was a metre tall concrete planter filled with earth in front of the main building, and she took cover behind it, knowing her father could easily see her when he came out, and she could quickly retreat into the building from where she was if forced to.

The unidentified helicopter rapidly approached, and one of the guards stepped out into the open and raised his ground-to-air transceiver to his mouth, warning the aircraft away. A second guard waved it away with light cones, but the helicopter continued to approach. The first guard replaced the transceiver on his belt and unslung his rifle. He raised it to his shoulder as he and the other guard started to back up towards the cover of a heavy-duty fork lift.

Tara heard one of the guards, she couldn't tell which one because of the distance, cry out in alarm, and then she saw all three of them fire towards the helicopter which was almost on top of them. It was less than fifteen metres from the guards when the pilot turned the aircraft's side towards them and Tara cried out in shock when a long tongue of flame shot out from the open side door with a stuttering roar. Being intimately involved in hand and aircraft mounted weaponry, she recognised that the fire was from a Gatling gun and realised that they had to be using tracer rounds because the weapon produced a continuous orange beam of light like a science-fiction ray gun. Glowing fragments of metal and concrete blasted in all directions as the beam swept across the helipad – and then it hit the foremost guard, who literally exploded in a spray of blood and shredded body parts. Tara wanted to shoot at the murderous helicopter, but knew her shotgun would be useless at her present distance, and the mini-gun would sweep her away like an insect before she could get within effective range. Not even her new strength and speed would help her dodge three thousand rounds per minute. She knew that she had to get her father away before they landed and Viktor came after them. In the moment it took for her to make that decision, the other two guards had been blasted to pieces as well and the Gatling gun fell silent. Staying low and grinding her teeth in rage, Tara ran back towards the tower building, and although she didn't realise it she was moving so fast that she was just a blur.

Without a conscious decision, her "sonar" came on and she darted through the door and around obstacles without slowing down, her breathing automatically adjusting for the need to continuously produce the ultrasonic sounds required.

Rowland was just coming out of his office wearing a backpack and with his auto shotgun in his hands when his daughter seemingly appeared out of nowhere in front of him. "Good god! Tara! How did – "

"The men are all dead. We have to go, right now!" Tara pushed her father towards the back of the building. There was a service exit at the rear left side that led to an access road and across that to the forest.

Her father obeyed without argument, but as he ran he said, "But what about Viktor?"

Understanding what her father meant, Tara said, "I don't think he can change into a werewolf at will. He may be a bit stronger and faster than normal in his human form, but nothing like the monster we saw unless he is hurt or frightened enough to produce a surge of adrenaline."

He had his hand on the access lever of the back door when the air shook with an incredibly loud explosion that came from the front of the building. "Flashbang grenade. They're coming!"

They were in the utility section of the building where the backup generator and the main fuse boxes were located. Tara darted to the wall and flipped the main breaker switch, plunging the entire complex into darkness. Still able to see with her sonar, she deactivated the backup generator as well before rejoining her father. "That should slow them down a bit." She took his arm in the darkness and led him out of the building. With her sonar she scanned her surroundings for something to jam the door, but there was nothing except the heavy metal rubbish skip that sat beside the exit. It normally required a fork lift to move it, but she had to do something or they were dead. "Don't move Dad. I'll be right back." She ran over to the end of the skip and put both her hands against the end and pushed. Her shoes slid on the concrete and the bin barely budged. She spread her feet and bent her knees, feeling her heart pound in her chest. If she didn't block the door soon it would be too late. Pressing her cheek against the painted metal and she heaved with all her might. The afterburner warning appeared on her HUD and suddenly the skip was moving, sliding across the concrete as if it was ice and coming to a halt directly in front of the door. The afterburner alert disappeared and the skip was an immovable mass again. She found herself panting, all her muscles trembled, and she suddenly felt ravenous. She realised that only seconds had passed and she hurried back to her father's side. "That should hold them for a moment. Come on, we need to go."

Although he could barely see in the gloom, it was obvious from the sounds what his daughter had done and Rowland shook his head in amazement as he allowed her to guide him into the forbidding blackness of the forest.

When they were about a hundred metres past the tree line, she heard a pounding on the door which only lasted a couple of minutes. "They're going to the front door and around the building," she guessed. With her sonar vision, she felt confident of outrunning her pursuers in the forest even if they had night vision glasses. It would be another hour or more before the sun rose enough to see, and the forest made it even darker. The only unknown factor was Viktor. They had no way of knowing what kind of powers he might possess apart from speed and maniacal strength. She judged that she was faster than he was in his lupine form, but she couldn't outrun the werewolf Viktor with her father in tow.

***

Hoch stopped at the edge of the forest. "We are too few to hunt them down in there, and none of us are woodsmen."

"I could catch them if I were …. "

"But you're not," Hoch said, wondering if the traitorous pilot would come up with the obvious solution.

Viktor looked at the darkness of the forest and back at Hoch. "All of you go back to the helicopter. I'll go after them alone."

Hoch nodded and silently turned and stalked away, followed by his men.

Viktor waited until they were well out of sight and then drew the pistol that Hoch had given him. He didn't recognise the make, but he knew it was a nine millimetre automatic. He hoped Hoch would not mind losing it. Gritting his teeth he pointed the muzzle at the side of his thigh well away from the femoral artery and squeezed the trigger. The hammer blow to his leg and the blinding pain made him drop the pistol and fall onto his uninjured side, but even as he fell he could feel the change and his lips pulled back in a triumphant grin that twisted into a snarl as his face started to elongate. Hair sprouted, and his body twisted and grew. Almost immediately he felt the bullet wound begin to heal and he barked a laugh when the bullet popped out of his flesh and fell on the ground. Bounding upright, he tested his leg and then sniffed the air. The craving for blood pushed logical thought into the back of his mind, and for a moment he was tempted to go after the fresher scent of Hoch and the others, but enough rational thought remained for him to understand that they were already in the air and out of his reach. Then the scent of a human female tickled his nostrils and he roared. Tara! He remembered the name and how she looked. This time he would have her. Dropping onto all fours, he loped off into the forest. He couldn't see in total darkness, but his night vision was greatly superior to that of a human, and combined with his keen sense of smell, Tara's trail was as clear as a marked path to him and he set off, running smoothly and silently through the forest in search of his prey. An irritating little voice in his mind told him not to kill Tara or her father, but the need to hunt was too great. He was going to taste raw bloody flesh and nothing was going to stop him.

***

Tara heard the crack of a pistol and the familiar growling roar of the werewolf. "Viktor's coming, and he's managed to change. I think he shot himself or had somebody else shoot him."

"That's crazy," Rowland gasped, his chest burning from the constant blind running through the trees and bushes, guided only by Tara's grip on his wrist and her whispered warnings of obstacles.

"Not if he's sure that he'll heal as soon as he changes. It looks like that part of the legends at least is true, although I wish the part about a full moon was as well."

"We don't ... know that ... it's not," her father said, breathlessly. "He might ... still ... involuntarily change ... during a full ... moon."

"Hope he does, the bastard. Right in front of a big game hunter's convention."

"You're not even panting," Rowland said.

She grinned in the darkness. "No I'm not. Wish this had happened before the last marathon. Watch out, there's a log coming up."

"We can't … outrun … him," Rowland said. "Or at least … I can't."

Tara stopped and grabbed his arm. "Oh no you don't. There's not going to be any heroic rear-guard actions today."

Her father shook his head. "I can't keep this pace up much longer, Tara."

"We don't have to. I have an idea, but I've been looking for the right spot, and I think we've found it just up ahead."

***

Tara flashed her small LED survival torch at her father who waved back, knowing that she could see him.

He was perched on a branch over fifteen metres up the bole of a huge old pine tree with a length of rope going around his waist and the tree, as a safety line. He had adjusted the sling of his shotgun so that he could comfortably point it straight down and wiped his hand dry on his trousers so that it wouldn't slip on the grip when he fired it. He could never have climbed up so far on his own. Tara had basically carried him piggy back up the tree, climbing it like a monkey.

When Tara was certain that her father was secure on his perch, she had executed the second part of her plan, which she had not described to Rowland because he would have shouted at her. She had climbed out on the branch until it was almost too thin to support her. Then gathering herself like a flying squirrel, she launched herself into thin air, arms and legs outstretched. The thrust of her legs was so strong that she actually flew upwards and then down in an arc as she crossed the six metre gap from the tree to another huge pine.

Without her sonar, the leap would have been impossible no matter how strong and agile she was, but even though her mind told her it was impossible, she rotated her body in mid-air and struck the tree trunk with feet and hands, the impact making the tree shake as if struck by a storm. Her fingers sank into the bark like steel hooks and for a moment she just clung there, letting her mind catch up with the fact that she had survived the leap and had not tumbled down to the ground like a sack of potatoes. She glanced around and picked the nearest branch that looked like it would support her weight. Once she was securely perched, she leaned back against the bole to catch her breath and calm down. As a test-pilot she was used to taking chances, but it was not the same when she was flying with nothing except her skin wrapped around her. When her hands were steady again and the claw-like tips had been re-absorbed into her fingers, she removed the silver chain from around her neck and selected two shotgun shells from the ammo bag. Using the Swiss Army knife that she always carried on her key-chain, she cut the chain into two sections. Then one by one she pried open the shot shells, dumped half the lead pellets and replaced them with a piece of silver chain before closing the shell up again. She had no idea if silver would have any effect at all on Viktor, but she needed every advantage she could get if she and her father were going to survive the next few minutes, and so far the legends had been right.

***

The werewolf entered the small clearing that was bracketed by two huge trees. The scent of both his prey was strong, and led straight to one of the trees. He circled the base of the tree, sniffing the ground, but there was no trail leading away from it. His huge fang filled jaws opened in a lupine grin. In the end the prey always climbed a tree or went to ground. He sat on his haunches and looked up. After a second his keen night vision caught the tiny incongruous movement high up in the tree. His grin changed to a snarl as he rose up onto his hind legs. Unlike a real wolf, he was quite capable of climbing, even though his rear legs would not allow him to cling to the trunk or a branch. He would go up there and rip them apart. Their only escape would be to jump to their death. His finger claws dug into the tree, crunching the bark and driving into the living wood like climbing spikes. An explosion above him made him lift his muzzle, just in time to receive a face full of lead pellets. Although the wounds began to heal almost immediately, the shotgun blast did hurt, and he quickly lowered his head, instinctively protecting his eyes. A second cluster of lead shot smashed into the top of his skull, then another, and he growled as he hunched down against the tree as if seeking shelter from the rain.

***

Her father's gunfire was her signal. What she was about to attempt was suicidal so she didn't allow herself to think about it and simply dived off of the tree. Although she had no evidence that it would work, it felt right and natural. If the alien species was a gliding predator, it made sense that it would attack its prey by diving at it from above. She was fast and incredibly strong now, but she still didn't fancy her chances in hand to hand or claw to claw combat with the monster that Viktor had become. She needed an advantage, and this was it. She plunged downwards feet first, her arms outstretched like wings, instinctively stabilising her flight and helping to aim the soles of her boots at the middle of the werewolf's shoulders. The thrust of her legs as she leapt from her perch had imparted an arc to her fall, and if she timed it just right she would smash into Viktor like a battering ram. Her boot shod feet had no tearing claws, but the sheer impact of her plunging strike would be deadly. She heard her father's shotgun fall silent and milliseconds later she slammed into the werewolf's body like an air-to-ground missile.

Viktor had no time to react, and the terrific impact smashed his face and head against the tree, sending it whipping back even as the blow against his shoulders and spine crushed his chest against the immovable bole, breaking his neck with a sharp crack and snapping ribs. Incredibly, despite the tremendous damage, he managed to whip his body around and lash out with his claws, and he felt a surge of savage satisfaction when he felt his claws cut into flesh, and he inhaled the scent of human blood even as his momentum spun him around to flop limply onto the moss covered ground.

Tara bit back a scream of pain when Viktor's claws raked across her belly, shredding both the tough fabric of her overalls as well as skin and flesh. The impact of her fall would have broken the legs of an ordinary human, but instead her knees flexed, absorbing the force and then her legs kicked her away from the werewolf in a backwards somersault that turned into an uncontrolled spinning fall when his claws had caught her. His blow would have eviscerated her if she had been standing still, but because she had already been moving away, his claws had just raked deep bloody wounds. Ignoring the agony of her torn belly, she continued to roll until she was sure that she was out of Viktor's reach and then sprang up onto one knee. She slid the auto-shotgun around on its sling and took aim. In her combined night vision and sonar, she could see the werewolf's body jerking and writhing, its broken bones already moving back into position, although the broken neck seemed to be giving it more trouble than the rest. Its head had just twisted back into place with a grating pop when she found her aim and fired, hoping that in its injured condition she might be able to inflict enough damage to keep it down long enough for her and her father to escape. Inspired by hundreds of zombie films and computer games, she automatically aimed for the head. To her amazement, the werewolf uttered a howl of agony as she fired shot after shot in aimed semi-automatic mode into its head. Hope flared in her chest. The silver chain! Somehow it really did affect him. She rocked back in alarm when the monster clambered to its feet with a hand pressed against its face. But instead of attacking her, it turned and staggered off into the forest.

Rowland could barely see anything except when Tara's muzzle flashes lit up the scene beneath him in strobing images that resembled some bizarre stop-motion animation. But the monster's scream of pain was unmistakable, as was the sound of it crashing its way through the undergrowth and snapping off low hanging branches in its flight. He immediately began hurriedly unfastening his lifeline and he jumped in fright when Tara's hand slapped against his ankle. "Bloody hell! You nearly gave me a heart attack. How did you … never mind." He found the image of his daughter scrambling up the tree like a giant spider disturbing.

"Ready to go?" Tara asked cheerfully. She was glad that he couldn't see the blood that stained the front of her ventilated overalls. To her relief, the wounds themselves had almost completely healed, although it still hurt to move. She was also feeling ravenous, with visions of rare steaks and juicy hamburgers insistently tormenting her. It made sense that she would be hungry, since all the energy to power her amazing exertions and healing had to have come from somewhere. More disturbing was the persistent aching of her gums around her canine teeth. Since the legends of the effects of silver on werewolves had proven true, it was not hard to believe that the vampire's legendary thirst for blood might also be real. Fortunately, she felt absolutely no desire to bite her father in the neck. She climbed up onto the branch next to him. "Come on then. Get on my back and I'll get us down – ow! What did you do that for?" she said indignantly when he slapped her on the back of the head.

"I nearly died of fright when you jumped off the tree like that. I thought that your plan was just to distract me, when you had actually decided to bribe Viktor with your corpse." He said, glad that no one was around to see him hanging from his daughter's back like a battered knapsack. He was even gladder that he couldn't see what was happening when they descended the tree at what seemed like free-fall speed. His relief when her feet touched the ground was quickly replaced by concern when Tara staggered and leaned drunkenly against the tree. "Tara, what's wrong?" He reached out to support her and his fingers found the jagged slashes in the front of her suit. "My god, are you hurt?"

"Viktor got in a good shot at me, but it's all right, I'm healing. That's not the problem. I'm feeling dizzy and shaky, and really bloody ravenous – and my teeth itch."

Rowland frowned and patted at his overalls. "Wait a sec, I recall I had … where did I put that bugger … ah!" His hand delved into a side pocket and produced a slightly crushed and bent chocolate bar.

Tara's nose twitched at the scent of the chocolate and peanuts. "Gimme!" she cried and snatched it from his hand, barely pausing to strip the wrapper off before stuffing it into her mouth even as she took his hand again and began walking.

Stumbling after her Rowland said, "I thought that um, people with your problem, craved only blood when they got hungry. That's what all the books say, anyway."

Struggling to speak through a mouthful of gooey chocolate, Tara said, "From my new memories, I think the bat aliens did drink blood. I have a memory of the pilot snacking from a flexible packet of what seemed like blood. Anyone infected with this thing and who didn't have the nano-interface would probably be driven to eat the way the aliens did. She chuckled. "The 'Fuel Critical' warning has been flashing in my HUD ever since my fight with Viktor." The painful gnawing pangs of hunger faded almost immediately after she swallowed the last of the bar, and the warning in her HUD changed to "Fuel Low". She smacked her lips and said, "That was good, but I'm going to need to eat again soon. Maybe I can catch something. Do they have rabbits around here?"

The sky was beginning to lighten and Rowland stared at the back of his daughter's head. She had never gone hunting before in her life and had learned to shoot at a firing range. He wondered what other changes the "medikit" had made and would continue to make to her mind. "There's a highway about ten kilometres in that direction," he said, using the glow of the rising sun to orient himself.

Tara slapped her shotgun. "No one is going to stop for two strangers carrying these and looking like they went through a car wash without a car."

"Perhaps I can hide behind a bush with the guns while you thumb a ride. Show them your cleavage or something. It always works on the telly."

Tara's eyebrows shot up in mock amazement. "Father, are you really telling me to use my feminine wiles to get us a ride? Perhaps I should strip off entirely. That should stop the traffic."

"I promise not to look," he said with a grin.

Tara sighed. "I'd be tempted to try it if I thought it might actually work. No, we're going to have to do it the hard way."

Even with the rising of the sun, the air was still uncomfortably cold, especially now that they had stopped moving, and Rowland blew into his hands and rubbed vigorously as he waited behind a bush like a really determined flasher. It had been almost two hours since they had started waiting for the right vehicle and he was worried that Viktor or his cohorts might catch up with them. Driven by increasing hunger, Tara had left him to go hunting in the forest. He jumped when Tara tapped him on the shoulder.

"This sounds like it. Get ready."

Rowland looked at her and did a double take. She was positively glowing with health and he could have sworn she looked younger and her cheeks ruddier. "Did you …?"

Tara nodded. "Hare. Big one."

Looking her up and down he said, "But there's no blood on you or anything. If you ate it raw, how did you…" She pulled back her lips in a mock snarl and he took an involuntary step backwards. "Bloody heck…" Although he had intellectually accepted the idea that his daughter now fit all the legendary descriptions of a vampire except for sensitivity to sunlight and the need to sleep in a grave, seeing the sharp extended canines in her mouth was a visceral shock.

"They're hollow and retractable, more like a snake's fangs than a bat's." She shrugged. "It was tidier than ripping the poor thing apart and eating it raw. You still get fur in your mouth though." She grimaced. "It's coming. Get on my back."

"This is really humiliating."

"I promise not to tell your mates. Now stop grumbling and hold on tight. This is going to be worse than the tree."

The huge lorry pulling a 40 foot (12.19 m) container rumbled into sight, slowing to turn the corner that they had deliberately chosen for the purpose, and when it was almost past, Tara straightened up from her crouch and began to run.

Rowland was surprised at how smooth it felt. He had been expecting it to feel like riding a motorcycle over rail-road ties. Her hair slapped against his face and got into his mouth, and he didn't realise how fast they were moving until the rear of the container loomed over them. Incredibly, she was actually catching up with the accelerating lorry while carrying a full grown man on her back as well as weapons, ammunition, and the laptop and external hard disks that contained all his files. He almost fell off her back when she sprang up and against the back of the huge container, aided by a grip on the container's locking bar. There were more nauseating movements and then suddenly they were both lying on the top of the container, and Tara wasn't even breathing hard.

"Are you all right?" Tara shouted over the roar of the lorry and the rushing torrent of air.

"Just fine. It was all quite invigorating really," Rowland said insouciantly.

***

"You've got to be joking!"

Rowland shook his head. "This is a small resort town Tara, and it's the week end. I'm afraid the Gucci boutique was closed. The only place open selling clothes was the ski shop. The only thing they had in your size was this, and only because someone placed an order and didn't come for it.

Tara stared at the skin tight Spyder race suit in horror. "I won't even be able to wear underwear in this thing."

"Stop grumbling. It's cutting edge technology and I had to pay nearly a thousand US dollars for that 'thing' as you call it. It's got that special gel impact padding on the knees and elbows, or at least that's what the saleswoman told me. You're fortunate it's in black and not the usual garish colours."

"And these?" she said, holding up the red and black ski boots with stylish clasps running down the side. "I'll look like a superhero wannabe!"

"At least they had socks, as well as these big sports bags that will hold the shotguns," Rowland said calmly. "I'd say we were lucky."

Still grumbling, Tara took her new clothing into the public rest room to change out of her torn and blood soaked overalls.

Rowland failed to hide his grin when Tara came out again. "Wow. You're always in overalls or baggy flight suits. I never realised how hot you are."

"Father! Is that really an appropriate thing to say to your daughter? People will think you're some kind of perv." Then she grinned and looked down at herself. "I do look pretty hot in this, don't I?" She didn't tell him, but when she had undressed and washed the blood from her body, she realised that all the tiny flaws, imperfections and childhood scars on her body had disappeared. Her skin was inhumanly perfect, and she would have bet anything that her innards were that way too. She wasn't sure if she was pleased or terrified.

***

The screaming agony of being shot in the face by that bitch Tara had made him stagger blindly into the woods, crashing into trees and bushes, and tripping over rocks. In the end he had ended the pain only by digging the piece of silver chain out of the flesh of his face with his claws. He had blacked out immediately after the last section of chain had come out. When he woke, he was back in human form, the bloody length of silver chain clenched in his hand. Although he felt sick and hungover, he nodded to himself. He had just learned something important. His new werewolf form was violently allergic to what appeared to be silver. He made a note to have the chain analysed. He felt too sick to continue the pursuit, and he would be too slow and weak in his naked human form even if he tried. Despite his misery, he smiled. It wasn't over yet. He knew where Tara and her father would be headed. He just had to get back to Hoch and then on to the city of Braşov. He looked down at the chain, which he remembered seeing around Tara's neck. She wouldn't be so lucky the next time they met.

***

Braşov was the seventh largest city in Romania, and had been home to the first aircraft manufacturer in the country, which was why Rowland had picked the city for his company's Romanian office. Situated along the busy Calea Bucureşti, it was centrally located as well as being near a couple of supermarkets and a hospital.

Rowland had the foresight to grab all the cash at the airfield, and after Tara had stuffed herself with enough grilled mincemeat rolls, musaca, and venison stew to feed an army, they had left the town in a four-wheel drive Dacia Duster that he had been forced to buy at an extortionate price, but only after Tara had filled the back seat with all the take away food and snacks that she could find.

During the eventful drive through the dubiously maintained Romanian road system and its obstacle course of potholes, maniac drivers, livestock, wagons, and numerous speed traps, Tara had come to like the skin tight suit. She had been forced to use her new found powers several times during the journey to get them out of trouble, including lifting the front of the car out of a pothole big enough to swallow the front half of the vehicle, and the suit had adapted well to both the stress and the odd changes to her body that had left the seams of her overalls in tatters. By adding a selection of T-shirts, sweaters, and jackets to her wardrobe, she was able to give herself a wide variety of looks. Her new musculature meant that she hardly missed her bra at all and the tightness of the suit reduced the amount of stare attracting bouncing to a bearable level and the tops hid the Olympic gymnast-class muscles that rippled all over her torso.

"Finally. We're nearly there," Rowland said as he turned the car into the Calea Bucureşti. They were almost within sight of their rented office when Tara grabbed his arm hard enough to make him wince.

"Stop the car. Pull over in front of that shop."

"Can't you wait? There's a better selection of food in the supermarket, and we're almost – "

"He's here!" Tara snapped tersely.

"Who's here?" her father asked in confusion.

"Viktor. He's here. I can sense him."

Rowland knew better than to question his daughter's abilities by now. "Damn! He's smarter than I thought. They must be waiting for us. We would have walked right into their trap if you hadn't..." He slammed his fist against the steering wheel. "What do we do now? Our passports are in the office safe, and we have to destroy all the files in the office." He had already called London and Whittle and the management there were packing up all the records and hard drives, and sending all the staff on holiday. He couldn't do anything about the main fabrication and assembly plant, but a report to the police of a fictional terrorist threat would make it a difficult target, at least for a while. He slapped his forehead. "What am I talking about? You are what they want most of all. But still, our passports..."

Tara shook her head. "I'm not letting Viktor get his hairy hands on your designs and technology. Who knows, in his present state he might be able to survive the nano-interface implant, and that would give him full control over his werewolf powers. We can't allow that."

Rowland bit his lip. "I hadn't thought of that. You're right. But how can we get to the office if they're waiting for us?"

"We can't. But I can. Park the car properly and go to that café over there and wait for me."

Rowland was used to seeing his daughter fly off in unproven and possibly dangerous aircraft, so he didn't protest. "Just be careful. You know what will happen to you if you're caught. You're strong, but they got Dracula in the end."

She kissed him on the cheek. "Don't worry. I may be dressed like a superhero, but I'm more Spiderman than Thor. Sneaky is best."

"Make sure you are. All right then. I'll wait fifteen minutes and then call the office."

Tara glanced towards the office building and nodded. "Once I'm in position I should be able to hear whatever is going on in the office, so I know if there's anyone in there with Krisztina when they respond to your call."

Rowland gave her a hug. "Love you."

She hugged him back. "Luvv you too." With that she set off towards the office. Simply walking down the road would be asking for trouble, so she made her way behind and through the intervening buildings as much as she could. She had donned a hoodie with a Batman logo on its chest, which she thought was ironically appropriate. They would be watching for a duo, so with the hood up and walking solo she hoped to avoid being spotted. It was unlikely that Viktor would be sitting around in his furry form, so her scent would not be a concern. When she reached the building next to their office, she went around to its rear, glanced around to make sure there were no witnesses, and then started climbing. There was no convenient drain pipe, but the building's façade had enough "architectural features" to provide a climbable surface, and moments later she was on the roof. Looking around, she was heartily glad that she had not become sensitive to sunlight. She crept up to the front edge and peered over. She immediately spotted the car parked across the road, the driver staring fixedly at the entrance to the building that housed the Harker Industries branch office. Looking straight down, she saw a man leaning against the wall and pretending to read a newspaper. She knew he was pretending because although he was holding the paper in front of him, his head was turned to watch the next-door building. She frowned. It bothered her that she hadn't spotted Viktor. On the other hand, his werewolf form wasn't the type to hide in ambush, but she still wished that she could have brought her shotgun. On the way to Braşov she had purchased a handful of cheap silver chains and made an entire box of customised shot shells.

She went over to the side adjoining the office, looked down to check for nosy pedestrians, and then across at the other roof. It would be stupid to make a spectacular leap only to be impaled on a pipe. The next roof was half a metre higher than the one she was on, but she felt sure that she could make the jump. She took off the hoodie, backed up as far as she could, took a deep breath, and started to run. The alien system had to be getting ever more integrated with her mind, because a countdown in metres and a red dotted line appeared in her HUD going from her feet to the edge of the other roof, and the ground-speed indicator came to life. By this time she didn't even notice it when the system made her utter the inaudible ultrasonic cries that powered her sonar and it felt as natural as breathing.

When she was a step away from the edge she made a small skip, landed on both feet and then sprang off the edge of the building, the thrust of her legs throwing her high and forward into the air with her arms outstretched forming a "Y" shape as if she had wing-flaps joining her arms to her torso and legs. She flew across the eight metre gap that separated the buildings, and for a second she felt a cold chill that told her that she had done something very stupid and that she was going to die, the same feeling she got when the plane she was testing stalled and a section of wing snapped and spun away from the fuselage. Then her hands hooked over the edge of the roof and her feet curled forward to absorb the impact of slamming into the wall. Concrete crumbled under her clawed fingernails, her bent legs thrust again at just the right angle, and she somersaulted over the parapet to land on both feet on the roof like a dismounting gymnast. "Damn. That was seriously impressive," she said to herself.

Her hand went to a pouch on her "utility belt", the military webbing belt that she had bought at a camping supply store and extracted a chocolate bar which she stuffed in her mouth. She grinned. Her female friends were going to die with envy when they learned that she could stuff herself with a dozen bars of chocolate a day and not gain a gram of weight. She patted her washboard abs complacently as she jogged over to the opposite end of the roof. Their office, which was two floors down, had a window overlooking a row of lower shop houses and she ought to be safe from observation. It would have been cool to climb down the wall head first, but that would have meant taking off her boots and socks, so instead she simply lowered herself over the edge and went down hand over hand, her fingers digging into the recessed joins between the dark brown blocks of the textured wall. She stopped when she was next to the office window and clung there as the clock in her HUD counted down the fifteen minutes. She could hear movement inside the office, but she couldn't be sure how many people there were. She jumped in surprise when the phone rang, sounding shockingly loud to her augmented hearing.

The ringing stopped, and Tara heard Krisztina's voice say, "Harker Industries" and then "good morning" in Romanian. "Oh, good morning Mr Harker! Is there something I can do for you? Yes, I'm fine. I have some letters and packages for you. Are you coming into the office?"

The tone of the last question sounded strange to Tara, almost hesitant or unwilling. She decided to risk a peek and shifted her body so that she could see into the office with one eye, but the curtain still blocked the view. Suddenly only the sounds in the office grew louder, while all the other environmental noises dimmed in her consciousness as if she had a microphone's noise cancellation function built into her head, and she heard the rustle of clothing and the breathing of a second person. She quickly pulled back from the window. Krisztina wasn't alone!

"Yes, yes, all right, goodbye Mr Harker. Take care and give my regards to Tara."

Tara heard the click of the line cutting off on the speaker-phone and then Krisztina spoke again.

"I did what you told me to. Please don't hurt me."

"I need you to do one more thing for me," a man's voice said in English. The accent indicated that he was American.

"What is it?" Krisztina asked, obviously trying to please.

"Die."

The crack of the silenced pistol made Tara jump, and she stiffened in rage and fear. The bastard had killed an innocent girl and Tara's friend! She heard the sound of dripping blood and of the man settling down in a chair. It seemed that he wasn't going away. Tara frowned. Why had he killed Krisztina when there was the possibility that her father might call back? But the more important question was how she was going to get hold of their passports with the murderer sitting in front of the safe? She couldn't think of a scene from a film where a vampire was faced with a similar problem. They usually just flew in through the window or walked in the door.

She was afraid that if she smashed the window it would alert the rest of the ambushers. So it would have to be the door. Then an idea came to her and she smiled.

***

The gunman calmly swivelled the chair and pointed his silenced automatic pistol towards the door. A glance confirmed that the dead secretary was not visible from the doorway. Three quick strides brought him to the wall beside the entrance. He knew it wasn't Harker or his daughter, since his team mates would have called to warn him. "Yes?"

"Delivery," a female voice said in Romanian.

"English?"

"Uh, de-li-vi-ree?"

"Leave it in front of the door," the gunman said.

"Sig-na-choor. You give."

The gunman rolled his eyes. "Fucking morons". He hid the arm holding the gun behind the door and then cautiously opened it wide enough to peer out. He frowned when no female face greeted him. "Hey! Delivery lady. Where the fuck are you?" He looked down and there was a large cardboard box sitting on the carpet of the hallway. "What the..."

Tara waited until he opened the door and glanced both ways along the hallway before dropping from the ceiling. Guided by her sonar, her grip closed accurately around the barrel of the gun and ripped it from his hand before he could react. Wary of her own strength, she punched him in the middle of the chest with the flat of her palm, sending him flying backwards into the office to crash against a drafting table. Both he and the table tumbled to the ground. Tara kicked the empty box into the office and followed it in. She turned to close and lock the door, and then spun around again, just in time to receive the darts from the Taser gun in her belly.

79

The man grinned evilly as he pressed the trigger button. "You hit like a girl," he said. For safety, the Taser was designed to deliver a ten second burst of fifty thousand volts at a frequency that makes the target lose control of their muscles. However the current could be made continuous simply by holding the trigger down. Needless to say, this was what he did.

Tara dropped like a rock, every muscle locked in spasm, barely able to breathe, her face and elbow slamming painfully against the floor.

Still holding down the Taser's trigger, the gunman strolled over and picked up his pistol which had fallen from Tara's nerveless fingers. "I wonder if your heart would stop before this thing runs out of batteries. They warned me that you were dangerous, but I was right about that Viktor character being a pussy. He just couldn't admit to being beaten up by a girl, so he made up some stupid story." He swung his foot and kicked Tara in the ribs, and then once more in the belly. "They want you alive, but nobody said you had to be able to walk. I don't think they'll mind much if I shoot out your kneecaps before making delivery."

It took all of her acting ability to maintain the convulsions when the pulsing shocks faded and then suddenly died. Her HUD reappeared and she almost grinned when the icon that indicated a system auto-bypass of a short circuit blinked. The alien medical nanites had adapted her body to the nerve scrambling current. She suspected that she would be immune to Tasers from now on. She was almost like the fictional Borg from Star Trek!

"Say bye-bye to your knees," the man said, pointing the swollen cylindrical end of the suppressor at her right knee. The pistol barked, still ear poundingly loud inside the confines of a concrete walled room despite the "silencer". His jaw dropped when the bullet hit the floor, penetrated the carpeting, and ricocheted to bury itself inside an innocent photocopy machine. "Wha..." Then he screamed and his knees sagged when what felt like giant bolt cutters crushed the bones of both his wrists into splinters. The gun and Taser fell half-way to the floor before they were snatched out of the air, and he stared in shocked puzzlement when the woman he had been about to shoot suddenly stood erect in front of him.

"I hit like a girl do I?" Snarling in fury, Tara punched out with all her strength using the hand that was holding the pistol.

The killer grunted and wheezed when the cylindrical silencer drove through his sternum like a hydraulic ram and crushed his heart into pulp. His eyes bulged and then he collapsed, folding up like an off-duty Muppet.

"Yuk!" Tara wrinkled her nose in disgust at the splatter of blood and bone fragments that clung to her hand. She grabbed a handful of tissues and carefully wiped down the pistol and Taser, even though she doubted that her vampire form fingerprints would be recognisable. She knew Krisztina had a tub of wet tissues in her drawer and she used those to clean her hand before adding them to the plastic bag she recovered from the waste paper basket. Her DNA in the rest of the office wouldn't matter because it was already all over the place, especially the desk and computer work station that she used when she was in Brașov. She had no idea what the police would make of the scene, but the gun had been used to kill Krisztina and trace residue of the gunfire would be on the dead man's hand and clothes. Since he was a foreigner and the dead girl an innocent local, she was willing to bet that the cops would not be trying too hard to find his killer. They would definitely not be looking for a young woman when they saw the man's injuries.

Once she was cleaned up as best she could

manage, she unlocked the safe and extracted the precious passports, the petty cash that was kept in the office, and a few other documents. She closed and locked the safe so the police would not be looking for stolen valuables and prepared to leave. She had avoided looking at Krisztina's body up till then, but now she took a long hard look to remind herself why she had killed the man and what her new enemies were capable of. She looked around with a sigh and went to the door. For once she was pleased that the corridors did not have closed circuit video cameras. She stood in front of the closed door and listened hard. She heard the hiss and hum of the ventilation system. It was a Monday morning, so there was the sound of people in the other offices, and all the sounds of computers and office equipment. However there did not seem to be anyone immediately outside the door. She opened the door a crack and when no one crashed in or shot at her, she slipped out and let the door click shut behind her. Being a secure office, it needed a key to get in, or someone to open it from the inside, so no one was going to accidentally wander in to discover the horror scene within. Even the cleaners required permission to enter and did not possess a passkey.

With everything safely in her backpack, she made her way out and away from the building the same way that she had come in, repeating the scary leap between buildings with more confidence this time. She risked a peek around the front and saw that the watchers were still in their car. Once more she wondered what had happened to Viktor. Perhaps he had been more severely hurt by the silver than she had thought. With hoodie back on and hood raised, she made her way back to where she had left her father, trying to look as unsuspicious and unvampire-like as possible. She giggled at the thought of trying to sneak around with a long black cloak and trailing a cloud of fog.

The smile vanished when she approached the café

where her father was meant to be waiting and saw the flashing lights of the police cars and ambulances. It seemed an impossible coincidence that it did not involve her father and she felt a rush of panic, with the example of Krisztina's death fresh in her memory. Had they killed him? She forced herself to breathe and to calm down. The gunman in the office had used a Taser on her instead of his gun, so the chances were that they had done the same with her father. She didn't dare approach the café since they might still be around waiting for her to turn up. Which brought her back to the question of how they had known he was here. Then it came to her. His telephone call! With enough money and influence it wouldn't be hard to bribe someone in the telephone company or even the police to maintain a tap and trace on the office phone.

Tara's Romanian was good enough to ask simple questions and understand the answer, so she stopped one of the crowd who had been gawking at the police perimeter. "Excuse me, what happened over there?"

The man shrugged. "Some kind of fight. Several people were hurt. I heard it was a kidnapping. They caught it on a security camera."

Tara thanked the man politely, even though she wanted to scream and tear things apart. She looked around and walked to a small grocery shop. She paid the owner to use their telephone and dialled her father's number.

"Hello? Is that you Tara? We have your father. Why don't we meet and we can talk. Otherwise something bad might happen to him."

Tara numbly put down the phone, thanked the storekeeper and walked away, trying to keep her pace casual, bored. Viktor's voice had answered her father's phone. They had him. She considered giving herself up as Viktor had suggested, but the idea didn't make sense. Both of them were equally valuable to whomever Viktor was working for. They wouldn't let him go. But on the other hand, they wouldn't hurt him either. They needed his knowledge and skills. Her eyes fell upon their car. They hadn't found it or made her father tell them where it was. He had probably put up enough of a fight that they had been forced to stun or knock him out and take him away before the police arrived to investigate the disturbance. That meant they didn't have his files. Without that, even her father would have to re-do a lot of his work, even if his kidnappers reverse engineered whatever they had managed to salvage from the downed DNIA prototype, which according to the security team's report from the plateau had not been a lot. She had to take the files and test data to safety. That would give her something to bargain with. That meant taking all of it back to England.

Chapter Five

The office of Harker Industries was located along Old Street in East London in the so called Tech City area. Most of the companies in the area were in the IT field, which Rowland had considered a plus, since it meant less snoopy neighbours in the same line of business, but at the same time providing good infrastructure and places for lunch.

Tara had been tempted to rent a car at Heathrow, but decided that the Tube would be less conspicuous. After all that had happened, it felt good to be back in London and in the familiar surroundings of an Underground train, even if she was surrounded by foreigners lugging suitcases and backpacks. She changed to the Northern Line at Kings Cross and got off at Old Street station. She had been forced to abandon all her weapons, and in order to move fast she only had one piece of luggage, which contained all the precious electronic files and a few items of clothing. It was past eight at night by the time she walked around the Old Street roundabout and past The Nelson's Retreat. The sight of the pub and the various little takeaways and cafés made her stomach rumble and she paused in front of the fire station, visions of a kebab making her mouth water despite the hot dog and Coke she had snatched at King's Cross station.

She frowned when her HUD's IFF indicator began to blink, indicating a friendly aircraft within transponder range. This was clearly impossible, since there were no flying Harker Industries aircraft in London. What on Earth was the system trying to tell her, she pondered. For a second the irrational hope that her father had somehow escaped and found cher made her heart leap, but she dismissed the idea, anger making her hands shake. She looked around and didn't see any familiar faces. She was about to turn back towards the pub when a black BMW 3 series skidded to a stop in front of her. She took a step backwards when the back doors opened and two men with balaclavas covering their heads and faces jumped out. When she saw the small sub-machine guns in their hands she spun on her heel and began to run. It seemed impossible that such a thing was happening in the middle of London, and this thought had made her hesitate just a moment too long. Despite her inhuman speed, she had only taken two steps when both men opened fire, blazing away in full automatic mode. Half a dozen bullets slammed into her back and legs, the impact and shock making her trip and throwing her to the ground. The wounds began to heal almost instantly, but the men continued to fire. A bullet struck her head, stunning her. She heard a man's voice shout in anger and realised that it was a suicidally brave fireman. There was more gunfire and a man's scream, and when nothing hit her she realised that they had shot the fireman. She tried to get up, but another shot struck her head and she collapsed back onto the pavement. Through the fog of pain and concussion, she wondered if they were going to cut her head off or just hammer a stake into her heart.

*****

The man who had died in Braşov had been Carl's friend and he growled in satisfaction as he fired another three round burst into the fallen woman. She didn't look that dangerous, and she definitely wasn't furry like that other pilot Viktor, but his orders were to not take any chances and to capture or recover her body at all costs. The people who had hired him for the job were generous and there was a new passport, a secret bank account full of money, and a private jet waiting for him and Hector, the other man in the team.

"I think she's down. You got the manacles?" Hector said, his voice fast and loud from the adrenaline of the moment.

"Yeah, I got them. There's a machete in my bag as well, just in case."

Hector laughed. "The owner of the Beemer isn't going to be happy when he gets it back with blood all over the interior."

"That's Bimmer, you peasant," Carl said, knowing that his partner wouldn't be offended.

"Si, I'm a peasant. A rich one now," Hector chortled cheerfully. "Get those cuffs on her arms and legs and let's get out of here before the cops arrive. I charge extra for killing pigs."

Carl knelt down beside Tara's quivering form, taking care to stay out of Hector's line of fire. "Shoot her in the head again if she struggles."

Hector nodded, switching his gun to single fire mode. "Don't worry."

Carl pulled one of Tara's wrists up and behind her and prepared to attach the electronically locked chrome steel manacles, ignoring the growing puddle of her blood that flowed around his knee.

"Let her go," a deep voice behind him said. "I insist."

Carl dropped the target's hand and raised his gun just in time to see a tall man in a conservative business suit step out of the shadows on the left side of the fire station. "Mind your own fucking business if you want to keep breathing." Tara twitched and without taking his eyes from the newcomer he said, "Hector, give her another round in the head." The man had not done the sensible thing and run away. "All right, if that's the way you want it..." His mouth remained open when the stranger blurred and seemed to disappear, only to re-appear behind Hector. "Hector! Look out behind..."

The stranger smiled at Carl as he put his hand on Hector's shoulder and the other hand gripped the Hispanic killer's upper arm — the one holding the sub-machine gun.

Carl gasped in horror when the man casually ripped Hector's arm out of his shoulder like a man would a drumstick from a roasted chicken and tossed it aside. The muzzle of his gun snapped up without conscious thought and he squeezed the trigger, but the man was gone and he saw Hector's eyes widen a fraction of a second before his bullets blew his partner's face away. He swivelled on his knee searching for a target. "Where are you, you fucker? Show your face again and I'll blow your ass away!" he cried. A rush of air made him spin to his left, and then he screamed in agony when the sleeve of his coat and shirt turned into strips as unseen claws shredded the muscles of his forearm. He tried to spring to his feet but then staggered, his sense of balance telling him that for some unknown reason the ground was tilting and swaying like a ship's deck in a storm, making him want to vomit. Shouting in panicked rage he pulled the trigger and emptied his magazine in a half circle, shattering the side windows of a passing bus and hitting the driver.

The bus swerved across the road and crashed into two cars going in the opposite direction and sending one of them rolling onto its side. Broken glass, blood, and engine oil sprayed in all directions.

Fire seared the backs of Carl's legs, and he cried out in terror when they would not support him. He realised that whatever was attacking him had severed his hamstrings. The sub-machine gun clattered against the concrete when he was forced to use that hand to prevent himself from falling and smashing his face against the pavement. He could see splashes and streaks of his own blood all around him and he was getting dizzy from the blood loss. He gasped in shock when an expensively shod foot stepped on his hand, crushing it against the metal of his gun and the balaclava was ripped from his head. An irresistible grip took hold of his hair and pulled his head back until he could see the top of the fire station against the night sky, threatening to snap his spine and bending his throat outwards. Dark eyes set deeply in a handsome but somehow disturbing looking face stared into his.

"I would like to spend more time teaching you better manners, but this little disturbance is attracting too much attention. The police and the SCO 19 with all their noisy firearms will soon be here along with the ambulances for all the injuries that you so rudely created, so I have to finish this. Give the Devil my greetings when you see him."

The man's mouth opened wide, revealing inhumanly long sharp teeth. Carl tried to scream again, but then his throat was gone and nothing came out except a hiss of air, and everything faded to dark.

The man, or male vampire, for there was no denying what he was, dragged the soon-to-be corpse over to Tara with one hand on the scruff of Carl's neck. He flipped Tara over onto her back and forced her mouth open with his other hand. "I'm sorry my dear, but you need this if you are to recover in time," he said, sounding like a family doctor prescribing an injection. He held Carl's torn throat above Tara's lips and allowed the blood to flow.

Only half conscious, Tara tried to struggle but she was too weak and dizzy from the multiple bullet wounds to the head on top of the massive damage the two sub-machine guns had done. She had no choice but to swallow the harsh metallic tasting liquid that filled her mouth. A strange, alien excitement filled her, and she seemed to feel her damaged flesh magically knitting together and some of her strength returning. Suddenly the forced feeding stopped and she felt herself being swept up by incredibly strong arms and thrown over a muscular shoulder. The rest of the escape was a blur of violent movements, the ground passing under her dangling head as if she was hanging out of the window of a speeding car. Then suddenly she was actually inside a car, and the warmth and cushioned seating lulled her into a deep, almost coma-like sleep.

***

The stopping of the car's engine woke her up. She had a headache and her body felt like she had just lost a heavyweight MMA bout. Her face and neck were crusty and sticky, and suddenly she wanted to throw up, although she was not absolutely clear why. Fortunately for the car's interior her stomach was completely empty and she just made embarrassing retching noises and worsened her headache. "I never thought I'd say this but, where am I?"

"You're in my car," her rescuer said, his voice smooth and cultured in the way only hundreds of years of breeding could achieve.

"Very funny. Now please answer my question. Should I prepare to start running?" She looked around but the night time view from the low slung car didn't reveal very much. "I don't hear any sirens." Instead of replying, the man opened his door and got out of the car. It slammed shut with the heavy bank vault sound that only the most insanely expensive of cars made. The door on her side opened and his hand appeared.

"Permit me. You are probably still a little unsteady on your feet."

Tara got out and saw that she had been riding in a Bugatti Veyron Super Sport. "This thing costs one point seven million pounds," she said accusingly, pointing at the vehicle. "Who are you, Bill Gates? You look too hot to be Bill Gates. Damn. I can't believe I just said that." Even as she spoke she realised that not only was she physically shaky, but she felt like she was drunk, and talked like it too. She told herself that she would blush later.

"Why don't we go inside where you can sit down and have a nice cup of tea and some aspirin." He lightly took her by the elbow and ushered her towards the door.

Tara realised she was standing at the front of a huge bungalow, which again indicated that her rescuer was madly rich. Now that she was feeling stronger, she wasn't too concerned about being alone with this man in his home ground. Her memory of events before she woke up in the car were still blurry and she wasn't sure how he had rescued her but assumed that he had a gun on his person somewhere, unless he had left it in the car. That or he was a master of the martial arts on the scale of a Hong Kong martial arts film. She realised that her HUD was not in evidence, but before she could worry, it seemed to respond to her concern and popped into existence again. She noted that the "friendly" IFF was a solid colour and not blinking, indicating that the "friendly" was very close. Her eyes widened when the front door silently swung open when the man approached it and just a quietly closed behind them. "Isn't that a bit dangerous?"

"The door only opens like that for me," the man replied. "I like gadgets," he said with a disarmingly youthful grin.

Considering that Tara had spent most of her adult life playing with big flying toys, she didn't feel in a position to criticise. She allowed him to lead her into the sitting room, which led into a spacious wood panelled study or office at the other end.

"There's a loo across the hallway, but I suggest you sit down and have a drink first. You still look a little wobbly."

"Thanks, I think I will. A Scotch would be most welcome right now."

This request seemed to interest him, and he studied her silently for a moment before going to a cabinet in the corner of the room which opened to reveal a small bar. He poured a generous portion of Scotch into a crystal tumbler and returned to hand it to her. "There you are. Drink it slowly." He watched as she took a large sip, and nodded to himself.

"I haven't thanked you for rescuing me. I don't know how much you saw ...." Tara deliberately left the sentence unfinished. If he had seen her being literally riddled with machine gun bullets and surviving, then he was probably full of questions. But if he had come upon her after she was already down he might have assumed that the bullets had mostly missed and that the blood on her head and clothes was from minor grazes. She wished that she could recall more of what had happened after she had been shot in the head, but it was all like a half remembered dream.

"How could I resist such a singular call for help?" he replied.

"Call for help? What do you mean? I don't remember shouting..." She froze, her attention going back to the glowing IFF symbol in her HUD. It couldn't be – could it? She started to stand up, but the dizziness returned and the whiskey hit her harder than it had since she was a teenager. Then she realised that she had been completely at his mercy for several hours now and he had not harmed her. "Who are you?"

"More to the point, my dear lady, is *what* are you?"

"I don't know what you mean," she said, struggling to make sense of the situation.

"Someone with access to professional assassins and military weapons seems awfully intent upon killing you. You shrug off bullet wounds that would have killed a platoon of soldiers. You heal when you drink blood but didn't try to attack me for mine, and most intriguing of all, you send off some kind of signal that only certain people can detect."

"Are you some kind of government agent, like the X-files or SHIELD or something?"

"From your appearances, I'm probably the only friend you have, and you haven't answered my question."

Suddenly Tara felt utterly exhausted, emotionally and physically. Since her father had been taken she'd had no one to talk to that wouldn't think she was mad, a monster, or a subject for dissection and study. She sighed. "My name is Tara Harker. Until a few days ago, I was a test pilot for my father's company, Harker Industries." She went on to tell him everything that had happened.

"Hmm. Fascinating. And do you really think that you are a vampire and, what's his name … Viktor, is a true werewolf?"

Tara shrugged. "I don't know what to think. The similarities to the fictional creatures are too great for it to be just coincidence. But I can't see how others could have come to be infected or treated by these medikit things. The alien ship was sealed underground high in the mountains of Romania – although that's another impossible coincidence."

The man rubbed his chin. "What do you think would happen to someone in the past who became infected with this 'vampire' treatment and lacked the advantage of your nano implants?"

Tara took another sip and frowned. "From what I know now, I would guess that he or she would become schizophrenic, thinking like a human one moment, then an alien blood sucking bat another. I admit that thought has been bothering me. There's no guarantee that I'll always be immune from that happening. The alien medical implant seems to be at least semi-intelligent and may decide to turn me completely into a bat thing as part of the 'cure'." She downed more Scotch, which was really excellent, and then looked at him. "You seem to be taking all of this very calmly. Or are you just humouring me and waiting for the men in white coats and butterfly nets to arrive?"

Instead of replying, the man reached into the collar of his turtle-necked shirt and pulled out a chain and pendant.

Tara recognised the cross shaped alien artefact immediately and covered her mouth. "Oh my god! Where did you get that?"

"I was lost in the mountains, injured and dying, when I came upon this cross in the snow. I took it as a sign of God's blessing and slipped it inside my clothes against my skin. You can guess what happened then."

She felt herself edging backwards in her seat. "But you don't have the nano-interface .... "

He nodded. "Your analysis of its effect was quite accurate. For a long time I was quite mad, or at least people would have called me mad. Fortunately I was lost in the mountains and I took out the uncontrolled rages and blood lust on the unfortunate wild life of the area and a few poor hunters and trappers who braved those desolate wilds. But I have always been stubborn and strong willed. Perhaps I am a genetic freak, I don't know. But after more than a year, I woke up one morning in a cave full of shrivelled – mostly animal – corpses, and I was myself again. Like you, the alien thing within me had come to an accommodation with my human nature. And like you, I retained the unnatural health and powers, but also my original personality. Unlike you, I had no alien memories or additional knowledge. After hearing your tale, I would guess that when the alien ship your counterpart was piloting was attacked, some of the things you call medikits must have fallen from the ship, scattered over the countryside to be found and used, or even traded as jewellery. Because of their shape and unknown materials, they would have been treated as great treasures by the ignorant peoples of that ancient time."

Tara nodded. "Giving rise to the legends of vampires and werewolves." She frowned. "Wait a minute, you said you picked that up in the mountains. The Făgăraș mountains in Romania?"

The man nodded and smiled. "Yes."

Her eyes narrowed and she stood up. "When exactly did you come across the medikit?"

"Ah. I was wondering when you would get to that. It was in the year of our lord 1474. I had escaped from the dungeons of the then King of Hungary, Matthius Corvinus. I was attempting to return to my family home, pursued by Corvinus's assassins, but they caught up with me just when I was almost home. I fought and killed them, but not without being grievously injured myself."

"1474?" Tara managed, speechless. She would have accused him of madness except that her own story was just as unbelievable.

He laughed softly, guessing her thoughts. "Forgive me. I have not introduced myself. I'm popularly known as Vlad Tepes, Vlad the Impaler, an affectionate nickname you might say. But perhaps you know me better by my Romanian family name – Dracula."

Chapter Six

"Dracula? Come on, don't be ridi…"

The man's lower jaw seemed to drop like that of a snake and his upper canine teeth grew and extended into sharp fangs. His eyes turned reddish as if flooded with blood, and the tips of his fingers turned into needle sharp claws. Then in a flash it was all gone, and he looked completely human again.

"Oh. Um, I don't suppose you're some kind of cosplay fanatic …." She sighed. "I suppose not. But Dracula. As if things aren't crazy enough."

"These days I go by the name of Dr John Seward. Yes, you'll have to forgive the little joke. It seemed awfully funny to Bram and I at the time."

"Bram Stoker? The man who wrote Drac … oh." Tara was getting tired of sounding like an idiot.

"Yes. I was the one who suggested the story and provided all the background research, as well as the funding and promotion that made his novel a success." He pointed at the sofa and sat down when Tara nodded. "My rescuing you wasn't entirely a coincidence. I had sensed you as soon as you touched down in Heathrow. I supposed it was Heathrow from the direction that your um, signal was coming from. When I saw the direction you were headed, I went to my office in Shoreditch to wait for your destination to become clearer. You can guess my surprise when you headed right towards me, or Old Street, at any rate."

"You have an office in Tech City?" Somehow the idea struck Tara as funny.

"I own one of the IT companies there, and the building it is based in." He raised an eyebrow. "Unlike in all the films, I didn't just lie around in ruined churches as the centuries went by. Remember that I was the equivalent of a King back in Wallachia, and one does get rather accustomed to the lifestyle." He waved his hand to indicate his surroundings.

"Why did you help me?"

"Why did Dracula the blood sucking monster help you or why did John Seward help you?"

"Is there a difference?" she replied, testing him.

"Dracula might have helped you out of curiosity, because you might be a potential ally, or because you had knowledge of a potential threat."

"And John Seward?"

"He helped you because you were a lone woman attacked by two armed killers, and because he had been preparing for this very thing for centuries." He folded his arms across his chest. "Both came to your aid because his honour required it. Many things may have changed in the man that was Vlad Dracula, but not that."

"History says that Vlad Tepes was a bloodthirsty monster."

"Vlad Dracula was a man of his time. He was ruler of a small backward kingdom faced on all sides by enemies with bigger armies and treasuries. The records that survive were all written by his enemies, and yet, to this day, the people of his land consider him a saviour, a hero, and a good ruler."

"And the impaling of tens of thousands including children?"

This made him laugh. "The entire population of Braşov my, largest city, amounted to a total of twelve thousand. And yet I was supposed to have impaled thirty thousand merchants in a single day who disobeyed my laws? I would have had to depopulate my kingdom to kill as many people as they claim. Would any army made up of feudal land owners and peasant farmers have been willing to do such a thing? As for the Turks, I was outnumbered at least four to one in every battle I fought. Are we to suppose that the Turks just stood around watching while my army laid down their arms and impaled the Turkish prisoners? As I recall it, we spent most of our time running to avoid being surrounded or overwhelmed. Yes, many of my punishments were harsh, but no worse than those carried out in London or Paris in the same era." He shrugged. "It was a harsh time." He pointed towards the office. "Do your own research if you don't believe me. The Internet is a wonderful thing."

Tara nodded. "I will. But the fact is that you did save me from death or worse, and I'm grateful. But what happens now?"

"We rescue your father. It is obvious that we cannot let both his nano-technology and that of the aliens fall into the hands of villains or governments – if there is any difference between the two."

"By God, you're right!" she exclaimed. The thought of an army – or worse – several armies, of vampires or werewolves was terrifying.

"They would never be able to contain it. I know more about the subject than any man alive and I've spent billions in research, but we are centuries behind in the required technology. It would be like a shipment of modern biological weapons falling into the hands of the warring nations of the Elizabethan period. They could easily learn to use it, but they would never be able to contain it."

"I suspect the … let's call them E-Nanites … are at least semi-intelligent." Tara added. "Who knows what kinds of directives might have been built into them by their creators." She chuckled. "They might even have an alien Digital Rights Management system, or they might be shareware." She watched the ancient vampire go over to the drinks cabinet and fiddle with a catch built into the lower section. It felt like madness to think of him as Dracula. She decided that John Seward was more palatable for the moment. "What are you doing?"

"Before we do any more planning or take any action, we need to get you back into shape and then find out what kind of capabilities you have and train you to use them properly." He held out a transparent plastic bottle containing suspiciously red looking liquid. "Drink this. There's more in the chiller."

She wrinkled her nose. "Is this human blood?"

"No, it's a synthetic nutritional liquid designed to suit our particular metabolisms. It tastes like strawberry. I do have some real blood stored elsewhere. In an emergency, blood still works the fastest when serious healing is required."

Tara popped the top and drank. It did taste like strawberry. There was an immediate reaction in her body, and she felt myriad points of pain ease and the shakiness begin to fade. "This is great! You ought to market it."

"Unfortunately some of the ingredients have not been approved for human consumption."

Her eyes narrowed. "You're not joking, are you? Oh well, I'm not human, so that's all right." She gasped when he darted close and gripped her shoulder hard.

"You *are* human. Don't ever forget that. Never think or say otherwise, even in jest." He turned away from her and seemed to be staring into the distance. "I've known too many good men and women who did forget."

"What happened to them?"

"Most of them I killed. Some were killed by monster hunters. And a few still hide out there in the world."

"What! You mean there are still vampires and werewolves walking around in the world?"

"None like us. The ones that were totally consumed by the animal or alien part did not survive long, although they often caused great suffering before their end. But there are others, fewer, who hide amongst the crowds pretending to be human. But like the infamous and fictional Dr Jekyll, they have no control over the alien being that shares their body. The vampires become overcome with blood lust and kill. Many so called serial killers are in fact vampires who have learned to disguise the nature of their kills. The werewolves survive by locking themselves up when they feel a change coming on, or live in the wilderness where their animal natures go mostly unobserved. These are the ones who gave rise to the legends. Quite a few, to my regret, are the result of my earlier years when I did not understand how the curse worked." He went back to the chiller and brought back another bottle of the red liquid. "But you need to rest. Allow me to show you to a guest room where you can wash up and get some sleep. While you do, I shall begin our search for your father and our unknown enemies."

"You're going out to prowl the night?"

He laughed. "Hardly. I'm a wealthy man with considerable influence. I have friends in the police and security forces who will tell me about your would be killers, and my corporation employs a reliable security firm who can do the footwork for us."

Tara gave him the name of the security firm that had provided the men in Romania and her account number and identification code. "They were supposed to recover everything they could from the crash site. Perhaps they found something that could be of use to us. Speaking of security, what about the security cameras where you found me? The police are going to have both our images on the telly by morning."

"I disabled them before coming to your aid, which is why I was rather late. I have discovered that with practise, my – our – ultrasonic projection can disrupt electronic equipment that is not hardened. Sort of like Dr Who's ultrasonic screwdriver," he said with a disarmingly youthful grin.

Reassured, Tara stretched and yawned, enjoying the lack of pain. "Um, do I need to sleep in … you know … a coffin, with the soil of my homeland and all that? Normal hotel beds seem to have worked so far." she asked as he led her upstairs.

Seward smiled. "Fortunately not. A normal spring mattress will serve perfectly well. And crossing running water is all right too, so you can take a hot shower or a good soak without worries."

"That's a relief. A coffin would creep me out."

"There's a call button in the bathroom and beside the bed if you need the maids to get you anything like more towels or if you'd like cook to make you a snack. You'll find some feminine clothing in the closets. Feel free to use anything that fits. Breakfast is at eight thirty. The breakfast room is just down the hall from the sitting room. The butler show you the way."

"Renfield?" Tara said jokingly.

"As it happens, yes," Seward said, laughing at her expression.

Chapter Seven

Ian Werner, CEO of Werner Aerospace and Robotics glanced at the LCD panel mounted under armoured glass in his desk. It displayed a constantly updated set of data secrecy and security parameters for his office and the building, including all external communications links. He had an entire division of the company devoted to data security, ostensibly marketing security products but in reality devoted to keeping the corporation's secrets secret. According to the display, his office in Washington DC and the data link to the Managing Director of the corporation's Biotechnology Division based in London, Carlos Rometty were secure at that moment. "Well?" he said to the image of his subordinate in the huge high resolution display on the wall across from his desk.

"We have secured Rowland Harker and some samples of his interface technology," Rometty reported briskly.

"Never mind that, what about this supposed alien technology rubbish in your last report? You had better be able to verify all of it, or you'll be retiring for reasons of health."

Rometty felt his palms grow moist even though he was sure of the value of his discovery. The kind of retirement Werner was talking about tended to be permanent and involved a quick cremation. "Just watch this video first Mr Werner, and then I'll explain."

Despite his threat, Werner was confident that Rometty wouldn't have mentioned alien technology unless he had something really significant to back him up so he simply nodded and waited. According to the scrolling text feed at the bottom of the screen he was watching raw footage from various cameras both from helicopters and the team sent to recover Harker's experimental aircraft. He watched silently as Viktor transformed, ripped the guards apart, and then changed back again. Then he saw images of the alien craft deep underground, both exterior and interior. Finally there were video and still images of the alien artefacts that Viktor had recovered. Then the screen cleared and Rometty's face reappeared. "Explain." He listened as the Biotechnology MD fleshed out the report and provided his comments and recommendations. "So, you managed to fuck up the capture of a single unsupported female in the middle of a London street."

"From Viktor Tiranul's debrief, we must assume that Tara Harker was also exposed to the same alien nano-technology, sir."

"We – and by that I mean I, don't have to assume anything. Do you have any reports of a hairy naked woman running around East London ripping people apart?"

"Er, no, Mr Werner. But..."

"In fact, did not the witness statements you obtained from your people in the local police force all agree that the woman had been shot multiple times and had fallen down? And did the police forensic reports indicate that there was at least one more person present and who likely carried the woman's body away?"

"Yes, Mr Werner," Rometty said, unsurprised that his boss had read the police reports even though he had not sent them to Washington yet. He had always known that there were others in his organisation who reported, spied, on him for Werner.

"According to the initial reports the dead men, your dead men, were killed with extreme skill and violence. Did Tara Harker ever receive military or special combat training?"

"No sir."

"Then what *we* shall assume is that your men were killed by a special forces team when then carried away Tara Harker or her corpse. Didn't you say that Harker had deployed an armed security team to the crash site and that their airfield was defended by trained military specialists?"

"Yes sir."

"Then the logical thing to do would be to locate the supplier of the military personnel and find out what they know, would it not?"

"Yes Mr Werner. I'll have our people get right on it. What about the alien artefacts?"

"We need to take great care with them. You have a functional specimen already on hand. I suggest that you find out everything you can about Mr Tiranul's condition and capabilities first, especially whether his condition is capable of being transmitted. After all, werewolves make other werewolves by biting them, isn't that what the legends say? I want his every molecule examined in detail. Is that understood?"

Rometty frowned. "You want to dissect him Sir?"

"If necessary. We don't need a zoo exhibit, Rometty. We need a product we can sell," Werner said. "Find out if his body can generate more of whatever changed him, and whether we can isolate it. The alien artefacts are limited in quantity and therefore priceless. We cannot afford to damage or waste them."

"Understood, Mr Werner."

"What about the alien ship?"

"According to the specialists, all the equipment, power and propulsion systems were somehow destroyed, literally turned to powder. They speculate that the ship was either attacked by an alien weapon, or the alien crew had activated some kind of self-destruct system when they realised they were stuck on Earth. They tried to take samples of the hull, but none of their tools could cut it. They recovered whatever loose material that they could find before Harker's security team arrived on site, and these are being studied as we speak."

"All right. Keep me informed." A touch of a

switch disconnected the video link, and Werner leaned back in his chair. "Get me Internal Audit," he said, and waited as the voice activated telephone system connected him.

"Internal Audit. This is Boucher speaking, Mr Werner. How may I help you?"

"Send an audit team to London. Mr Rometty is handling a very delicate situation and I want to be sure that everything is handled according to corporate policy."

"Yes sir. A team will be despatched immediately."

"They are to report directly to me and to me only."

"Yes sir. Your eyes only sir. Understood."

Werner touched a switch on the arm of his chair, cutting the connection. "Wendy." His secretary's name activated the secure intercom, and a moment later she came into his office. It was a given that she was beautiful and that she wore a short skirt, but in truth Werner expected the women who worked for him to be beautiful as well as completely competent, so he hardly noticed.

"Yes Mr Werner?"

"Find out who is next in line in London under Rometty, and get me his personnel file." It was possible the second in command was a woman, but one of the perks of being as rich and powerful as he, was that he could ignore political correctness with impunity. In fact he ignored most things he didn't like with impunity – or they conveniently went away.

"At once, Mr Werner." Wendy looked like a supermodel and dressed like a stereotypical hot secretary, but she also had a master's degree in engineering and earned more money than anyone else in her class at university, so she was more than happy to make coffee and to tolerate with a smile visitors trying to peek under her desk. More than one of her boss's visitors had been fatally distracted by her looks, not all of them male.

As soon as Werner had cut off, Rometty buzzed his own secretary. "Miss Cartwright, have Mr um … Tiranul come in please. Miss Cartwright?" He pushed back his expensive mesh backed executive chair and stood up. "If that stupid girl has gone to the loo again I'll..." He pulled the door to his office open, and the tirade he had been mentally preparing died in his throat. The whole of the waiting room had been painted with splashes of crimson and rust red. Furniture had been ripped apart as if someone had gone mad with a sword. Worst of all was Miss Cartwright's head which sat upright in the middle of the floor, surrounded by a circle of blood that soaked into the elegantly patterned beige carpet. Her body lay across her desk, ripped open from neck to groin and some of her organs had obvious bite marks. Large, inhuman looking bloody footprints tracked across the floor towards the exit, and now that he was listening he could hear a chorus of screams coming from the rest of the floor. It was obvious that Viktor Tiranul had overheard Werner's instructions and had strongly disapproved. "Oh shit." Then he noticed the note in his secretary's hand. Prodding it with a pen he managed to flatten out the blood soaked paper. "HQ audit team en-route. All access and support required." Rometty recoiled as if he had spotted a snake. "Fuck!" Using the pen he jabbed a button on his ex-secretary's complicated telephone unit.

"Security. Mr Rometty, there is a dangerous intruder in the building. Please stay in your office until we have..."

"I know we have a dangerous intruder you stupid twat! Have your men get their useless arses up here immediately. All of them."

"But sir, the intruder..."

"Are you fucking deaf? Get up here now!" Rometty screamed, spittle flying from his lips, the pen snapping between his fingers and staining his fingers with ink.

***

Ignoring the shotgun pellets that rained upon him from all directions and the uniformed guards that were running towards him, Viktor – or the werewolf that was Viktor – headed directly towards the gate.

The guard that manned the guardhouse bravely stepped out in front of the charging monster and fired his pump action shotgun, once, twice, his body rocking smoothly with the recoil. He saw the lead shot strike its target and his eyebrows shot upwards in disbelief. The werewolf was upon him before he could pump the shotgun action for a third shot. He hunched and launched a butt strike at his hirsute attacker and grunted in satisfaction when he felt the solid impact. The creature roared in his face, and ripped the weapon from his grip as if it was an adult chastising an obstreperous infant. Refusing to give up, he planted his feet and threw a punch straight from his shoulder, and cried out in shock when a clawed paw intercepted his fist. Another set of claws dug into his elbow and his entire body lurched forward when the *thing* pulled his forearm towards its jaws. He screamed in terror and agony when the monster's teeth closed upon his arm, cut through the skin and muscle to shatter the bones, and severed the limb just below the elbow.

The werewolf retained sufficient cunning to know that there was no time for it to linger over the prey and it swatted the guard aside, its claws stripping the flesh and muscle from the guard's chest before sending the dying man smashing into the guardhouse and knocking the wooden structure down in a shower of painted splinters.

With a single bound it landed on the top of the razor-wire festooned gate and then sprang ten metres away, past the curving access road, several factories, and into the green countryside of Hemel Hempstead.

Escorted by the remaining members of the on-site security team, Rometty watched in frustration as Viktor loped away across the open fields.

"Should I have the men mount up and go after it sir?" The guard commander asked.

The Managing Director shook his head. "No. With luck no one should tie that thing to us, but they definitely will if vehicles bearing the Werner logo and armed men wearing our uniforms go racing all over the countryside taking potshots at a monster. You and your men need to secure the facility in case it comes back. I'll make arrangements for someone to handle that thing and to clean up the mess." Rometty made his way back to his office, stepping gingerly around and over the remains of his secretary. He closed the door with a sigh of relief. At least his office still appeared normal. Then he looked down and cursed when he saw that he had tracked a trail of bloody footprints into the room.

He sat down and entered the password into his private and very secure address book application and placed his thumb on the scanner without any request from the software. If anyone tried to access the database with just the password the program would suffer an "unexpected fault" and corrupt the database beyond recovery. He selected a number and clicked on the "dial" button. When a voice answered, he said, "We need the cleaners and the exterminators. A pest has made rather a mess at our facility." He was confident that the line he had used was clean, even from monitoring by Werner's own data security team. That was against corporate rules, but as the Managing Director he had some wriggle room.

"On the way," the voice said and hung up.

Rometty closed his eyes and sighed. With luck,

the cleaners would be done before the Internal Audit team arrived and he would have Viktor's corpse to show them. All the witnesses would agree with complete truth that Viktor had suddenly gone berserk and had to be put down. He straightened his tie and tapped the intercom. Normally he would have had his secretary do it, but since she was severely indisposed, he was willing to make an exception this time. He made a mental note to have HR find him a new secretary.

"Yes? What is it?"

"I need to speak with Dr Maeda."

"He's very busy. Call back later."

"This is Rometty. Tell him I want his arse in my office within five minutes or he's fired."

"Uh, OK I'll tell him."

Rometty shook his head. He had some of the biggest brains in the field of biotechnology in his employ, but they often behaved like they lived on another planet. Four minutes later there was a tap on the door. "Come."

Dr Maeda stuck his head around the door. "You wanted to see me?"

"Come in and close the door." Rometty waited until the scientist was standing in front of his desk and fidgeting impatiently before he said, "You are to proceed with human testing of the samples immediately."

"Human testing? But that is against all protocols. We won't be able to publish our results or market any resulting medical product," the researcher protested agitatedly.

"Let me worry about that. Once we've reverse engineered the thing we can make up the necessary research papers if we want to. But our first priority are the possible military applications."

"But what about the test subjects?"

Rometty held up his hand. "Suitable volunteers will be found. Your job is just to discover how this thing works. Leave the marketing and legal aspects to the specialists."

Dr Maeda looked and behaved like a cartoon mad scientist, but he was no fool. "Ah. Volunteers. Yes of course. I shall set up the tests immediately and await the arrival of these um … volunteers."

There was always a good supply of drug addicts, the homeless, and criminals that no one would miss, and Rometty knew just the people who could gather a suitable group of them for Dr Maeda to perform his tests on. With luck, he would have some promising initial results on hand by the time the "Internal Audit" people arrived.

***

One of the effects of the alien modifications to Viktor's physiology had been more acute hearing even when he was in human form, although nothing like the incredible auditory ability he possessed as a werewolf. He had been sitting outside Rometty's office and he had been able to hear and understand enough of the discussion between Rometty and Werner to know that he had been a fool to trust these people. Since the initial transformation, he had been subject to violent rages at the slightest provocation, and it had become increasingly hard for him to control his temper. Every powerful rush of rage-fuelled adrenaline brought him to the brink of transformation, and when he heard Werner discuss him as if he was a laboratory rat, it had enraged him beyond control and he was unable to stop the change. But he had also developed greater cunning, and he accomplished most of the change in near silence instead of roaring his defiance to the world. By the time the unfortunate secretary had looked up it had been far too late for her, and a slash of a clawed hand had prevented her from uttering a sound.

110

Without Hoch and his gunships, the guards and staff had barely presented any obstacle at all, their pump action shotguns firing too slowly to be any real threat, and Viktor, still in werewolf form, had headed north and soon found himself wandering the English countryside, still angry and increasingly hungry. He sniffed the air. Food. He needed food.

***

"Hurry up daddy, I'm hungry."

"Don't be rude. Let your father clean up before he comes to the table."

"Jenna's in a hurry. Her new boyfriend's coming over," said Meg, sticking her tongue out at her older sister.

"Boyfriend? Since when did you have a boyfriend, Jenna?" her father asked, drying his hands on a towel and tossing it on the sideboard.

"Don't do that, Dan," Susan said warningly.

"Sorry dear," he replied in a long suffering tone as he recovered the towel and headed for the kitchen.

Jenna was bouncing up and down in her seat with impatience by now, but the stern eye of her mother prevented further outbursts. What made it worse was the family rule that no cellphones or tablets were allowed at the dinner table, so she couldn't even check if Trevor had texted her.

Meg, who was too young to be subject to the torments of teenage romance, grinned and giggled at her sister's discomfort all the way through the meal, and was so distracted by this entertainment that she even ate all her vegetables without protest or threat.

Dan frowned. "The chickens sound unusually restless tonight."

"That fox might be back again," replied Susan.

Feverishly counting down the seconds to the time

111

when she could reasonably ask to be excused from the table, Jenna jumped when the doorbell rang. "It's Trevor! MayIbeexcusedplease – thanks." She was half-way to the door before her father's mouth could fully open to say yes. But she came to a complete halt in front of the door and checked her hair, tugged at her blouse and jumper, and then assumed a casual, bored looking stance before reaching out for the latch.

Meg rolled her eyes but was prevented from shouting something that would have seriously embarrassed her sister by a firm prod in the ribs from her mother. "Spoilsport," she muttered rebelliously.

Jenna opened the door. There was a flash of furry arms and she screamed as she was dragged out through the entryway.

Susan turned in her chair. "Jenna?" She was half-way out of her seat when her eldest daughter came flying through the doorway again, a huge furry shape wrapped around her body. "What..."

"Mommy, mommy, look what Trevor bought for me!" Jenna squealed happily, all attempts at dignified disinterest forgotten. With both arms she held out a giant teddy bear that was almost as tall as she was.

Looking embarrassed at the fuss he had created, Trevor cleaned his shoes on the mat and stepped into the house. "Evening Mr Buckley, Mrs Buckley. My brother went on holiday and helped me get it for Jenna. I hope you don't mind."

Jenna's father nodded. "Good evening, Trevor. Nice bear."

Jenna snatched the huge stuffed toy away when Meg tried to grab hold of a leg. "Oh no you don't. I'll put this in my room before we go out. Come on Trevor!" she cried dashing up the stairs.

Trevor looked to her parents for permission.

Susan smiled indulgently while Dan just nodded and gave Trevor a warning finger.

The young man grinned and nodded his thanks, and then ran up the stairs to catch up with Jenna.

"He seems a nice young man," Susan said, swatting playfully at Meg when the girl stuck a finger in her mouth and made gagging noises.

Dan leaned back in his chair. "At least he knows to keep his hands off of Jenna in front of us. That last boy was like an octopus." He frowned when a loud female squeal came echoing down the stairwell. "On the other hand..." He got up with a disappointed sigh and went over to look up the stairs. "Jenna, is everything..." His question was cut off when a loud thump on the stairs made him start and twist his head to look up. He blinked when something wet splattered against his face. Then there was another thump and something rolled and slithered down the stairs. His first thought was that one of the kids had slipped and was rolling down towards him, so he stepped forward and held out his arms. But what he caught was too small and light to be a teenage body, even Jenna's slim one. It wasn't furry, so it couldn't be the giant teddy. Then he realised that whatever he was holding was wet. Sticky and wet. And the smell. He recognised the smell. Terror gripped his chest when he realised it was the smell of freshly spilled blood. Fear became horror when he finally recognised the object to be a leg. A human leg, torn off the body at the hip. In the numbness of shock he saw that the leg was hairy and thick with muscles, so it couldn't belong to a girl. A girl! "Jenna!" he screamed as he threw the leg over the bannister and pounded up the stairs as if he was running on level ground, his bad knee forgotten.

Jenna's room was wrecked, like the images from TV news reports of typhoons and earthquakes, except that there was blood, more blood than existed in the whole world, running down the walls and forming puddles on the floor. Dan's foot slipped on a chunk of raw glistening flesh and he almost fell. Frantically he turned around and around. The mattress had been thrown from her bed and he could see that there was nothing under it. He pulled open the door of the closet, but it only revealed shockingly crisp and clean clothes. The curtain flapped in the draft blowing in from the splintered window. Jenna was gone.

Chapter Eight

"Nothing? Nothing at all?" Tara said as she buttered her toast.

John Seward inhaled the fragrance of his butter roasted Singapore coffee, a taste for which he had developed during his extensive travels, sipped, smacked his lips and sighed. "Not a trace. I've been having my blood tested ever since they invented microscopes and blood tests. I've long suspected that whatever it is, it self-destructs as soon as it leaves the host body, except when it directly enters another living body."

Tara chewed her toast thoughtfully. "That makes sense. You wouldn't want the stuff lying around to be eaten by animals and insects, or trying to revive a truly dead body." She grimaced. "The last thing we need are zombies on top of werewolves and vampires." She grinned when Renfield placed a bacon-egg-and feta tart before her. "Thank you, Renfield. Have I said how much I love being able to eat like a pig?"

"I believe Madam has mentioned it once or twice," the butler replied, absolutely straight faced.

"Mmm, this is really good. Where was I …"

"Zombies?" Seward suggested.

"Yes that, but I was wondering why everyone who is infected becomes so aggressive. Surely the aliens who created the medikits were a bit more civilised than that?"

Seward cut into his steak and eggs Benedict. "You have to remember that civilisation, culture, taste..." He forked a piece of steak and egg into his mouth and smiled. "All of it is learned behaviour. A baby is as savage and uncaring as any wild animal, lacking only the physical ability to be dangerous. These 'medikits', except for the one you so fortunately stumbled upon, were designed to heal the body, not the soul. I surmise that when it repairs the brain, it restores the damaged parts to what might be called a factory default. It may even do a backup of existing memories and physical skills, such as walking or riding a bicycle, but when the host body is not the one it is designed for, it must somehow be programmed to do its best not to damage the original design."

"But if that's the case, why change the recipient at all?"

"I'm only guessing, but I would say because it only has one complete template and set of specifications built-in. So it can only be certain that it has 'fixed' a complete werewolf or vampire, not a human."

"So this confusion forces it to change the patient back and forth between the two forms?"

"Based upon my own experiences, I would say that the recipient's own strength of will and intelligence play a part even when he, in my case, doesn't have a convenient nano-interface like you did. The only setback being that it becomes an extended case of trial and error. If the recipient actively tries to interact, the e-nanites will cooperate and try to provide feedback and controls."

Tara nodded, prodding at her tart with the tines of her fork. "But someone who thinks he has been turned into a monster or possessed by a demon will only become worse by fighting it and providing the wrong kind of expectations to the e-nanites. That makes sense."

Seward nodded. "I was always exceptionally strong willed and determined to have my own way. Even the best or worst efforts of the Turks and the Hungarian King Matthais Corvin were unable to sway or break me when I was their prisoner. It took decades, but I eventually came to an understanding with the thing that had possessed me. All of its powers became mine to control."

Unexpectedly, Renfield stepped up to Seward and said, "I rather think you should see this, Mr Seward." He pointed to the wide screen television mounted on the wall. The news presenter's expression was an omen of the bad news that was to follow. The warning that there would be scenes that "some viewers may find disturbing" confirmed it.

Tara listened to the report in grim silence. "Viktor. It has to be."

"You don't think it could be someone else infected with the e-nanites? After all, they made off with an entire shipment of the stuff," Seward asked, interested to hear her logic.

"I don't think so. Whoever attacked the farm showed too much control and coordination. It didn't just charge through a door and window. It climbed up the outside of a building and quietly broke into the empty room and waited in ambush. Of course it was the girl's bad luck that she went back upstairs instead of going out, although the werewolf might just as easily have pounced on them outside if that had happened. And of course it took the girl, instead of killing her, which means at least some of Viktor's human drives are reasserting themselves. When Viktor first saw me in his werewolf form he just attacked."

"Perhaps you weren't his type?" Seward quipped.

"I doubt it. He was constantly hitting on me before that day."

"All right, if it is Viktor, that may be a good thing. At least we're not looking at a mass outbreak of lycanthropy."

"Yet," Tara added. "I have to do something. The police think it's a madman with a chainsaw or an axe murderer. They'll get ripped to shreds if they are unlucky enough to find him, and some might even get infected themselves." She looked at Seward. "I'll understand if you don't feel obliged to go with me."

His eyes seemed to darken. "I have lost many things over the centuries, but not my honour. We are the only ones who understand the threat and have the ability to stop him. Renfield..."

"Yes, Mr Seward?"

"Do you remember where I put those silver crossbow bolts?"

"Of course sir. And I took the liberty of replacing the old crossbows with new carbon-fibre compound crossbows; woodworm, you know," the butler said, straight faced.

"You have silver arrows?" Tara asked.

"Silver tipped. The last time I actually had to use them was over a hundred years ago, but it pays to be prepared. It's getting harder and harder to carry firearms around, but bows are still legal and less high profile. I actually have memberships in several archery clubs, and I have a number of championship trophies lying around somewhere. I also have some silver inlaid hunting knives, but those would be harder to explain if we're stopped and searched."

"I'll pack a picnic hamper and make sure the Range Rover is ready." Renfield said.

***

The werewolf that was Viktor opened its jaws in a lupine grin. It had all been so easy. At first it had been drawn to the farmhouse by the smell of cooking, and then when it was closer, it caught the scent of live prey. It remembered the taste of human flesh from the ones on the plateau, the ones who had tried to hurt it. It remembered the blood flowing down its throat and the strength that it had felt. It was hungry from its exertions and from healing the injuries the guards at the new place had inflicted. It could have killed all the men with the weapons, the shotguns, but there were many humans in the building, and somehow it understood that more would come and with better weapons. It would choose the right time and its own hunting ground. It also remembered the scent of the human female in the office.

118

He had killed her because she was going to raise an alarm. But her scent had aroused other needs in him. Normally the smooth hairless form of the human females would not have aroused its interest, but the *other* that shared its mind found her attractive and her scent alluring, and because they were one, he felt it too.

When he had arrived at the farm, drawn by the sound of human voices, he had caught the scent again. Mixed in with the farm smells, the cooked flesh, and the live humans, was that other alluring scent. At the back of the farmhouse he had lifted his head and sniffed, searching with an olfactory sense that was almost as clear as what he saw with his eyes or heard with his ears. His whiskers told him the breeze that carried that smell came from higher up in the farmhouse, so he had climbed. The *other* memories told him that the smooth rectangular shapes in the hard wall could be opened. He had entered the upstairs room like a huge deadly shadow. He sniffed at the sleeping pad. The scent was strong, heady, irresistible.

The werewolf had been about to go through the door and down the stairs where the prey was gathered and where they stupidly made so much noise, when he heard footsteps, the voice of a female, and then the scent. Her scent. The one whose den he was hiding in. He retreated into the shadows of the corner, away from the window and out of sight of the door. The door knob rattled and the door swung open. It prepared to spring, but then shrunk back, confused by the entrance of the large, wrong-smelling animal. A second later he realised that it was not a living thing at all and he silently snarled. She had still not seen him, her view blocked by the head of the fake animal. He allowed her to take another two steps into the room. A swipe of his hand eviscerated the false animal and threw Jenna across the room and onto her bed, stunned and confused. Then he spun around and leapt out of the room just in time to catch the male human as he reached to top of the stairs. This one smelt liked food. He lashed out with a clawed hand, ripping out its throat and painting the wallpaper behind it with a long dripping feather of crimson. He sank his teeth into the human's shoulder even as his claws tore open its belly.

There was a sound at the foot of the stairs and the werewolf snarled, baring blood painted fangs. Then it opened its mouth in a grin, ripped the entire leg off of the dying human's body, and threw it down the stairs. It tore out the prey's liver tossed it down its throat, and then with its hunger momentarily satisfied, it turned back to the room. The female was just beginning to stir, stunned from the impact of her head against the wall. He grabbed the false animal, flung it aside, and then threw the female over its shoulder as it headed for the window while footsteps pounded up the stairs. Its arm lashed out and destroyed the window frame, the need for silence long gone, sending a hail of glass fragments spraying out into the garden. With the stunned girl firmly embraced in its arm, the werewolf sprang straight out of the room, its powerful legs sending it arcing across empty space to land half-way across the large garden and easily absorbing the shock of the landing. Effortlessly it threw its fur covered body into a sprint. It sprang over the hedge, Jenna's head and limbs bouncing against its torso, and disappeared into the night.

***

Jenna's head hurt when she opened her eyes. It was still dark, but there was just enough light so that everything was not blackness. The countryside wasn't like the city with its ever present street lights. Unless the sky was clear and the moon bright, the night was an inky blackness. Since she could make out the trees and grass around her it had to be just before dawn. She couldn't remember how she had got here, and at first she thought that she had gotten totally blasted, but she had none of the familiar symptoms of a hangover, and she didn't feel like hurling, just the sodding headache. She knew she was in terrible trouble if she had spent the entire night out with Trevor. She shivered, and then her apprehension became fear when she realised that she was completely naked. Could Trevor had slipped her some kind of drug? It wasn't easy to get stuff like GBH out here, but there was still stuff like benzos and drunk pills around if you looked for it. She began to feel angry. She would kill that sodding bastard if he had done this. Her hand went gingerly between her legs, but found no soreness or stickiness, so perhaps she hadn't been raped. Perhaps it was some kind of stupid prank. She slowly pushed herself into a sitting position, wincing at the feeling of the grass and earth against her bare bottom. "Trevor? Are you there? What the fuck do you think you're playing at? My dad will kill you for this." When there was no response her tone suddenly changed. "Trevor," she called, her voice lilting playfully. "Now that you've got me like this, why don't you come out and we can … talk."

There was a rustling sound from the darkness behind her and she slowly turned, her hands coyly covering her breasts and loins. "There you are. I thought you'd never …" The glow of the sky coming through the trees was bright enough now that she could make out the silhouette of the approaching figure, and she could see that it definitely wasn't Trevor. Fear became sheer terror when she realised that her kidnapper was covered entirely in fur. The creature stepped into a faint beam of dawn-light that abruptly illuminated its loins like a spotlight. Jenna's eyes were drawn downwards – and she began to scream.

***

121

Even in a world jaded by TV and internet images of violence, having someone literally ripped apart in a farmhouse and a teen-aged girl kidnapped presumably by the same murderer, who then escapes by leaping out of an upstairs window while apparently carrying said kidnapped girl, was enough to quickly attract international media attention. The police sergeant called to the scene was unfortunate enough to be caught on camera throwing up after viewing the internal-organ strewn crime scene and featured on numerous news specials. A leaked police video went viral on the internet. Plain-clothes detectives streamed to the scene and because it was assumed that young Jenna might still be alive, reinforcements in the form of volunteer search teams, helicopters, and sinister looking armed police in body armour and bearing automatic weapons soon arrived as well. No unexplained vehicle tracks were found at the scene of the crime, so a search cordon based upon the ability of a strong fit man to travel on foot while carrying or dragging the kidnap victim was marked out on maps and search quadrants assigned. Crime scene investigators quickly discovered odd looking animal tracks, but since they were not those of a horse, or some dangerous climbing creature such as a leopard, they were quickly dismissed as irrelevant. Bloodhounds were brought in, but they proved strangely reluctant to pick up the scent, whining pitifully with tails firmly tucked between their legs. The word "terrorism" was whispered and quickly denied by the authorities, which only made the public even more watchful for bearded foreigners bearing swords and meat cleavers. A local butcher of Sikh extraction wisely decided it was a suitable time for a holiday in Spain.

***

The frantic search efforts and the even more frantic efforts of the news services to capture newsworthy video clips became plainly visible as the Range Rover passed around Hemel Hempstead. "We're going to need a reason to be here you know, or the police and the locals will be awfully suspicious of two city dwellers turning up right at this time," Tara said.

"I've taken care of that. After we heard the news, I had my personal assistant make enquiries with several estate agents in the area. She'll have emailed me a list of properties and agents. Have a look at my inbox," he said, handing her his smart-phone. "If anyone asks, just say we're newly-weds looking for a nice country home, which will explain us not watching the news."

Tara grinned. "Is that a proposal?"

"Well you must admit, we do have rather a lot in common." He glanced at her and saw her face darken. "Did I say something wrong?"

She shook her head. "No. It's just that thoughts of marriage reminded me of my father. I have to find him."

"Until we learn more about your mysterious attackers and hopefully their employers, Viktor remains your best chance of finding out the whereabouts of your father, especially since he seems to have parted ways with his allies."

"I know. It's just so .... "

"Concentrate on the task at hand. Don't let yourself get distracted by worries about matters you can't control or affect."

Tara nodded, and then pointed. "That looks like a police checkpoint up ahead."

"I may be forced to kiss you in order to protect our cover," Seward said, arching an eyebrow humorously.

"With hundreds of years of experience, is that the best line you can come up with?"

"As Voivode of Wallachia, my problem was usually that of avoiding the ambitious women who wanted to kiss me. Of course, after becoming a vampire I have been able to rely upon my mystical hypnotic powers in order to have my way with any woman I desire."

"Really? We have hypnotic powers?"

"No. And garlic doesn't do anything to us either. I just had Bram Stoker put that in because I disliked garlic in my food at that time."

"Damn. There are a few hot guys I wouldn't mind having my wicked way with."

"You should be able to stun and disorientate people using a variation of the ultrasonic sound that your sonar uses. You just have to experiment a bit to find the right tone." He looked at her again as he slowed in response to the checkpoint. "Besides, I wouldn't think you would need any powers other than those granted to you by nature in order to make you irresistible to most men."

She narrowed her eyes and smiled. "Now *that* was a much better line."

***

"What do you mean *nothing*?" Rometty snapped.

"Precisely what I said. We managed to activate the alien device and it applied the cross shaped cartridge which Tiranul claimed was some sort of healing device, but none of the test subjects demonstrated any changes at all. Blood tests reveal no foreign micro-organisms, active chemicals, or artificial particles whatsoever. Nothing at all other than the presence of inert trace elements in too small amounts to be significant. There were no improvements to pre-existing conditions or the chemical addictions that most of them seemed to possess."

"What about the healing that Tiranul claimed? Or increased hair growth?"

"Nothing."

Rometty ground his teeth at the smug tone that the Japanese researcher used when repeating that word. He tapped his fingers on the desktop as he thought. "Tiranul's changes only manifested under conditions of severe stress. Have you applied the appropriate stimuli to the subjects?"

Dr Maeda shrugged. "We tried flashing lights, loud and sudden noises, pin pricks to the soles of the feet, changes in room temperature. Nothing."

"Fool, I said severe stress, not foreplay. Commence destructive testing at once."

"D-destructive testing?" Dr Maeda said, stuttering in surprise.

"I want them tested to destruction if necessary. Is that clear enough? Get me some results!" Rometty shouted, slamming his fist on the table. The audit team's flight would be landing in an hour, so he needed something, no matter how slight, within three or four hours at the latest.

***

Seward had parked the Rover at the side of the road when Tara's HUD had shown faint IFF signals marked as an enemy "aircraft". They were well beyond the police search perimeter, and the countryside was dark and silent save for the sound of the wind and occasional animal and insect life. There was almost no sound from traffic or the glow of headlights since most cars had been diverted or turned back by the police, or the news of a mad killer running wild in the countryside. All sensible residents were safely locked up in their homes, or so they hoped. Seward knew from experience that a werewolf could break into any building short of a fortress using brute force. Fortunately, werewolves didn't climb that well, and sheer walls were still an effective defence. "We'll have to go on foot from here. It should be safe to bring out the crossbows. If we're stopped or meet anyone, we'll say that the car broke down and we are carrying these because we heard the news and were afraid."

Tara nodded, knowing that Seward would be able to see or at least sense the movement despite the darkness. Unlike the powerful link that she had with Seward, her ability to detect Viktor, if it was indeed him and not some other unfortunate who had been infected, was much more limited. "That way, I think."

"Let me lead the way. I've had much more hunting experience. Stay on my right and try not to shoot me in the back."

She started to take offence when she notice the grin on his face. She chuckled and smiled back. "I'll do my best." To be fair, Seward had no reason to trust her competence when it came to medieval style combat, or hunting and tracking. He began to jog in the direction she had indicated, and as they glided silently through the countryside, she marvelled at the speed and confidence with which they were able to move in the darkness. She was even able to avoid treading in the numerous cow patties.

Seward led them in a zig-zag course, constantly refining their direction guided by Tara's HUD, occasionally going around buildings, ditches, and impenetrable clumps of trees. Several times they took cover and froze when a search helicopter flew overhead.

"Can you sense Viktor at all?" she asked, marvelling that she wasn't winded in the slightest. In fact it felt wonderfully free and invigorating. The small backpacks that Renfield had supplied fitted tightly and didn't bounce or chafe at all, although she could feel the water in the canteen slosh and the numerous energy bars roll around inside.

"Vaguely. I don't have a visual guide like you do,

but over the years I've developed feelings, senses that I can't properly describe. Being constantly hunted by vampire killers is an excellent incentive to build up your survival skills. The modern age has actually been quite a relief and a bit more restful. Especially after Hammer made vampire films so very popular. I've developed quite an affection for Christopher Lee and his portrayal of me. Nowadays, everyone knows about vampires, but no one actually believes in them any more – almost no one, at any rate."

"Wait! The track is getting stronger. That way!" she said, pointing. "Maybe five miles."

"Yes, I can feel him now. Hurry," Seward said, breaking into a run.

Tara imagined a long silk cloak trailing behind his tall athletic figure and grinned as she followed. In the corner of her mind she couldn't help noting that he had a nice tight bottom too.

Ten minutes later, a shriek of female agony rang out across the fields. It would have been too faint for any normal human to pinpoint, but Seward's head swivelled like a tracking gun turret. "There!" He sniffed the air and then led them in a curving path towards their prey. "We have to approach from downwind or he'll catch our scent."

It took them another three minutes to cover the remaining distance, and Tara burst through the trees into a clearing behind Seward, only to be faced with a scene of nightmarish horror. Although Seward had been silent as a ghost, his footsteps seeming to not even bend the grass, Tara didn't have his skill and the tiny rustling noise she made caused the werewolf's head to snap around, it's blood soaked muzzle curling in a snarl. They had arrived too late, and Jenna was nothing but butchered meat. Tara saw the damage to the girl's loins and felt an overwhelming urge to throw up.

Seward raised his bow and fired, the cable

whipping through the complex arrangement of pulleys and hurling the silver tipped bolt as fast as a bullet.

But fast as the ancient vampire was, he was almost too late. Warned by the sound of their approach, the werewolf snatched up his victim's limp corpse and held it in front of himself like a shield. The bolt struck and pierced Jenna's torso and went on to tear a deep scratch in the werewolf's forearm.

Tara recovered from her shock and disgust and fired a second later, trying to aim and shoot around the dangling corpse. Her bolt hit Jenna's skull at a shallow angle, bounced off and sliced the werewolf's cheek and ear.

Roaring in pain and rage, the werewolf ripped the corpse in two and hurled the gory pieces at his attackers.

Seward dodged the clumsy missile and yanked the string of the high powered crossbow back with his fingers, a task that would normally have required a hook, cable, and crank, and reached into his quiver for another bolt.

The mass of raw flesh hit Tara's bow like a battering ram as she dodged, ripping it from her hands. She dived and rolled, snatching up the crossbow again and imitated her partner in reloading.

The distraction had given the werewolf the time it needed to dive into the trees, its furry form blending into the blurry grey shadows of early dawn. However it had not escaped unscathed. The silver arrow heads had done their work and disrupted its alien metabolism, and it began to change back to Viktor even as it bounded away.

Although the blood and other fluids coating her hands and arms made her skin crawl, Tara unhesitatingly charged after Viktor, her reloaded crossbow scanning the path in front of her as if it had a mind of its own. But something was wrong. She frowned when the IFF signal began to fade. She realised that she could only detect Viktor when he was in his werewolf form, unlike

Seward, whose vampiric attributes were constantly present. She slowed, and realised that Seward was just behind her. "I've lost him," she whispered.

"If he's changed back, he'll be slower and weaker. As soon as the sun rises I'll be able to track him the old fashioned way."

Before she could reply, Viktor's voice floated out from the semi-darkness. He spoke softly, and the trees and bushes made it impossible to pinpoint anything more than a general direction. It also seemed as if he was moving as he spoke. "Tara, I know where your father is."

Tara froze. He had been present when they took her father, so it was completely possible that he spoke the truth. "Where is he? Is he all right?"

"A trade, Tara. You give me a head-start and I'll tell you where to find him."

"How do I know I can trust you to tell the truth?"

"The bastards wanted to cage me, cut me up like a lab rat. Why do you think I'm out here? I don't owe them anything. I intend to have my revenge on them in due time. Helping you get your father back will be a start."

"How do you know you can trust us?" Seward called out, his head tilting from side to side in an attempt to pinpoint Viktor's location.

"I'll write the location in the dirt and you stay where you are for at least twenty minutes. Then you can come and find it. If I hear you move before then I'll double back and erase it, and you'll never find him. It will take you hours at least to find me, and now that I know about your little bows and arrows, our next meeting won't be so one sided. After my escape, they will most likely move your father to a safer location, so you don't have much time to save him. Do we have a deal?"

Tara looked at Seward, agonised by the need to decide.

"He's your father. The call of blood is a strong

one. You must decide."

"Perhaps I can go to my father and you can go after Viktor."

He shook his head. "They've already proven that they are well armed and dangerous. You'll need help to rescue your father, who might be injured or drugged. If you agree to the deal, I'll go with you. When your father is safe, we will resume our hunt for Viktor."

Tara sighed, her shoulders slumping. She knew that she had no choice. Viktor knew how close she and her father were, and knew how she would decide. "All right, you bastard. You have a deal. But if you're lying, I swear that I'll not rest until I have your shaggy hide for a rug."

"Temper, temper, Tara. Remember, I'll be listening and smelling. Take a step from where you are, and your father is gone. I won't tell you a thing, and good luck in even catching the werewolf me alive. Goodbye."

Seward waited silently until five minutes had passed, and then gestured with his bow. "Let's go."

"But he said..."

"He'll be long gone, and we still have to find the spot where he wrote the location." It took almost an hour for them to find the exact spot in the dirt where Viktor had inscribed his message even though it had become light enough for Seward to follow his tracks, because the werewolf had woven a complicated path back and forth through the trees as they had talked, and his tracks repeatedly crossed and went over each other.

Tara knelt down and stared at the words, desperate not to make a mistake. "Werner Biotech Research".

Seward pulled his smart-phone from his backpack and performed a search. "I know that name. They are one of my competitors. Ruthless bastards. Several of their products have proven to be dangerous, and they indulge in a lot of industrial espionage, although nothing anyone can prove in court." He flipped his finger across the screen as he read. "Ah hah! They have a research and development facility in Hemel Hempstead, not too far from here."

"Lets get back to the car then," Tara said, relieved that Viktor had apparently not lied.

"You realise that we can't just barge in and demand they give your father back."

"I know that."

"What I mean is, are you ready to do whatever it takes to free him? It is likely that people who are just doing their job are going to get hurt."

"Are you suggesting that I call the police?"

"No. Without evidence of any kind, at best they would just take your report and toss it in the bin. With good lawyers this Werner group could even get a restraining order against you. Don't underestimate corporate power in today's world. But once you go in, you'll be on the wrong side of the law. Have you considered the possibility that you might even have to kill someone?"

Tara clenched her fists and nodded. In her mind she replayed the moment the airfield guards were literally shredded by the helicopter's Gatling gun, innocent Krisztina's dead body, and then the white hot agony of the machine gun bullets slamming into her own back and head. "They started the killing first. Even Jenna's death can ultimately be laid at their doorstep." She turned to look at him. "I'm sorry. I've been taking it for granted that you'd want to go along with this madness. My father isn't your responsibility, and I've no claim upon you. You've already helped me more than I could reasonably expect. Just help me get to Werner's facility and I'll do the rest myself."

"Don't be ridiculous. I chose to help you, and I won't walk away now. Besides, there is still the matter of the alien artefacts to be considered. I don't fancy the idea of either the military or the corporations getting hold of the ability to create and use monsters. Besides, I suspect that everyone is going to underestimate the capabilities of the e-nanite system. Over the centuries I have come to the conclusion that it possesses a degree of AI, a sophisticated artificial intelligence."

"Then you'll help me?"

He nodded. "I will. But let me suggest that before we barge in anywhere, we make an effort to link your attackers with Werner. While we wait for my contacts in the police force to get into the office this morning, we can scout the Werner facility from the outside."

They had reached the Range Rover and Tara pressed her forehead against the chill metal of the vehicle. Then she looked up and managed a smile. "Vlad the Impaler is suggesting caution?"

His face hardened. "I was a successful military leader, fighting forces greatly larger and more powerful than mine. There is a time for caution – and there is a time to strike fear in your enemy's heart. You may yet regret allying yourself with Vlad Dracula."

"At least you haven't shot me in the back."

"And I never will. Backstabbing was never my style," he replied, smiling at her.

They were standing very close, and Tara became intensely aware of how good looking he was, and how his eyes seemed to magnetically draw her attention. Feeling suddenly breathless, she took a step back and shook herself. "I thought you said you didn't have hypnotic powers."

Seward just smiled and tilted his head towards the Rover. "Perhaps we should get going."

Tara took a deep breath and narrowed her eyes suspiciously. "Perhaps we should."

***

The test subject screamed and convulsed, his

struggles so violent that he bled at the wrists and ankles despite the padding of the restraints.

Dr Maeda put down the insulated electrodes and grunted in annoyance when the subject went limp and stopped breathing. The instruments monitoring his vital signs indicated that he was dead. This was the fourth subject that had died under extreme stimulation despite the application of the alien treatment. It had not been hard to discover how to activate the alien device and to make it apply the symmetrically cross-shaped cartridges to the test subjects, two male and two female so far, but annoyingly, nothing at all had happened as witnessed by the three other corpses in the body bags on the other side of the laboratory. He knew Mr Rometty would not be pleased, and his employer seemed particularly unstable today. In addition, the euphemistically named "Internal Audit" team would be arriving at any moment and Maeda did not savour looking incompetent in front of representatives from Head Office.

He ordered his assistant to take the corpse away and used the intercom to call for the next test subject, a woman this time. Glancing at the appropriate folder on his computer monitor, he saw that she was a street walker, a common prostitute. Surprisingly, she was young and attractive, and the initial tests had revealed that she was free of any infectious diseases and she had not been a heavy drug user. Despite being totally ruthless when it came to his work, Maeda was not insane and was quite boringly heterosexual, so he looked towards the entrance with pleasant anticipation when he heard the patient trolley coming down the hallway. The automatic doors silently slid open to reveal the naked woman strapped to the shiny metal surface of the trolley.

The attendant pushed the trolley to the position marked by painted lines on the floor and then turned and left, all without meeting the doctor's eyes. Dr Maeda did not encourage familiarity when dealing with the staff.

Maeda pressed the button that sealed the laboratory doors, and then turned to his new subject.

"Who are you people? What am I doing here? Look, if this is some kind of kinky game, I'm willing to go along. You don't have to use these," the woman said, pulling at the thick straps that held her wrists. She tried to smile seductively at the white coated Asian man, which was difficult given the absolute terror that gripped her mind. She had seen enough slasher films to know that she was in serious trouble.

Maeda picked up a scalpel and placed his rubber-gloved hand around her throat. "You will remain silent. If you speak again, I shall destroy your vocal cords and render you permanently silent. Is that understood?"

The woman went cross-eyed, focusing upon the glittering stainless steel blade that hovered above her face and nodded vigorously, her chin thumping against Maeda's hand.

Maeda activated the voice recorder, the same kind used by a forensic pathologist when performing an autopsy. In his mind, there really wasn't any difference between an autopsy and what he was doing. "Subject number five of DT series one. Caucasian female. Initial medical examination and test results indicate no presence significant diseases or physiological dysfunction. Blood-tests reveal traces of alcohol and cocaine in non-significant levels. Examination of her genitals indicate recent sexual activity, but no vaginal or anal lesions. Now activating video cameras prior to application of the extra-terrestrial dermal injection system."

The woman began to struggle again when she saw the strange glowing device that hovered above the surface of the steel trolley that Maeda pulled towards her. She struggled even harder when the white coated man swabbed her upper arm with alcohol and brought the blade of the scalpel towards her. "Aaaoww! That hurt you fucker!" she yelled when Maeda cut a neat shallow "X" in her skin roughly two centimetres across.

"As confirmed in previous tests, the alien device only responds to actual physical injury, although it is possible that it would also respond to a serious disease of some kind. Therefore, two intersecting incisions have been made upon the subject's left upper arm in order to initiate a response." Even as he spoke, his free hand shot out to grip her throat again, half throttling her in warning. He touched a shaded indentation on the device and nodded when a particular light came on, followed a moment later by the extension of the flexible arm, tipped by one of the cross shaped cartridges. Normally they would have been too precious to use in this manner, but since they had five crates full of them, Rometty had deemed it acceptable for a limited number to be expended in experimentation. This was the last that Maeda planned to use in this way.

Despite the girl's best efforts, the device succeeded in placing the cartridge against the skin of her arm where it adhered firmly. Her struggles subsided when nothing else happened and there was no unpleasant sensation other than a cool tingling.

"The applicator cartridge has adhered itself to the subject's skin. All previous applications required half an hour before the cartridge could be detached from the subject. The video cameras and instruments will be set to continuously record until the process is completed." Maeda turned his attention to the girl. "I shall leave you now, but I'll be back in half an hour. I suggest that you try to get some rest until then." He stepped back and out of the view of the cameras and then let himself study her naked form. Apart from signs of malnutrition and some bruises which were the result of her capture, she was really quite attractive, and he eagerly anticipated the next phase of the test. This time he intended to apply the pain and physical damage much more slowly in order to give the alien system the best chance to respond. He tapped on the keyboard of the medical computer, made some technical notes and checked her vital signs, then strode out of the laboratory in search of a Cornish pasty and a cup of tea.

Just as Seward had feared, Maeda had made a fundamental error regarding the nature of the alien implant. Once applied, it did not blindly attempt to heal its host. It immediately recognised that it was in a being that it had not been designed to treat, and as basic principal, did nothing. This rule was only overridden when the host was in danger of imminent death. Its designers had foreseen the possibility that only the wrong kind of healing unit might be available in the battlefield, and so in an ultimate emergency, the nanite colony would intervene. Even then, it would do the very minimum required to maintain life, basically placing the host in an induced deep, almost death-like coma pending the arrival of proper medical attention. Only if the host's condition continued to deteriorate and no appropriate treatment appeared would the nanites take further action. Their next step was to attempt to obtain the patient's consent to emergency treatment. It this proved impossible, and death was imminent, the nanites would intervene, using its basic medical template, which in this case was the werewolf form of the alien species it had been designed to treat. This had the unfortunate effect of grafting the werewolf physiology on the host. Under normal circumstances this was not a complete disaster, since the application of healing nanites appropriate to the host's species and hospital treatment could in many cases reverse the changes, if it was not left for too long. The other significant factor was that this was a shipment of medical nanites intended for the military. It was assumed that they would be used under battlefield conditions. Hence they were designed to boost physical strength, all the host's senses and mental acuity, create an increased mood of aggression, and restore or improve combat related "muscle memory". In a totally alien species which did not understand what had happened, these were the optimal conditions to create a monster, especially if the will and intelligence of the host was weak.

***

Subject One opened his eyes. It was totally dark and it was hot and hard to breathe. At first all he felt was confusion and pain. He tried to move his arms and discovered that they were constricted by something smooth and slick. It was as if he was inside a big rubbish bag, except that it was made of much stronger material. He tried to speak, and it hurt. He realised that his jaw was injured, as was his tongue, and it seemed as if some of his teeth were missing or broken. With this realisation came even more pain, and he began to struggle against whatever was holding him. Flashes of memory suddenly returned. He remembered being beaten and tied down. The air in the bag was growing foul and he started to gasp. He remembered a face – a Chinese or Japanese man in … in a white coat. Then it all came flooding back, the burns and cuts and shocks. Rage and terror pounded through his being and it felt like his heart was going to explode. He had to escape or he would die. Fresh pain washed through his body as bone, muscles, and tendons began to twist and change. Broken flesh started to heal at an incredible rate and his skin itched madly.

The prostitute who was now Subject Five heard sounds of energetic struggling, the rustling and ripping of tough plastic, and the squealing and rattling of a medical trolley. "Hello? Is somebody there? Can you help me?" She went silent when she heard the sound of heavy breathing … no, it was more like the panting of a large animal. She tried to twist her head around to see,

137

but she was too tightly restrained for her to move that much. There was more ripping and rattling, then a soft moaning that somehow changed into a low, angry growling. She bit her lip and pulled at the straps, trying to remember all the escape tricks she had ever read or seen. Then she heard what sounded like feet landing on the ground … but the clicking noise made it more like the paws of a large dog jumping onto a tiled floor. Why would they allow a guard dog into a laboratory? The growls grew louder, as if the animal was gaining strength. Then she heard the click of an electronic lock and the hiss of the laboratory's doors sliding open. She almost cried out in relief. The mad scientist had come back!

The pasty had hit the spot and Maeda strode into the laboratory, whistling cheerfully, eager to get to work on the attractive woman. He pressed the button that locked the doors behind him and would require the entry of a code number and a scan of his hand to open again. "All right, how are you feeling Subject Five? Do you feel any unusual …" He saw the way she was struggling, her naked body glistening with sweat and frowned. "I thought we had an underst…"

"Look behind you!" she whispered fearfully.

"What? What do you mean? And why are you whispering like that?" Then Dr Maeda heard the rumbling growl behind his back and he realised that he had been terribly stupid. "Bugger. I forgot something. Don't go anywhere, I'll be right back," he said, slowly backing towards the door.

"Wait, you can't leave me here with whatever-it-is."

"You're already infected. You're just as dangerous as it is." He was forced to turn and look when he heard the click of claws on the floor moving towards the exit. "Oh my." The werewolf was much larger and menacing in real life than when he had watched the videos of

Viktor. The most disturbing thing about it was the obvious intelligence in its eyes.

The werewolf glanced at the security lock and then back at Maeda. Its jaws opened in a toothy grin, plainly daring Maeda to try for the door. Some of the deeper wounds that Maeda had inflicted upon Subject One could still be seen as patterns of disruption in the sleek flow of the werewolf's fur, and the creature traced one of them with a huge, razor sharp claw, and then tilted its head.

Maeda reversed his direction and backed towards the trolley that held Subject Five. Next to it was a tray bearing a collection of implements that could be used as weapons. He reached behind himself when he felt the tray touch his back and his shaking fingers felt the rounded cylindrical shape of the cattle prod. He knew it wasn't an ideal weapon, but it might keep the thing off of him long enough to unlock the door. Gritting his teeth, he snatched up the powerful electric shock device and extended it in front of himself like a rapier. He pressed the trigger button, making a miniature lightning bolt jump from one contact to the other at the tip of the prod. The werewolf backed away, obviously wary of the weapon. Maeda grinned and edged towards the door. "Not so fierce now, eh?"

The werewolf reached out a paw, then quickly withdrew it when Maeda zapped it with the cattle prod, roaring in anger.

Maeda entered the security number by touch, keeping his eyes on the werewolf's movements and holding it off with the threat of the prod. He sighed in relief when the pad beeped and a synthetic voice said, "Please place your hand on the scanner." He held out his hand, fingers and palm flat, and that was when the werewolf struck. His eyes widened in surprise when the monster gripped the end of the cattle prod, completely ignoring the high voltage flowing into its hand. The prod was ripped from his grip, and then the werewolf was upon him, moving faster than he had imagined possible. One hairy paw closed around his throat, huge claws digging into the sides of his neck and lifting him up onto his toes. The other grabbed his extended arm by the wrist. The beast's black nose was close enough for Maeda to smell the creature's foul breath and he saw it look at the security pad and then back at him. That was when he realised he had been outsmarted. The werewolf had deliberately allowed him to enter the code number into the lock before attacking, letting him think that it feared the cattle prod. Then the creature grinned and looked at his hand. Maeda's face paled. "No!" His screams echoed from the laboratory walls when the werewolf's teeth crunched into his elbow and severed his arm.

The werewolf that had been Subject One licked Maeda's blood from its lips, savouring its taste. Still holding the screaming scientist off the ground with one hand, it kicked up a hind foot and raked its claws across Maeda's belly, ripping it open and disembowelling him with a single stroke. It pulled Maeda's face close to his, snarled its hatred, and then let the dying scientist drop to the floor. Subject One sniffed the air and growled. The scent led him to the other body bags. They did not smell completely right, but he could sense the kinship in them. He ripped the bags open and studied the contents. Subject Two, a woman, was already starting to twitch, while Subjects Three and Four were still healing from their fatal injuries. It sniffed again, and it turned its attention to Subject Five, who was still uninjured and fully human.

The young woman who was Subject Five watched in frozen horror as the hairy monster, the werewolf, walked up to her. She had seen what had happened to Maeda, but despite her best efforts at escape she had only succeeded in further tearing the skin around her wrists and ankles. Her naked skin crawled and she bit her lip until it bled when the werewolf placed a clawed paw upon her belly and leaned its huge head down to sniff at her. She almost screamed when it pressed its nose into her crotch and snuffled vigorously. Its nose was wet and cold, and she shuddered when its long tongue reached out and licked. It raised its head, tilted it quizzically, and whined. "Nice doggy?" Subject Five said, forced by her terror to say something. She was sure she would go mad if she remained silent any longer.

The werewolf was confused. This thing on the table was not its own kind, but something inside of it insisted it was a female. But it was too different in form to be properly sexually attractive. And yet there was something in its scent.

The helpless woman shuddered when the creature's saliva dripped onto her thigh and the claws on her belly sank ever so slightly deeper into her flesh, but not quite breaking the skin. The thing's jaws opened and she thought that it was going to sink its teeth into her leg. Then its belly rumbled, loud enough for her to hear it. The werewolf's head turned and it sniffed. Then suddenly it was gone, and she heard the sound of teeth tearing at flesh and fabric and she realised that it had decided to eat the scientist instead of her. Normally the sounds and the thought of what was happening would have made her violently sick, but right now all she felt was relief.

The werewolf ate until it was sated, having consumed a good portion of the corpse, its accelerated metabolism breaking down and absorbing the meat with incredible speed and using it to build up the creature's body. Licking the gore off of its muzzle, it turned its eyes to Maeda's severed arm and then to the lock.

***

Seward set down his cell phone. "That was Danny Craig, my head of security. The police have identified your would be assassins and their records show them as freelance guns for hire. Mercenaries."

Tara took the binoculars from her face and frowned. "So they're a dead end."

"Not quite. According to SO15, that's Counter Terrorism Command, which incorporated the old Special Branch, these men are known to have worked through a hiring agent, who handles negotiations and payment on their behalf. The police couldn't touch the agent because there was no evidence at all that he was involved in your case." He held up a finger to forestall Tara's response. "But, my own people paid him a visit, and when he discovered I was interested, he was most forthcoming."

"Why would he be frightened of you? Does he know that you're..."

Seward smiled. "Of course not. Including you, there are only three people in the world who know my true identity." He laughed at his own words. "It makes me sound like a comic superhero, doesn't it? Come to think of it, a fancy costume and a mask would certainly make people look in the wrong direction if my – our – abilities were discovered."

Tara tapped her fingers impatiently on the dashboard. "The agent?"

"Oh yes. No, he doesn't know that I'm – who I am – but I've had dealings with him before. A few years ago someone tried a bit of kidnapping and bombing in an effort to force me out from a business deal. Business is business, and I normally don't get worked up about it, but when some of my employees were badly hurt, I made an exception. As in your case, the villains were recruited by this agent. When he woke up one morning to find himself out in the countryside, and faced with the sight of every one of the men he had recruited to attack me impaled on a stake while still alive, he became most cooperative. Especially since there was an empty stake next to them, the significance of which did not escape him."

"Y-you did that?" Tara asked, shocked despite herself.

Stone faced, Seward said, "Before you judge me, consider what you would do in order to save your father and to prevent him from suffering the fate that they had intended for you."

Tara had a vision of her father's body shattering under a hail of bullets, and suddenly she felt a rush of anger that made her canine teeth ache and the tips of her fingers begin to change into claws. She forced herself to calm down, and she only spoke when all the changes faded completely away. "Was that all me, or has my character been changed as well as my body?"

"I doubt that, and remember I know what it feels like to completely surrender to the vampire or alien aspect. But, the alien system is very responsive to our needs and desires. It's a case of being careful what you wish for. But as for personality, I have not noticed any changes that couldn't be explained by time and experience. By modern standards, I was not and am not a very nice person. None of us were. My contemporaries when I was Voivode would have found the Geneva Conventions to be hilarious."

Taking a deep breath, Tara nodded. "So what did this 'agent' have to say?"

"According to him, the commission came from a 'cleaner', a corporate problem solver who works for a shipping company which is owned, through a series of obscure subsidiaries and nominees, by Werner." He nodded towards the facility that they were observing.

Tara gripped his arm excitedly. "So Viktor was telling the truth!" Then she pointed. "Look, there's a vehicle leaving the facility." In her haste she knocked the binoculars onto the floor of the car. "Dammit! I can't see if my father's in the vehicle." She squinted in frustration, knowing that the passengers would be out of view once the car turned the next corner in the road. "Hey! I can see them – as if they were right in front of me. It's two of the group who drove in an hour and a half ago. My father's not with them, unless he's in the boot." She turned to glare accusingly at Seward. "Why didn't you tell me we can do that? I've been staring through those bloody binoculars for hours."

"I didn't know if you could do it, or if just telling you would do any good. I'm not the one with the nano-interface thingy."

"So now that it's confirmed, can we go in and rescue my father?" Tara said.

Seward got out of the Rover with fluid grace and gestured towards the Werner facility in invitation.

"Aren't we taking the crossbows?"

"They'll have security cameras. We can claim to be animal-rights activists or something if we're spotted, but it would be hard to explain wandering around a legally operating research facility carrying crossbows and silver tipped arrows."

With her newly discovered hawk-like vision, it was simplicity itself to spot the security cameras and to find a blind spot. Well, she mused, it was a blind spot if the intruder could jump up most of the height of a telephone pole and then leap across the gap from the pole in order to cling to the wall of the closest building eight metres away, and then crawl up to the flat roof.

When Seward landed beside her on the roof, he said, "This was how people came to believe that vampires could fly or melt into mist. There were few really tall buildings in those days so it was easy to jump up and onto roofs or out of windows, seemingly disappearing into thin air, kind of like those fantasy kung-fu films."

"We're standing on the office and IT wing of the

complex. The senior management, laboratories, and storage spaces, basically the confidential stuff, are over there," Tara said, pointing to the larger block of buildings at the other side of the property. "No cameras up here."

"Watch out for staff coming out onto the roof for a smoke," Seward said as he ran across the building beside her.

"This is almost too easy," she said as they leapt side by side across to the main building containing the reception area, meeting rooms and conference halls, the offices of the administrative and accounting staff, and the staff canteen.

"You'd prefer angry peasants with pitchforks and torches?" Seward said, scanning his surroundings with all his senses to see if they had been detected. The roof of the main building was harder to navigate, being covered with antenna, dishes and cables as well as the obligatory air conditioning towers. He watched fascinated as Tara flowed over and around all the obstacles with a sureness that only her sonar enhanced senses allowed. He was more than capable of the same, but it was different to see it in someone else. Especially since that someone had such a good figure and was wearing a skin tight body suit.

Tara was just about to leap across to the laboratory wing when her enhanced senses caught a tiny movement on the roof. She didn't need the "Incoming Missile" warning in her HUD to tell her to dodge, and she threw herself sideways and down, slamming hard into the reinforced concrete parapet. There was a sharp crack of sound and the rumbling whoosh of a projectile just missing her head. "There's a sniper on the roof!" she shouted.

Seeing that Tara was the sniper's target, Seward didn't hesitate, but instead accelerated until he was a blur of motion and launched himself across the gap between the 	buildings.

The sniper gaped in amazement at the figure flying towards him even as his training and instincts tried to swivel the muzzle of his silenced precision rifle towards the rapidly approaching target. But the rifle and telescopic sight were not made for snap shooting. He fired and missed, and he was still working the bolt to reload when the flying figure landed beside him. He tried to scream in terror when he saw the inhuman red eyes and needle sharp fangs that looked nothing like the special effects in the cinema, but for some reason no sound came out of his mouth.

Dracula dodged the jets of blood spurting from the severed veins and arteries, and waited until the blood stopped pumping before he reached out with claw-tipped hands to grip the sniper's head.

Tara landed upon the roof just in time to see her companion tear the sniper's head off of his body and skewer it on the long barrel of the dead man's rifle before wedging the stock between a couple of pipes so that it stood erect in gory warning. "Oh my god!" Tara gasped, almost slipping on the puddle of blood that covered the roof around the headless corpse. She stepped backwards in shock when Seward wheeled around, fangs bared and claws ready to strike. Worse still, she felt her own fangs and claws begin to form in response to the threat.

The monster that was Dracula spun away, and when he turned back he was Seward again. "I apologise. He tried to kill you, and old memories and habits are hard to suppress."

Tara recalled the legend that Vlad's wife had thrown herself to her death in order to escape capture and dishonour at the hands of his enemies. She waved off his apology. "You just caught me by surprise." Nodding at the head-on-a-stick she said, "That's going to be a bit hard to explain though."

He smiled. "Everyone knows that terrorists

commit all manner of atrocities. Convenient things, terrorists." He nodded at the blood soaked rifle. "With luck, no one noticed the shots."

Just at that moment, alarms began to blare all over the complex. Tara raised an eyebrow. "You were saying?"

Seward held up a finger. "Wait. Listen to that."

Although it would have been inaudible to anyone else, when Tara concentrated she could hear the PA system inside the building. She frowned in concentration and recited, "Containment breach in Laboratory Three. A dangerous specimen is loose in the building. Institute full lock-down procedures." She looked at Seward. "Some kind of disease or biological weapon?"

"I don't think so. It's too much of a coincidence. With Viktor's departure, I believe our friends downstairs have been experimenting with the e-nanites, and they're not pleased with the results. Fools! I wonder how many werewolves they've just created. As if we didn't have enough trouble on our hands with Viktor running about the countryside. Sooner or later he's going to accidentally infect someone too. This is rapidly getting out of control."

"My father's trapped down there with those werewolves!" Tara exclaimed.

Seward pointed at the door that lead up to the roof. "It looks like I was wrong in not bringing the crossbows."

***

"I must protest this high handed removal of the alien samples from this facility without my express approval," Rometty said angrily.

"Your protest is noted and Mr Werner will be informed," Brad Dennel, leader of the Internal Audit team said. "You could hardly expect that we would allow

147

such an important discovery to be concentrated in a single location. The fact that you did not immediately send samples to Head Office upon receipt will also be noted in our reports. My men will ensure that the samples are securely transferred by a trusted courier, and while they are out they will also look into this mysterious person who prevented the elimination of Tara Harker. Through our contacts in the NSA we have been able to access images from a traffic camera near the scene. It meant nothing to the local police because they do not know about Tara Harker, but a face recognition system was able to pick her out as a passenger in a car leaving the vicinity of the abortive attack. We'll identify the owner of the car shortly. Mr Werner is also concerned that you did not make stronger efforts to capture her alive."

"According to Viktor's debriefing report, the woman is dangerous, and this information was passed on to the capture team. It seems that they chose to interpret it as a licence to employ lethal force. If they had survived the operation I would have had them properly … reprimanded."

Dennel waved Rometty's excuses aside. "I'll look into that later. Right now, I need to talk to this Viktor so that I can assess him personally, and I need to know what your researchers have discovered to date."

Rometty had been dreading this question. Despite his senior position in the company, he knew he could lose everything in a heartbeat if Mr Werner decided that he had acted improperly. The Internal Audit teams were like the Inquisition. They ensured that senior staff remained loyal, eliminated the incompetent, and made things and people who might embarrass Werner Aerospace and Robotics disappear. "I'm afraid Viktor Tiranul is unavailable at the moment."

The big American frowned disapprovingly. "Unavailable? Explain."

"Viktor had some personal matters to attend to. He should be back in a day or so."

"Lying to an Audit team is viewed very seriously by Mr Werner," the Auditor said. "We have seen your security videos and we know what happened."

Rometty shrugged. "He'll be recaptured. Remember, it – he – was a part of our team in Romania and was here voluntarily. We had no reason to think that he would become … difficult."

"Until he learned that you wanted to cut him up," Dennel said sarcastically.

"I admit that was an oversight. No one imagined that his hearing was so good while still in human form."

"It's your job to imagine these things. Now because of your carelessness, we may have lost sole access to the alien technology. Mr Werner is not pleased."

"Viktor is Romanian, with no friends or relatives in Britain. He has little or no money, and his papers including his passport are still here. How far can he go? We'll get him back."

"Not if he becomes the subject of a public manhunt," Dennel said. "What about Roland Harker? Is he cooperating?"

Before Rometty could reply, the blaring of the laboratory containment breach alarm made him jump.

Dennel frowned. "Laboratory Three?"

Rometty went pale. "That is Dr Maeda's laboratory. He's the one assigned to test the alien samples."

"I don't recall Head Office giving approval for the alien samples to be tested," Dennel snapped.

"Well, with Tiranul's escape…" Then the alarm changed, announcing the escape of a dangerous specimen and total building lockdown. All exits from the building would be locked and the floor which held the breached laboratory would be sealed off, including the ventilation system.

"What the hell is wrong now?" the American shouted angrily.

Rometty pressed the button on his intercom for Security. "What's the problem?" he asked, trying to sound calm.

The security guard who answered sounded winded and scared. From the sounds in the background it was obvious that he was using his radio, which was being relayed to the intercom system. "Dr Maeda's dead! The thing tore him apart, as well as one of my men who was patrolling the corridor. He's the one who triggered the lockdown, but it trapped him inside the section with the … the creature. It looks just like the one which escaped earlier. I can see it through the security door, and it can see me." There was the sound of pounding. "It's trying to break through," the guard said nervously.

Rometty rolled his eyes. "Those doors are airtight and bulletproof glass. Don't be..." Over the intercom came the sound of more crashing and pounding. Then he heard the crash of a shotgun being fired. "Why are you shooting, you fool! You'll damage the door!"

"It jumped up and tore into the ceiling," the guard shouted, deafened by the noise of the shotgun being fired inside the narrow confines of the corridor. "And that's not bulletproof … sir." The shotgun crashed again, and then there was the sound of another man's voice and then two shotguns fired in quick succession. "Wait, I think we hit it. I saw something through the hole. I can see..."

Rometty never discovered what the guard saw, because the man's transmission was interrupted by a ripping sound, the thud of something heavy falling, more gunshots – and then screams of absolute horror and agony. There was a loud crackle and thud of something striking the microphone, and then the transmission went dead.

There was the smooth click of lubricated metal as

Dennel worked the slide on his automatic pistol. He lifted his cuff to his mouth. "Sam, we have trouble. Go weapons free. Meet up with me at Rometty's office and bring the case with you," he said, authorising his subordinate to shoot anyone or anything that got in his way. "Can we get out of the building?" he asked Rometty.

"Only by unlocking the doors from the main security station on the ground floor. That's so that I can't be forced to open the exits by the staff if there's a biological contamination. The door to the station is armoured and the guard inside is under orders not to let me in unless I'm alone.

Dennel nodded. He knew that in the event of a bio-hazard, Head Office had instructed the guard not to allow anyone in or out until the Decontamination Team, which was situated outside of the complex, was on site – not even Rometty. Fortunately it was obvious that the problem was not a disease or poison, so the guard should cooperate. And if not, he had something in the bag that Sam was bringing that would take care of the door to the security station. He had asked Rometty because local management had been known to install their own bolt holes in violation of regulations.

A rap on the door announced the arrival of Sam, and Rometty let him in.

The "Auditor" entered and nodded to Dennel. "Hey Brad. Sure sounds like the shit has hit the fan. I brought presents," he said, throwing the long heavy case he was carrying with both hands onto Rometty's desk. He unlatched the lid and threw it open to reveal a mass of weaponry. There were two TAR 21 assault rifles, two Kriss Vector .45 SMGs, and an assortment of accessories, blades, and explosives, as well as magazines and ammo for the guns.

In the meantime, Rometty had picked up a remote control and after entering a password, was able to display the feed from all of the security cameras, one floor at a time on his wide screen. He switched on the intercom's general PA channel. "This is Mr Rometty. Anyone sighting the escaped experimental animal should notify me immediately. There'll be a bonus for anyone who contributes to its capture."

"Experimental Animal?" Dennel said in a sarcastic tone.

"Well I can't just announce that a werewolf is loose in the building, can I?"

The intercom buzzed. "Mr Rometty, this is Watson in Enzyme Research. I heard a noise and when I stepped out of my lab I think I saw..."

"Watson? Watson? What did you see? Come on, talk to me, you bloody fool." He jumped when a low vicious growling came over the intercom. "Shit!" Rometty cried, cutting the line and jumping back, as if that could keep the creature away. "Watson's lab is on the third floor. The werewolf is headed upwards – it's coming here!"

"You can't know that. It's probably just going after targets of opportunity," Dennel said calmingly, but that didn't stop him from lifting a TAR 21 from the case, inserting a magazine, and racking the charging handle to load it. He checked the safety and put the rifle down on the table beside him.

Sam did the same, but selected a Kriss Vector instead, preferring the more compact weapon for use in the rooms and corridors. "Close range stopping power," he said in explanation for his choice.

With his eyes still locked on the TV screen, Rometty went behind his desk and extracted a Smith and Wesson .357 M&P R8 revolver from a drawer.

"Nice gun," Dennel said.

Rometty nodded. "I prefer revolvers," he said absently.

Sam pointed to the screen. "There! I saw it."

Sweating in fear, Rometty clicked on the remote and the image from that particular camera filled the screen. The high-definition camera made the creature look like something out of a horror film as it stalked down the corridor. "Shit, that's the fourth floor. It's definitely headed upwards!"

The werewolf sniffed and then snarled, revealing its long, startlingly white fangs. Then it suddenly spun to face the door of the service closet that it was standing beside. It tilted its head and then sniffed again. Its hairy muscular arm shot out like a battering ram and its paw punched through the plywood and with a single heave of its shoulder it ripped the door off of its hinges and threw it aside, revealing the terrified crouching form of a blonde haired woman in a lab coat and who was still incongruously clutching a tablet computer in her hand. Her mouth opened in a silent scream, the security system not having audio, and she struck out at the werewolf with the tablet when it hooked its claws in the fabric of her coat and hauled her out of the closet. The tablet struck the creature on the nose, and the roar that it uttered made the video image vibrate. A slap of its hand sent the tablet flying to smash against the opposite wall.

"Fuck!" Sam exclaimed when the werewolf grabbed her forearm and ripped it completely off with a twist of its paw like a child disassembling a doll.

Dennel's face hardened in concern when the werewolf turned to look directly into the camera lens and snarled. "It knows we're watching." He picked up the Tavor. "We can't stay here. Since it's coming up, maybe we can slip past it using the elevator emergency override."

Rometty selected another camera, this one on the third floor. "No we can't," he said and pointed.

"Son of a bitch!" Sam said when he saw each of the lift doors jammed open with a dead body lying half-way into the cage. "That thing is smart."

"All right then. It's coming up the left side of the building. We'll go all the way down the hall and used the other set of emergency stairs. Rometty, you bring along any passkeys or ID that might help us open doors. Sam, you stuff a sling bag with C4 and detonators. We might need to blow our way through a door or wall. I'll take more ammo."

Rometty clipped the pistol holster onto his waistband and added a couple of custom 8 round speed-loaders in leather pouches on the other side.

Dennel cracked open the door and peeked out into the newly cleaned reception area and saw Rometty's replacement secretary look up at him. "All right, lets go."

Rometty looked at the secretary, who was staring at all the fire-power on display. "You better come with us, Miss..."

"Palmer, Emily Palmer, Mr Rometty," she replied automatically. Numbly, she considered switching off her workstation, then changed her mind and picked up her handbag. Having also seen her share of slasher films with her boyfriend, she inserted herself behind Sam, leaving Rometty to take the rear. As they went out the door into the corridor, she remembered the quite illegal canister of pepper spray that an ex-boyfriend had brought back from the US. She delved into her handbag and brought the spray can out, holding it in front of her.

Sam glanced over his shoulder and saw the pepper spray. "Watch what you do with that. You squirt me with it and I'll shoot you."

Emily quickly took her finger off of the spray button and lowered her hand to waist height.

The little column came to a halt when Dennel held up his hand as he approached the side corridor that led to the lavatories and the emergency staircase. He quickly peeked one eye around the corner, and when he saw that the side corridor was empty he gestured with his hand

and resumed his advance.

Emily had just stepped into the open when a male scream echoed out of the emergency exit, the sound loud enough to penetrate the heavy fire door. She jumped in fright and collided with Sam's back when she scurried forward.

"Watch it!" Sam hissed angrily.

"It's coming. Run!" Rometty snapped, walking crabwise with his pistol pointing back the way they had come. When they were half way down the corridor, he suddenly grabbed Emily's arm. When she squeaked in alarm he hissed, "Our scent. It will catch our scent. Viktor could follow a scent like a bloodhound."

Dennel looked back and nodded. "We'll wait for you at the corner," he said and began to run, followed by Sam.

Confused, Emily watched the two Americans run away and looked uncomprehendingly at Rometty and his tight grip upon her arm. In panic she started to raise the pepper spray, which was in her other hand, but gasped when Rometty grabbed her wrist and directed her aim back the way they had come. "We need to hide our scent. Spray the corridor," he said, moving her hand in a circle in demonstration before dodging around her. Realisation penetrated her panic and she shielded her face with her forearm as she began to spray the noxious capsaicin based compound over the carpet and into the air.

"All right. That will have to do. Now run!" Rometty snapped and suited his words with action, not looking back to see if his new secretary was following.

There was a crash of splintering wood just as Emily darted around Dennel's body and into the side corridor where she saw Sam holding the emergency door open and waving to her.

Dennel remained where he was, his rifle held against the wall and pointing down the main corridor. He tensed when the werewolf burst into sight, its paws and arms dripping with blood. For a second it looked in his direction, but then it sneezed and hacked and retreated in the direction of Rometty's office. As soon as the creature's back was turned Dennel pulled back and ran towards Sam. "Lets go."

Sam carefully let the fire door click shut and then followed his partner down the fire stairs.

***

The rooftop access door locked itself just as they reached it, the metal of the door vibrating from the blaring alarm going off just behind it. The lock was strong, but the door itself was made of aluminium sheeting, and the metal shrieked and crumpled when Tara braced her feet and pulled sideways on the handle. "I could get used to this," she said with a grin.

"Just be careful the next time a guy gets grabby in a bar, or a woman bumps you with her trolley in the supermarket. With great power..."

"Comes great responsibility, blah, blah. I know."

"Actually I was going to say that it comes with ample opportunities to make a fool of yourself – and to bring out the peasants with the pitchforks," he said dryly. He smiled and gestured towards the stairs. "Ladies first."

"How gallant," she said with a raised eyebrow. She heard him chuckling as she cautiously made her way down to the sixth floor, her every sense extended to the maximum. She could hear the sounds of people moving and breathing, hushed whispers and a few voices shouting in panic. As usual, the occupants seemed split between those who desired to do something, anything, even if it didn't make much sense, and those who wanted just to huddle in a corner in the hopes that somebody else would fix the problem. One useful thing she did learn was that the lock-down only applied to the laboratories and the actual exits. That meant they could

156

freely move and search between floors – and so could the werewolf or werewolves. She was about to step out into the main corridor when Seward stopped her.

"Cameras," he whispered.

"Can you disable them?"

He peeked up and down the corridor. "Two of them. One at each end. Maybe more inside the units. I'll have to get closer." He reached inside a pocket of his coat. "Here, put this on."

"Venetian masks?" she asked in amusement, looking at the elaborate gold mask studded with zircon gems of various colours.

"Leftovers from a charity masked ball I held recently."

"Well they're certainly more classy than balaclavas," she said as she put it on.

"Wait here until I've put the cameras out of commission. That way they won't have any video of you, just the testimony of frightened witnesses. Always keep them guessing."

Even though she intellectually knew how fast Seward could be, it was still a shock when he seemingly almost vanished. She felt a rush of air as he went down the corridor after disabling the nearer camera to take care of the other one. Moments later he was back.

"All done. Shall we go?"

Most of the doors were identified with signs as well as numbers. Most were either filing and storage or the offices of the support services, with photocopiers and laser printers busily chugging away, the machines blissfully unaware of the panic, or filled with half disassembled equipment and boxes of parts. The staff that Tara saw peeking out of doorways didn't seem inclined to question the two masked strangers until their luck ran out and a uniformed security guard stepped out into the corridor.

"Hey! What are you doing out here? Didn't you

hear the lockdown alarm..." Then he noticed the masks and levelled his shotgun. He had seen what the unknown intruders had done to both guards and civilians alike, and was in no mood for restraint. He took aim at the larger of the two masked figures and fired.

Tara darted forward and to the side. Her sonar augmented vision let her "see" Seward spring up and out of the line of fire. She reached the guard at the same time as Seward, who had rebounded from the ceiling like a giant rubber ball and crashed down onto the guard, clawed hands striking the hapless man first and raking across his face and throat. She snatched the shotgun out of the man's hands as he fell, but realised that it was unnecessary. "Why did you have to..." Her rebuke was cut short when she saw the ragged hole in the waist of Seward's coat just above the hip. "You're hurt!"

Standing astride the dying guard, Seward turned his red-eyed gaze towards her. "I suggest you look away." When she didn't he shrugged and crouched down to close his jaws over the guard's torn throat.

From her own experience after the ambush, Tara understood that drinking blood allowed the e-nanites to most rapidly heal physical damage to their bodies because that was the vampire-like aliens' natural diet. Seward could have healed even by eating chocolate bars, but it would have taken hours, and they did not have the time. However, that didn't make it any easier for her to watch, especially knowing that she might have to do the same if she was injured. Besides, the guard had fired at Seward without bothering to identify them or giving them an opportunity to surrender. If Seward had been an ordinary human, he would have been the one lying on the ground dying.

Seward stood up, mopping the blood off of his lower face with his handkerchief. His fangs had retracted, but there was still a tinge of red in his eyes which stared challengingly at Tara from behind the gaudy mask.

"I can still see the bloodstains," she said, surprised and not a little concerned by her own lack of strong emotion. She suspected that either the alien pilot's emotional matrix was mixing with hers or the medical nanite system was suppressing her responses. Perhaps it was both, or perhaps she was more ruthless than she cared to admit.

Seward acknowledged her comment with a silent nod. She was unlike any vampire he had ever known, and he was still trying to understand her personality and the way she was ultimately going to react to everything that had happened to her. He suspected that her father's peril had kept her going in crisis mode up to now, but it would be different when her father was either safe or dead. He hadn't known anyone he could be totally truthful with, except for Renfield, for a very long time; it would be a pity if she went insane or turned into a classical "vampire" because she couldn't accept the changes that had been wrought in her. He pulled a packet of "wet wipes" from his coat and used them to clean the bloodstains off of his face. Although these days he rarely took blood from living creatures, human or otherwise, there was always the possibility he might need to, and walking around with half his face covered in blood was guaranteed to spoil the "successful entrepreneur" image that he tried to cultivate in line with his latest persona. "Keep the shotgun. You're less likely to hesitate with it that than with claws and fangs if the time comes that you need to fight." He removed the shotshell pouch from the dead guard's belt and handed it to her.

Now that they had made a spectacle of themselves, there was little chance of stealth, at least on this floor, so Tara picked an office and hammered on the door with her fist. "I know you're in there, so don't make me kick down the door. We just want to ask you some questions. No one will be hurt if they don't attack us."

After a moment of stunned silence, the electronic lock clicked and a frightened female face peeked out. "Please don't kill me. I'm just a clerk." The very fact that she wasn't gibbering in fear indicated that she hadn't seen Seward's vampiric activities.

With a reassuring smile Seward said, "We just need some directions. This lady is looking for her father. Where would um, guests be kept in this building?"

"Th-this is a research facility. We don't have guest rooms."

Seward saw that Tara was about to drive the butt of her shotgun into the woman's face and kicked her ankle. "All right then, what about somewhere with a good strong door? Some place that you might keep a large animal specimen, say a big dog or chimpanzee?"

"You're not from PETA are you?" the clerk asked suspiciously. Her eyes widened in fear when Tara shoved the muzzle of the shotgun under her chin.

"Just answer the sodding question or they're going to be needing a new clerk," Tara said, struggling to prevent her teeth from growing into fangs.

"F-fourth floor. Animal specimens not actually being used for testing are kept there."

Seward patted her cheek. "Thank you. Now be a good girl and go back inside; lock the door and don't come out again, or my friend will shoot you in the face."

Tara pointed. "That way's nearer. The lifts don't seem to be working. I haven't heard them move since we got here."

***

Subject Five bit her lip to stop from screaming. She had been lying strapped down naked on the chilly metal trolley for what seemed like days. She had been sniffed and pawed by a werewolf and survived, although the scientist person had been eaten. Now she could hear the other two dead bodies beginning to stir in their plastic cocoons. She had visions of zombies, but then she heard the growling. Shit, she thought, just what she needed – more werewolves!

***

Dennel and the others had just reached the fourth-floor landing when the fifth-floor fire door crashed open and a huge furry form hurled itself over the railings and swung arm over arm down the stairwell like a giant monkey to land with an acrobatic flip on the stairs just behind Rometty. With a triumphant roar it lashed out at the Managing Director with its paw.

However, demonstrating unexpected agility and reflexes, Rometty dropped and slid down the stairs onto the landing before rolling over and taking aim with his pistol.

Unfortunately for Emily, Rometty's manoeuvre left her standing in front of the werewolf. Its claws ripped right through her blazer, blouse and bra straps, and raked diagonally across her back. The impact of the blow hurled her forward to land right on top of Rometty, who barely managed not to blow a hole in her stomach.

With the line of fire clear, Dennel and Sam blazed away on full automatic at the pouncing monster. Both of them emptied their magazines in seconds and although many of their bullets had clearly hit the werewolf, they seemed only to have the effect of making it even more angry as it landed astride Emily and Rometty's bodies. Dennel spun and tore open the fire door. Holding it open with his shoulder even as he reloaded, Dennel shouted, "Back up Sam, I have the door."

Sam had already stuffed a fresh magazine into his odd looking compact weapon and he fired in short controlled bursts at the werewolf's face as he walked backwards out into the hallway.

Dennel fired as well, but on full automatic mode and succeeded in driving the werewolf back a step by the sheer impact of his bullets. He stepped back and pulled the door shut. Letting his rifle hand from its sling, he grabbed the door handle with both hands and braced a foot against the wall to hold it shut.

Spotting the red cabinet of a fire hose and axe, Sam smashed the glass with a snap kick and snatched the axe off of its brackets. Dashing over to where Dennel was holding the door, he shoved the haft of the axe through the door handle, jamming it shut.

Red faced with effort, Dennel released his death grip on the door and took off running, with Sam pounding along right beside him, abandoning Rometty and Emily to their fate.

***

Seward stepped into the fourth floor corridor, and was surprised to see two heavily armed men running madly in his direction. From their looks of surprise, they had not been expecting to see Seward and Tara either. From the quality of their suits and weapons, Seward guessed that these men were not mere security guards but some kind of corporate trouble shooters or mercenaries. Given the way they were running and their sweating faces, they had obviously found more trouble than they had bargained for. Seward extended his arms out to his sides. "We're looking for Roland Harker," he shouted in the voice he used on battlefields when he wanted to be noticed. He saw the barrel of Tara's shotgun extend past his shoulder out of the corner of his eye.

"Get out of the fucking way, you idiot!" Dennel cried, stumbling to a halt. He would simply have barged past the oddly masked man if not for the shotgun in the hands of the woman beside him. He glanced over his shoulder and then said, "You don't understand..."

162

"You have a werewolf chasing you," Seward said. "Tell us where Harker is and we'll let you pass."

"Fuck you," Dennel snarled and started to raise the muzzle of his rifle, trusting Sam to take care of the woman and her shotgun. His companion was a pro and at this range would be able to take her down by firing from the hip with his stubby submachine gun before she could even pick a target.

As a test pilot, Tara was very familiar with how her senses seemed to speed up in a life threatening crisis, but she was still amazed when everything went into slow motion except for her and Seward. With her eagle sharp vision she saw the muscles around Sam's eyes tighten and the tendons on the back of his hand twitch when he made the decision to fire, and she had all the time in the world to step out of his line of fire and to bring her own muzzle into register with his head. But instead of squeezing the trigger, she rammed the weapon forward, striking him between the eyes with the steel circle of the shotgun's barrel. She almost laughed when his eyes rolled comically upwards and the funny looking gun fell from his nerveless fingers. With her opponent down, she swept the muzzle around to point at the man confronting Seward.

Seward had moved even faster, and with one hand he had grabbed the barrel of Dennel's rifle and twisted it downwards in a jerking whip-crack motion, snapping the American's wrist and tearing his trigger finger right off of his hand. The rifle's sling snapped, but not before the force slammed Dennel to his knees. Seward's other hand shot out to grip Dennel's face, claws digging into his temples and hair line with irresistible force.

Dennel screamed in shock and pain. He wasn't even sure how he had ended up in his current position. All he knew was that his kneecaps felt as if they had been smashed, his wrist was definitely broken, and worse still, his trigger finger was either smashed or entirely gone. He couldn't see because of the hand over his face and something was gripping his head like a vice – something with sharp spikes. He felt blood trickle down the side of his face. "Wh-what do you want?" He couldn't see what Sam was doing, but his partner had definitely not fired, so he assumed that Sam was also down, impossible as that seemed. Dennel had fought and killed all over the world, but he had never faced anything like this, and he experienced something he had not known for a long time; stark terror.

"Roland Harker. Where is he?" Seward repeated in a patient tone.

In the shock of the werewolf's escape and attack, Dennel had forgotten all about the captive bio-engineer and industrialist, but he remembered now. "Th-this floor. Room 405. But the door is locked and I don't have the key code." Then he remembered something else and he tried to struggle until the claws holding his head dug through flesh and ground into the bone of his skull. "Aaagh! The werewolf! It's going to get through the fire escape door at any moment!"

Seward released his grip on Dennel's head. "Take your friend and go." He trod on the rifle when the American tried to reach for it with his left hand. "I'm being generous and leaving both of you your pistols. Now get going before I change my mind."

Dennel climbed painfully to his feet and went over to help Sam, who had a circular imprint on his forehead and was having trouble standing up. He didn't waste time swearing or uttering threats but simply staggered away as fast as the two of them could manage.

"Getting soft in your old age? I expected you to tear their heads off," Tara said as they jogged towards Room 405, trying to understand her strange and mercurial companion.

He smiled coldly. "I was tempted. The people in this company seem awfully keen to shoot perfect strangers. However with luck they can better serve as a distraction for the werewolf who they claimed is chasing them. I'd rather not fight it if we don't have to. Ah, 405."

The door was locked, and there was no sign on it to indicate a mundane purpose. A cracking sound from the jammed fire exit prompted her to pound on the locked door in front of her. "Father? It's me, Tara. Are you in there?"

"Tara? Did they get you too?"

"Dad! Stand back. I'm going to break down the door." She tried pushing, first with her hands and then with her shoulder, but although it creaked, the door and lock held.

"Kick the lock," Seward suggested.

Tara stepped back, inhaled, and kicked out hard, striking the lock panel with the sole of her boot. The heavy wood of the door around the lock exploded into splinters and the lock itself shot into the room and smashed against the back wall like a cannonball, missing her father's head by a foot and showering him with concrete and brick dust. "Whoops. Sorry."

"Tara! Thank goodness you're all right. I've been out of my mind with worry."

She rushed in and wrapped her father in her arms. "Me too. I've been imagining them doing all kinds of horrible things to you."

Roland grinned. "Fortunately, they seemed more interested in the alien artefacts than with me. I suppose they don't know about..." He stopped talking when Seward shook his head vigorously, pointed at the ceiling, and then at his ear. "Ah! Yes. Walls have ears and all that." He studied Seward for a second and turned to his daughter. "I don't believe I know your friend."

"Introductions later. We have a more pressing problem," Seward said.

In her happiness at finding her father safe, she had forgotten all about the werewolf. A louder, more ominous cracking sound prompted her to grab her father's arm. "Come on dad. We have to go. Right now. The werewolf is about to break through the door."

"Werewolf? Is Viktor here too?" Roland asked as he followed his daughter out of his former prison cell.

The handle on the fire door snapped and the axe fell to the ground with a thump.

"In here!" Seward cried, trying the next door down the row and finding it unlocked.

Tara saw the werewolf step out into the corridor just before she entered the room behind her father. When Seward slammed the door shut she hurriedly turned on her heel and activated the lock. "This isn't going to hold it," she said, tapping the door with her fingernail.

"With luck, it won't have to," Seward replied, his ear pressed against the wall.

***

The werewolf stopped outside the door and angrily slammed one paw against it. It had seen the people scurrying into the room and it wanted to tear them apart, even though it wasn't really hungry. Then it sniffed, and the scent made it curl its lips and snarl. There was something wrong with the scent, something that warned of danger. It sniffed again, and its head slowly turned to look up along the corridor. It crouched and sniffed the floor. This was a more familiar scent. The scent of the two humans who had hurt it and escaped. Ignoring the locked door, it loped down the corridor towards the other fire door and its jaws opened in a canine smile when it came upon the blood and a severed finger. It was back on the trail of its prey. When it had finished with these two, it would go back and find the other human who had hurt it in the landing.

***

Seward grinned. "I told you those two would be useful. The werewolf's gone after them. Time to go."

"Father, this is John Seward. He saved my life back in London when more of Werner's people, this facility belongs to Werner by the way, shot me."

Roland held out his hand. "It appears I owe you a debt of gratitude, Mr Seward."

"It was my pleasure, Mr Harker. Your daughter and I have a lot in common," Seward said with an amused gleam in his eye.

Roland's brow wrinkled in thought. "Your name sounds remarkably familiar."

"A lot of people say that."

"I think we ought to get going," Tara said hurriedly, not at all eager to explain to her father that he was talking to Dracula.

When Seward stepped over the shattered fire door into the landing, the first thing he saw was the limp form and bloody form of Emily lying face down on the stairs. "She's still alive. That's a surprise, given that she was trapped in here with the werewolf."

"Perhaps it was caught up in the chase. Wolves can be like that," Tara said.

"Whatever the reason, she's jolly lucky," Roland said, kneeling down beside her. He gently turned her over after making sure she didn't have any broken bones and her neck and spine seemed intact. "Good lord!" he exclaimed when Emily's eyes suddenly opened to look at him.

"Is it safe to wake up?" Emily asked. "I'm Emily, Mr Rometty's new secretary. Why are you two dressed for a costume party?"

"You mean to say you were awake all this time?" Tara said.

"I thought the werewolf might ignore me if I played dead." She looked at each of them anxiously.

"You do know about the werewolf, don't you? I think it escaped from one of the labs on the third floor." She sat up, wincing at the cuts on her back and the collection of bruises that she had gathered from being thrown down the stairs and on top of Rometty.

"It's busy chasing down two rather unpleasant Americans," Seward replied with a satisfied smile.

"That would be Mr Dennel and Sam, I never did get his last name. They're from Head Office in America sent to check up on us. There would have been two more of them for that werewolf thing to eat except that they went off to London. I heard them talking on those silly radio things in their sleeves. Said they were going to handle some business in London, and then take care of a busybody who had interfered in the Company's business, oh and they also wanted to find a woman. Right rude they were about her too. 'Fucking bitch' this and 'fucking bitch' that, pardon my French."

It too a moment for her listeners to absorb the stream of data that flowed from her, seemingly without the need to draw a single breath in the process. "They know who you are!" Tara said with a gasp.

Seward nodded grimly. "Time for us to leave." Neither sight nor sonar revealed any sign of the werewolf, so he led the others down the concrete stairs, only to be brought up short on the third floor landing by huge swaths of blood painted on the stairs leading down to the second floor and the sound of roars and growls or more than one creature echoing up the stairwell. He held a finger to his lips. He peeked over the railings to the landing below them and quickly pulled his head back. The second floor fire door had been ripped off of its hinges and there was a werewolf on the landing tearing into a corpse with its fangs. He made clawing motions with his hands and pointed straight down, then held up one finger.

The third floor fire door was jammed half open by

another corpse, a man in a lab coat and wearing yellow rubber gloves. The back of his neck had been bitten and the white vertebrae were clearly visible. Tara peeked out into the corridor and then gave the others a thumbs-up. She tip-toed through the doorway stepping carefully over the corpse. Followed by the others she moved away from the fire-escape. "What do we do now? The upstairs werewolf was chasing the Americans down the other set of stairs and one or more werewolves were waiting below this one."

Roland caught a movement down the corridor. "Look, there's someone or something there."

Since the werewolves seem to have originated on the third floor, it seemed strange that there were any survivors. Seward shrugged. With two or more werewolves behind them, they had little choice but to advance, so he took the lead and crept down the middle of the corridor, keeping an eye out for surprises from either side.

"Doesn't sound like a werewolf," Tara whispered.

"You can hear something?" Emily asked. All she could hear was the thunder of her own heartbeat.

"It's coming from Laboratory 3," Seward said, pointing at the signs on the doors and walls. When they reached the door to the lab, which was locked in an open position, he signed for the others to flatten against the wall and out of sight. He leaned forward and peeked into the room. Pulling back he whispered, "There's a man in there. Doesn't look like a scientist. He's gathering up things from the lab into a bag, including some of the alien artefacts. There's also a woman strapped to an operating table."

"Let me look," Emily whispered back and pushed herself forward. When she returned she said, "It's Mr Rometty, my former boss. I quit when he left me for dead back in the fire escape. Be careful, he has a big gun." She giggled. "That didn't come out quite right. I actually haven't seen his..."

"We know what you mean Emily," Tara said, rolling her eyes at her father. "John and I will take care of him, and then the two of you can come in."

"I will?" Seward said.

"I'll take him alone if you can't be bothered," she replied with an arched eyebrow. She edged towards the door and took a final peek. Rometty was looking down at the bound girl, and it seemed the perfect time to make her move, so she looked over her shoulder to nod at Seward, and then rushed into the laboratory.

"I'll shoot if you come any closer," Rometty snapped.

Tara came to a skidding halt. Rometty had the muzzle of his pistol pressed against the girl's temple, and despite her speed, it was likely that he would be able to pull the trigger before she could stop him. She guessed that he had been about to shoot her anyway, but that didn't make any difference.

"Nice mask. Miss Tara Harker, I presume?"

Tara nodded stiffly. "There's no need for that. Just put that box down and we won't stop you from leaving."

Rometty tilted his head curiously. "Interesting. You show no signs of changing like those poor fellows out there, but it's obvious that you've been enhanced. Viktor couldn't confirm that you had received the alien treatment, but I would say it's a safe assumption." With his other hand he unfastened the restraints that held the wrists of the girl on the table. "I might be doing this girl a favour by shooting her. She's been exposed to the werewolf toxin too, although I can't explain why she is still human," he said patting her naked belly. He made the girl sit up so that he could reach her ankles while keeping the gun against her head. When her legs were free he put a hand on her shoulder so that he could guide her. There was the sound of angry roaring from outside of the lab. "I believe it's time for me to leave. If any of you so much as twitch I'll blow off the side of this poor girl's face." He pushed his hostage. "We're going to the lifts. Be a good girl and once we're out of here I'll let you go."

Tara watched helplessly as Rometty guided the girl out into the corridor, and then over to the bank of lifts which were all jammed by bodies or parts of them. With the girl's help he was able to kick the torn corpse out of the lift and the door slid smoothly shut. The slam of the fire door at the far end of the corridor drew her attention. She put her head through the lab door, only to see the American, Sam, running towards her.

"It's right behind me!" he shouted. No one needed to be told what the "It" was.

Roland, who had entered the lab along with Emily when Rometty had departed, had been examining the contents of the laboratory, which resembled an insane cross between a medieval torture chamber and a modern place of research, with sick horror. His eyes were suddenly drawn to the label on a large glass bottle. "Silver nitrate," he read aloud. He remembered Tara's account of her battle with Viktor and he began to look around. "Aha!"

Sam had just run past the open entrance to a lab when he came to a sudden halt. He pointed and shouted, "Behind you!"

Tara twisted her head around just in time to see the first of the pair of werewolves step into the corridor. She hurriedly pulled her head back and forced the heavy sliding door shut against the mechanism, even though she didn't have the locking code. "Two werewolves incoming!" She snatched a chisel shaped tool from a workbench and jammed it between the door and the track with a thump of her fist that bent the handle.

Seward went to the window and hit it experimentally with the bottom of his fist. The thick glass vibrated with a low pitched "bonk", but seemed otherwise unimpressed. "Bulletproof," he said in disgust. "There's got to be at least one … aha," he said, spotting the openable window. Throwing open the latch, he pushed the heavy window out and peered down. Like many modern buildings, the exterior was flat and lacked climbable ledges or drainpipes. "Tara, you'll have to piggy-back Roland and Emily down. I'll hold the werewolves off. Just give me a shout when you're done and I'll join you. But first..." He ran over to the remaining alien packing crates and began tossing them out of the window.

Tara looked at the door. "But..." She wanted to say that even he couldn't fight two werewolves at the same time without weapons and armour, but she realised that he already knew that. "Thank you," she said as she ushered a frightened looking Emily towards the window.

Roland had grasped the situation and was already standing by the opening, the strong draft blowing his hair into a tangled mess.

The thought of chivalry never crossed her mind as Tara stooped in front of her father so that he could clamber up onto her back. "I'll be back for you in a moment," she said to Emily. The secretary watched in stunned amazement as Tara moved towards the window. Tara saw the woman's open mouthed expression and chuckled. "I work out a lot."

Seward thought longingly of his ancient armour, shield and longsword as he stood in front of the door with the shotgun in his hand. Half a dozen slim stoppered test tubes that Roland had given him rattled in his pocket, and one more was inside the barrel of the 12 gauge shotgun. He had stuffed a wad of note paper in to stop it from sliding out when he swung the muzzle around. Most of the torture implements and medical instruments were too small to make effective weapons, but he had been delighted to find a machete lying on one of the shelves, and it was now tucked in his belt. His sonar let him see that Tara had just disappeared out of the window when there was a heavy impact against the door, making the items on the shelves rattle.

The door rocked on its tracks as the werewolf tried to slide it open, and there was a roar of fury when the steel sheathed door refused to budge.

Seward knew that the wedge wouldn't hold for long, and he raised the shotgun to his shoulder. The rattling and pounding grew more intense and several of the screws holding the door tracks sprang out and flew across the room. He had been a seasoned warrior even before he had become a vampire, and the thought of death after so many centuries did not concern him greatly. His only concern was to hold the doorway until Tara and the others could escape. The door boomed like a giant gong and crumpled like a sheet of aluminium foil. He dodged aside when the door came tumbling through the air in his direction and his finger smoothly pulled the trigger.

The shotgun crashed deafeningly in the enclosed space and a column of glass, silver nitrate, and lead pellets blasted out of the muzzle at over a thousand feet per second to slam into the upper chest of the leading werewolf, which used to be Subject Two and a woman. For a moment it took on an almost comically surprised expression, and then it staggered backwards, roaring in pain. However, unlike Viktor, the minds of both subjects were so drug addled and weak that the werewolf persona was actually dominant in each of them and while the silver served to disrupt the healing ability of the e-nanites, the shot werewolf remained in its non-human form.

Seward pumped the shotgun's fore-end to reload, and then dropped another of the silver-nitrate filled test-tubes down the muzzle. He took aim at the injured werewolf's head, hoping to take it out of the fight quickly, but instead the one behind shoved the wounded one at Seward with piston-like force. He suddenly found two sets of sharp claws shooting towards him and he was forced to abandon his shot in order to dodge. Fast as he was, a claw managed to rip the lapel of his coat. Now he was bracketed between the two werewolves. Using his sonar to guide him, he ran backwards and sideways, keeping level with the injured monster. He fired as soon as he had a clear shot, hitting it between the shoulder blades. "Hah!" he grunted in satisfaction as the werewolf went down.

However this action allowed the other werewolf to charge across the room. Seward sprang straight up into the air to avoid its claws, but the werewolf's slashing blow caught the heel of his shoe, and the force of the blow sent him tumbling. He crashed into a glass fronted cabinet, sending shards of glass and vials of chemicals and medicines flying in all directions. He managed to pull free of the wreckage, blood dripping from a slash on his cheek, just as the werewolf bounded across the intervening space, its hairy body completing the destruction of the cabinet. Without time to insert another test tube, Seward fired point blank into the werewolf's face, sending it staggering back against the wall. But when he racked the shotgun the cartridge jammed instead of ejecting cleanly. It would have been a simple matter to extract the jammed cartridge except for the fact that the werewolf had already recovered and bounded towards him on all fours, jaws gaping wide. Instead, Seward shifted his right hand to the butt of the shotgun and rammed it forward like a stubby spear, driving it directly into the werewolf's maw and knocking the monster gagging and choking back onto its haunches. However Seward didn't escape unscathed. Dagger-like claws raked his left forearm, tearing off the sleeve of his coat and shirt and digging bloody furrows in his flesh.

Seward somersaulted forward, over the werewolf's back drawing the machete in mid-air. He landed with his back to his hirsute opponent, his useless left arm pressed against his side although the wounds were already knitting and healing. He whipped around like a ballet dancer, the blade of the machete an extension of his arm and guided by his sonar. Its razor edge struck the side of the werewolf's neck just as it managed to pull the blood drenched barrel of the shotgun out of its throat. The heavy carbon steel blade slammed into the werewolf's flesh like the spinning propeller of an aircraft, driven by Seward's inhumanly strong muscles, severing the werewolf's neck and sending its head rolling across the floor. Not even the e-nanites could repair that kind of damage unless someone held the head back in place almost immediately.

Clawed arms closed around his body, trapping his arms at his sides, the talon-like claws sinking into the muscles of Seward's chest. He gasped in shocked agony and anger; anger which was directed at himself for allowing his focus on his opponent to blind him to other possible threats. He dropped the machete and despite the pain of the claws, doubled over to pull his neck out of range of the werewolf's jaws. The manoeuvre was just in time and he heard the click of the creature's fangs as its jaws snapped shut just short of his spine. He bent his elbows, his own claws forming and extending as his eyes turned red and his fangs extended past his lips. He sank his claws into the backs of the werewolf's paws, ripping and tearing at flesh and tendons, and he felt the crushing grip loosen. He broke free of the werewolf's deadly embrace, dived forward and rolled.

Seward sprang to his feet just in time to meet the werewolf's charge. Skill, blinding speed, and agility met huge fangs, raw strength and savagery as they battled toe-to-toe in the middle of the laboratory, smashing furniture and equipment as if they were children's toys. Seward grabbed a hairy wrist, twisted and spun, sending a full sized defibrillator machine flying out of the door to smash against the opposite wall.

But the werewolf, itself covered with cuts and gashes from Seward's claws, rebounded from the floor and threw itself at Seward, heedless of the blows that its enemy threw at it.

The impact of the werewolf's body pushed Seward backwards into a corner formed by two heavy work tops. Unable to dodge, he was forced to meet the creature head on. His hands and claws locked around the werewolf's wrists, and he held its rear paws away from his belly with a foot planted firmly in the monster's groin.

But the werewolf was stronger with more powerful arms and shoulders, and its snapping, saliva dripping jaws edged closer and closer to Seward's face.

Despite the imminence of defeat and death, the being known to the world as Dracula, was not one to surrender meekly to his fate. His face twisted and stretched, forming a devil's mask of needle sharp fangs of his own as he prepared to rip and tear at his enemy. Then, unexpectedly, he felt the pressure of the werewolf's arms falter, and its face took on a look of surprise. Seward's head twisted and darted forwards in a fluid and completely inhuman movement, and his fangs closed around the werewolf's throat. With a twist of his neck he ripped the werewolf's throat open and threw it backwards with a thrust of his leg. Pushing himself off of the synthetic marble counter he snatched up the machete. Propelled by the power of both legs he sprang into the air and literally flew towards the hunched, choking werewolf. He twisted in mid-leap and landed on both feet, facing the creature's side. With both hands he slashed the machete down and across with all the strength and skill of a swordsman who had had centuries to practise.

The werewolf's head rolled across the laboratory floor like an out of control bowling ball, only stopping when it collided with Tara's shins. "Yuck!" she cried, skipping aside.

Panting and with his hands on his knees, Seward examined the handle of the huge amputation knife that had been driven into its back. "It appears I owe you my thanks."

She pointed at her face. "You've lost your mask." Then she shuddered. "It's going to take a while to get used to that face of yours."

"Face? Oh, sorry," Seward replied, and then his face rippled and twisted and the red faded from his eyes. "As for the mask, there aren't any security cameras in the lab. From the looks of this place, I'd bet that they wouldn't want any embarrassing videos of what went on here turning up on the Net."

A muffled roar came from outside the lab. "Should we..." Tara said, pointing towards the noise.

"No. I'm hurt and we're not equipped. Besides, we don't know how many of them there still are wandering around the building, and we have Emily and your father to worry about. With Viktor at large and all the survivors in the building, I think it's too late to hope we can cover it up."

Tara covered her mouth. "I forgot about the other two Werner thugs back in London."

"I haven't. But first I need to find a nice clean pig or cow."

"Pig?"

"Well I could suck the blood of the next attractive maiden we come across if you insist on being traditional," Seward said as he climbed out of the window.

"Oh." Her eyes widened. "We can um, do pigs?" She made a fanging motion with her fingers.

"Any warm blooded animal will do, though it's not quite as good as human blood."

"Do you still do that?"

Seward chuckled. "There have always been women, and men too, who like the idea of … being with a vampire. Nowadays, they even have clubs, websites, and munches. So yes, I do, but not by force, and it's all very safe, sane, and consensual. We, you and me, don't carry infectious diseases, and the e-nanites are not present in our saliva, unlike in the case of werewolves; don't ask me why. We can pass the e-nanites on to someone else, but only if the person drinks our blood and is near to death. Otherwise the e-nanites self-destruct in the digestive tract."

Roland rushed towards his daughter. "Tara! Thank goodness you're all right. We've been hearing the most horrific sounds coming from − John, you're hurt! Your face … and you've got cuts all … we need to get you to a hospital."

Seward shook his head, urging all of them into motion. "No hospital." He sniffed the air. "I think there are some cows over that way."

"Cows?" Emily asked.

Tara sighed. "It's a long story."

***

Emily gazed at Seward in awe. To everyone's surprise she had not been freaked out by the sight of Seward sinking his fangs into the neck of a cow and sucking her blood, and she had chosen to sit in the passenger seat next to him for the drive back to London. "I love vampires," she said. "Not the Goth, sparkly type, but the scary ones. I've watched every vampire film ever made, and I have a huge collection of books and graphic novels on my tablet and my phone."

Seward met Tara's eyes in the rear view mirror and she grinned. With an ample supply of blood and the time it took to get back to the Rover, he was fully healed and looking disgustingly healthy. With his slightly messy hair and ripped shirt, he looked like the cover of an erotic romance novel. She couldn't help but feel a little smug that she was now capable of healing and retaining her youthful looks too. And she was going to take great delight in chucking all those anti-wrinkle creams into the bin.

Looking pensive, Emily said, "I suppose I'm out of a job now. I'm certainly not going to work for that beast Rometty again."

"I'm certain you won't have any trouble finding another secretarial position," Tara said consolingly.

Emily twisted around to look at Tara, the seat belt doing interesting things to her cleavage; something that Seward was quick to notice. Her movement also hiked her skirt up and he noted that she had excellent legs.

"Oh I'm not really a secretary. Mr Rometty's normal secretary had a run-in with that other werewolf, Viktor was his name I think, the one who escaped. They needed a replacement urgently, so my supervisor sort of volunteered me. I'm actually a research assistant to one of the Company's big brains. I have a master's in biochemistry. I guess I've always been kind of a nerd."

The thought of the apparently scatter-brained young woman as a scientist made Tara's head spin with cognitive dissonance. As a woman and a successful test pilot, she knew she really shouldn't feel that way, but Emily was such a convincing dumb-blonde; even though she was a brunette. "I'm sorry, I just assumed that you were .... "

"Eye candy for Mr Rometty's office? Don't worry about it. I like looking good and I enjoy being looked at. None of that 'rapey male gaze' rubbish for me. Oh, and did I mention that I just love vampires?" she said, batting her eyelashes at Seward.

He chuckled. "You may have brought it up once or twice. Don't worry about your job. I think I should be able to find you a suitable position."

"Really?" she said breathlessly. "I'd be ever so grateful for any position that you might put me in."

Tara sniggered.

Roland had been examining one of the alien injector modules. Holding it up to Tara he said, "See this indicator here on the underside? I think it indicates that it is still fully charged. The one that was used on you had the marker in the other position. I have no idea what these markings mean, but they are different from yours. It probably indicates the intended species." He frowned. "We really need to take back the rest of these things that Rometty made off with."

"You don't think they should be handed over to the authorities?" Seward asked.

"Good lord no. That's why Tara and I were in Romania in the first place. When I first mentioned my research into nanite technology, this awful chap from some ministry or another turned up and offered to fund my work in exchange for my handing over all my results to the MOD. When I asked around, I discovered that several of my friends and colleagues had been made similar offers and had later completely disappeared. These things hold the potential for immortality and things like super soldiers. I shudder to think what the military and those of our good friends the Americans would do with this technology."

"But you would trust me with it?" Seward said.

"You've known about it for centuries and I don't see the world overrun by vampires. So yes, I think I can trust you to do what is best for mankind," Roland said.

Tara silently wondered what her father would think when he discovered that he was placing his trust in Dracula.

***

"Hey look, I can see smoke," Tara said, lowering

180

her window and leaning out as they drove through the genteel surrounds of St John's Wood. Spotting flashing lights and the red bulk of fire engines, she said, "Wait a minute, isn't that …. "

"My house," Seward said grimly. "Looks like we're too late." He found a spot to pull over and stopped the car. "I think it's best if the police don't get a look at all of you, so stay here while I go and find out what happened. The keys are in the lock. Keep the windows up and the doors locked. I'll be back as soon as its safe. There's a phone built into the Rover, so I'll call if I can't come back."

"If it was those thugs from Werner, the so called Auditors, they might still be about. I'll go around using a more sneaky route and have a look at the bystanders," Tara said.

Seward firmly closed the door to the Rover and began to stroll down the road towards the commotion until he was stopped by a policeman. "That's my house." He was immediately ushered to the middle of the activity where a senior police officer was consulting with a fireman. He endured the expected barrage of inane questions, including veiled suggestions that he might have committed arson on his own property, all the while suppressing the urge to rip out the officer's throat. Finally he was given the information that he most wanted, and it took all of his self-control not to reveal the insane rage that exploded in his breast and to remain outwardly calm as he listened.

"I'm sorry to have to inform you that four people were killed in the blaze."

"Four … how is that possible? The house has … had a sprinkler system and fire retardant partitions and doors."

The policeman's eyes narrowed. "All the bodies were found in the same room, and there are indications that the door was locked."

Seward clenched his teeth in fury, and he lowered his head and pressed his lips together to hide his canines which were growing into fangs. He had been holding on to one of the hand rails of the fire engine, and he felt the stainless steel tube crumple under his grip. Then his head lifted and he leaned towards the startled policeman. "You said four bodies. Did you find a survivor?"

"Why yes. A man. Badly injured, but still conscious. He says he's your butler." The policeman looked Seward over, suspicion plain on his face. "From his injuries, he was savagely beaten. Do you have any enemies who might have done such a thing?"

Seward scowled. "I'm a rich man and an industrialist. So undoubtedly there are those who wish me ill. But I had no warning that anyone planned such an … atrocity. Now may I see my friend, my butler?"

"He's in that ambulance over there. Please don't go anywhere, Mr Seward. I may need to talk to you again."

Seward nodded. "I'm not going anywhere until this is resolved."

"We'll do our best to apprehend whoever did this Mr Seward, but understand that it may take some time – unless you can give us somewhere to start."

Shaking his head angrily Seward replied, "I've already said I don't have any names to give you. Now please excuse me, I have to see to my friend." Without waiting for the officer to reply, he strode off towards the ambulance.

Renfield had splints on his arm and leg and half of his face was grotesquely swollen and bleeding, but he still managed a smile when he saw Seward approaching. "Master Seward," he mumbled through puffed lips.

"I think his jaw is fractured. Don't make him talk," the paramedic cautioned before stepping back.

Seward put his hand lightly on Renfield's shoulder. "I'm sorry Renfield. I failed you and the others."

"Nonsense sir. You had no way of knowing. They wanted to know where Miss Harker was and why you helped her. I told them that they should go back to buggering their mothers, which seemed to upset them for some reason. They were professionals and heavily armed. Be careful sir. They might still be around."

"I'll make them pay, Renfield. I swear it," Seward said softly, aware of the many eyes watching him.

Renfield smiled again and winced. "I know you will, sir. That is why the bastards were puzzled when I kept laughing as they were assaulting me. They said they were leaving me alive so that I could give you a message. They said, you should learn to mind your own business, and that if you didn't want the same to happen to you, that you should hand Miss Tara over to them. They put a note containing the URL of an on-line forum where you can leave a message and what to say."

"I know exactly what I wish to say to them." Seward took out his phone and called one of his personal assistants to arrange a first class room in a private hospital for Renfield where he could arrange for round the clock security. Renfield's family had served him for centuries, and was the closest thing to a true friend and confidante that he had. House Dracul always took care of its retainers as if they were family. He leaned over and kissed Renfield on the forehead. "Rest and get better, my friend."

"Give them hell, Lord Dracula."

"I intend to, Renfield. They shall curse their mother's wombs for giving them life when I am done with them. This I swear."

***

"I think it's him, the one in the traffic camera video you showed me. No, I don't see any woman. He looks to be alone. He's talking to the man they pulled

183

from the house, that butler bloke." He listened and nodded. "Yeah, yeah, I understand. I'll follow him when he leaves and I'll let you know if he meets up with anyone else, and where he goes. Yes I'll call you back the moment I have anything." He jumped in surprise, then hissed in pain at the crushing grip on his wrist. "Who are..." The man grunted in pain when Tara forced him to his knees and snatched the phone from his hand. "Don't move." She opened the back of the phone and pulled out the battery. Werner's people seemed to have a lot of influence and resources, so she wasn't taking any chances that the phone could be traced.

As soon as he saw her attention was focused on the phone, the man tried to make a run for it, but instead performed an undignified pratfall when Tara's hand darted out, grabbed his collar, and pulled hard in the opposite direction. She had seen the remains of Seward's home, the body bags being loaded into the coroner's van, as well as the broken form of Renfield next to the ambulance, and she was in no mood to be gentle. She dropped a knee on his chest, driving the breath from his lungs, and clamped a clawed hand over his mouth. Before he realised what she was doing and could resist, she hauled his hand up while letting her teeth grow into fangs, and bit off his little finger with a shake of her head.

With his mouth sealed shut, the man made screaming sounds through his nostrils, his legs and uninjured hand scrabbling at the grass and dirt. She spat out his finger, let him see her red eyes and needle sharp teeth, and then said, "Are you going to be good?"

The man nodded vigorously and with total sincerity.

"That's good. Otherwise I might suddenly get in the mood for oral sex." She smiled at him, her long canines gleaming in the sunlight.

The man shuddered and looked ready to faint.

"You're going to get up and come with me to meet my friends, who might have some questions for you. As you know, one of them is the owner of that house, and those dead bodies were his friends and employees. I won't vouch for your safety if he thinks you're not being cooperative. Do you understand me?"

His nod was so forceful that he risked dislocating his spine, and a dark wet patch formed in the crotch of his trousers.

***

"Renfield should be all right with rest and treatment, but the others never had a chance. Up to now, I opposed Werner and his organisation because I believed that the alien nanites shouldn't be in the hands of people such as they. But now it is personal. They have attacked my home and killed those who looked to me for protection. There can only be one answer to such barbarity, and I intend to give it to them." Seward lashed out at an unoffending tree, his claws sending splinters flying through the air like shrapnel and forcing Roland to dodge. He took a long, shuddering breath. "I apologise. The deaths of my people has … upset me."

Seemingly unalarmed by his display of rage, Emily touched his arm. "I'm sorry."

Regretting his loss of control, Seward bowed to her and smiled ruefully. "My temper still gets the better of me, even after all this time." He turned to Tara's captive, who was clutching his bleeding, handkerchief wrapped hand and watching them apprehensively. "Who do you work for?"

The man shrugged sullenly. "I'm a freelancer. I don't know anything. I just do what I'm told and paid to do."

Seward had driven around until he had found a suitably derelict spot where they could interrogate the

185

man in private. He edged closer. "I'm in a very bad mood at the moment, so I suggest you don't play games with me. Who hired you?"

The prisoner squirmed. "Look, these blokes are real hard cases. Mostly ex-military, paras, SAS, that sort of thing. They'll kill me if they find out I've grassed on them."

Seward smiled at him, and his gaze and voice were distant, as if he was seeing something else. "Have you ever seen a man impaled? Skewered like a shish kebab but still alive?"

"What? What the fuck are you talking about?" He winced when Seward's hand clamped down on his shoulder.

"I used to be really good at it. They would scream for days, crying out for their mothers." He glanced around. "I'm sure I could find a suitable stake. A length of pipe would probably do..."

The absolute sincerity in Seward's voice convinced the freelancer that he was serious. He looked desperately from Tara to Seward, and then at Emily. "You can't let him..."

"I've never seen somebody impaled before," she said, her eyes wide and fascinated.

"You're mad! The lot of you. You're stark raving..."

Tara leaned close. "Not mad. We're monsters; and that's much, much, worse." She let her canines extend slightly and smiled at him as if he was dinner.

"All right! All right, stop it. I'll tell you all I know. It's not much. It's supposed to be anonymous and all that, but a bloke in my line of work gets to hear things, you know what I mean? Anyway, from what I hear, they are supposedly one of those 'security consultancy' firms. You know, bodyguards and heavies for hire. But word is that they mostly work for only one boss."

"Werner," Tara said.

"So you know about them. Yeah, they have a number of different companies, but all of them are really owned by Werner."

"Why were you watching my house, and what do you know about … what happened," Seward asked.

Another shrug. "Damn if I know. I get a call telling me to get my arse over to an address and to bring my camera. I was just supposed to watch and report."

"I heard you tell them that he had arrived," Tara said, nodding at Seward.

"They sent me pictures of a man and a woman and said to watch out for them." The man nodded slyly at Tara. "The other picture was of you."

"Where can we find your employers?"

"Don't look at me. I just have a telephone number. I get paid in cash at a pre-arranged drop."

Seward's grip tightened and his claws pricked the man's skin. "If you can't help us you really aren't of much use, are you?"

Sweat ran down the freelancer's face. "Hold on! Wait a minute! I didn't say I couldn't tell you anything. "I know they have a place, a sort of HQ, in London. I heard them talk about it in the background and from … sources."

"Address?" One of his claws drew blood.

"I don't know. Honest to god I don't. But I've heard them call it 'The Warehouse'. The way they said it made it sound like a name and not just, you know, any old warehouse."

Seward felt Emily nudge his side. He glanced at her and then back to the man. "All right. I'm going to follow up on your information. In the meantime, I'm going to find some place to store you away. Somewhere nobody is going to find you. If you've lied or left anything out that gets us killed, well, you're going to get very lonely, and hungry."

The man swallowed. "It's the truth, on my

mother's grave."

Seward tied the man's hands behind his back and his ankles together with twisted wire, then blindfolded and gagged him with an old scarf and some duct tape from the Rover, and then dumped him in the back of the car. Coming back to the others he looked at Emily and raised an eyebrow. "You had something to tell us?"

Emily nodded. "Werner has a warehouse and distribution facility in London. I've had to contact them to follow up on orders of supplies for my boss, my real boss, not Rometty. And I remember the address and phone."

"I've never seen somebody impaled before?" Tara said, raising an amused eyebrow.

"What? I'm not squeamish, and Rometty left me to be eaten by a werewolf. Besides, I figure that he deserves whatever's coming to him if he's part of the gang that left all those people to burn to death in Mr Seward's house," Emily replied. Seward handed her a pen and paper and she wrote down the details of the warehouse.

Seward kissed her on the forehead. "Thank you, Emily. I truly owe you one."

Starstruck, Emily looked embarrassed but also well chuffed.

"Someone's definitely got a fan," Tara whispered to her father. Then she saw the concern on his face. "What's the matter dad?"

"I assume you intend to go along with whatever Seward plans to do?"

"I ... yes, I do. For several reasons. One is that they kidnapped you and most likely are still after both of us. Second, John saved my life and nearly died rescuing you when he didn't have to. And third, I agree with John that we can't let Rometty run around with a bag full of the medikits. Who knows who he might sell them to. The last thing the world needs are werewolf terrorists or street gangs."

"It's just … these people are really dangerous, Tara. They've shown that they won't hesitate to kill – and they almost killed you!" Roland said, clearly upset.

"But they didn't, and that's all because of John. I'm stuck with this new uh … life, and he knows better than anyone how to survive."

"Can we trust him?" Roland whispered. "I mean, he just threatened to impale that man, and we really don't know anything about him."

Tara had been dreading this moment, but it wasn't fair to her father to keep him in ignorance. "Actually we do. We've known about him all our lives." Speaking in hushed tones which she knew Seward could hear perfectly well but might make her father more comfortable, she explained who he really was, and gave Roland a summary of what she had learned about him and the true history of vampirism.

"You mean he's actually Drac..." Roland began.

"Dad!" She held up a shielding hand and pointed at Emily behind it.

"But he's a..."

"Whatever he is, I am now too," Tara said slowly, giving weight to her words.

Roland visibly made an effort to relax. "He does seem to be a nice enough chap, and he's certainly suffered because he tried to help us." He shook his head in amazement. "It's just incredible, meeting Dra … I mean such a famous character in person. It's as if Sherlock Holmes suddenly walked up and shook my hand."

"Excellent. We'll be waiting." Seward put away his cell phone.

"So what do we do now?" Emily asked as Tara and her father moved closer.

Seward tapped the phone in his pocket. "I've arranged for another car and for some help in taking care of our friend," he said, nodding towards the Rover. "I have a number of houses and apartments in an around the city, owned under different names and which cannot be traced to John Seward, who for the moment at least, shall have to disappear."

Fifteen minutes later a silver Mercedes E-class pulled up behind the Rover, followed by a white Ford Transit van bearing the logo of an Indian restaurant. A man and a woman got out of the Mercedes and walked up to Seward. The woman held out the keys for the Mercedes. "Good to see you again, sir. The car's been swept and is clean of bugs or trackers. The GPS has been disabled. And here are the keys to the flat. The staff have been notified to expect you, and a security team is watching the area."

The man held out a briefcase. "Replacement ID, corporate credit cards, passports and cash in Sterling, Euros, and Dollars, plus a new cell phone and a Glock 21 with silver tipped ammunition and clip holster."

"We'll take care of the Rover and it's occupant and the van will escort you to your destination," the woman added.

Seward took the keys and briefcase. "Let me know if you learn anything new from our guest. Here are the keys to the Rover." Turning to Tara and the others he nodded at the Mercedes. "Let's go before we start to draw unwanted attention."

When they were in the car and moving down the road, Tara said, "Won't the Werner people be watching all of your known contacts and properties?"

"I've established a large number of different personas over the years. None of which can be linked to the others. These people don't work for John Seward, and the place we're going to is not registered in that name either." He held up the briefcase. "The corporate credit cards aren't linked to my name and won't draw attention even if we have to make large purchases such as another car.”

“Who does own the flat then?” Roland asked.

Seward chuckled. “This particular property is legally owned by the estate of the late Mr Abraham Van Helsing and is presently the subject of a highly complicated ownership dispute. Anyone trying to trace its actual ownership is in for a very perplexing time.”

Chapter Nine

The pair of "auditors" drove up to the main entrance to the Werner Biotechnology complex then went past it to the front of the Research wing.

"Something's not right," Jackson Turner said, pointing at the entrance. "The emergency lockdown light is on."

His partner Mike Garcia waved his phone. "Dennel's not answering. Neither are Sam or Rometty."

Turner racked the slide of his pistol, loading a round into the chamber before re-holstering it. "Let's take a closer look. We can't just say that we saw the lockdown, turned, and went away without checking it out."

Garcia opened his door and got out of the car, his hand hovering near the butt of his pistol in its shoulder holster. "I don't see anyone at reception." He looked up, squinting against the glare. "Can't see any faces at the windows either."

"Where's the emergency team with the Hazmat gear and shit?"

"According to the file, the response team is based in London. It would take them a while to get here, and we don't know when the lockdown occurred. It could have just happened, whatever it is," Garcia said, not knowing that Rometty had cancelled the response so that he would have more time to work out an explanation for the disaster that would show him in the best light and throw all the blame on Dennel and Maeda.

Turner put the edge of his hand against the glass of the main door and peered under it into the lobby. "Hey! I think I see a leg sticking out from behind the reception counter."

"Where?" Garcia asked, imitating his partner.

A tremendous impact against the sealed bulletproof glass doors jolted both men and sent them staggering backwards.

"What the fuck is that?" Turner cried, pointing his gun at the blood soaked creature that was smashing at the doors in a maniacal attempt to get at them. Blood streamed from his nose which had been broken by the flexing of the door.

Equally bloody from a split lip, Garcia shouted, "It's the werewolf!"

"But Rometty said it ran away, and you saw the security video of it jumping over the fence," Turner said, nervously eyeing the rattling doors.

"Then if it's not that Viktor character … oh shit." Garcia looked up just in time to see another fanged and furry face slam against a window on what the American called the second floor of the building. "That stupid bastard Rometty must have made more of them."

"Dennel and Sam are trapped in there with them. We should..."

Garcia shook his head. "They're not answering their phones and they haven't tried to call for help. They're probably dead. Besides, we can't get in."

"Oh fuck, the Hazmat team. We've got to stop them from unlocking the doors!"

Garcia looked higher up the face of the building and his face paled. "Screw that. There's an open window up there. I don't know about you, but I'm not hanging around until those things find it. We can notify Hazmat when we're at a safe distance."

Turner had seen the video of Viktor tearing the guards to shreds in Romania and nodded in agreement. "Let's get the fuck out of here. You drive and I'll call DC and notify Mr Werner."

***

The lone guard locked in the ground floor security centre had been in a state of panic by the time Rometty

193

had arrived at the door. Over the banks of security monitors he had watched as the werewolves had killed person after person including his fellow guards. This was like no situation he had ever been trained to face and was more like a nightmare or a horror film. The idea of being the last living person trapped in the building with the werewolves was unbearable, so when Rometty had knocked on the door he had unhesitatingly opened it to him, all protocols and orders from corporate headquarters to the contrary.

From the security room it was simple for Rometty to program the main doors to only open to his personal code and the system to continue full lockdown until deactivated by the proper code. After dressing her in a spare security T-shirt, he took a pair of handcuffs from the equipment locker and put them on Subject Five, who was too terrified to object. When the guard had confirmed that the werewolves were all safely away from the main entrance, Rometty had led the other two in a dash out of the building. He had watched the doors seal themselves behind him, and then headed for his car, dragging the woman with him. He would have taken the guard as well, but the man had run for his own vehicle and driven away as soon as Rometty had opened the perimeter gate with the coded remote control in his car. He shrugged as the guard's car disappeared down the road. He would have to submit a report of a guard suffering a nervous breakdown and violently attacking other members of staff. Combined with unbelievable tales of werewolves, it would guarantee a lengthy stay in a psychiatric hospital for the guard. He turned and smiled at the shivering woman in the passenger seat of his Bentley. "We're going to take a nice drive to London now. You'd like that wouldn't you," he said, nodding for her. As he drove he wondered how the werewolves would respond to Sarin gas.

Sitting in the stolen car, Viktor smiled in triumph. Even from this distance he was able to catch the scent of the newly created werewolves that were running wild inside the facility, and he watched as the auditors beat a hasty retreat. For the moment the werewolves were none of his concern, although he fully intended to return later and perhaps influence their fate. But for the moment more important business called out to him. He had stolen a car and had ensured that the theft wouldn't be reported for a while through the simple expedient of murdering the middle aged couple who owned it. Even in his human form, Viktor had willingly embraced the predatory nature of his alter ego. Everyone was potential prey. After escaping from Tara and her new ally, he had moved around the forest for a while until he was sure that they were not tracking him, and then he had stolen the car and headed back towards the Werner Biotechnology facility.

He had arrived only to see that Rometty's car was gone and two of the Auditors hastily departing. Werner owed him a great deal, and Viktor fully intended to be paid in full. It was logical that if Rometty had been forced to abandon the facility because of an outbreak of werewolves, he would have taken at least some of the cruciform nanite dispensers with him, and Viktor wanted them. At the very least he was going to squeeze a generous payment out of Werner for work done. He started the engine and pulled out onto the road in pursuit of the departing Auditors who seemed to be headed for London. He thought about that old film "An American Werewolf in London" and smiled. He would show Rometty and Werner what a Romanian werewolf in London could do.

***

Seward drove south towards Hyde Park, his eyes constantly checking the rear view mirror in case they had somehow been followed. He did not put it beyond his opponent's capabilities to be able to access the city's security camera network or even arrange satellite surveillance, but it seemed unlikely that they had managed to identify this new car so quickly.

"Where are we going?" Emily asked.

"I have an apartment in Mayfair. You and Roland should be safe enough there, until I've taken care of matters," he said, patting her reassuringly on the knee. He glanced at her speculatively when she placed her hand on top of his and slid it higher up along her thigh.

Roland said, "If you can get me some equipment I can have a look at these medikit things. Even if we can't analyse the e-nanites themselves, we can at least try to confirm that the units are designed for only two species. For all we know, there might be more. If vampires and werewolves are real, who knows what else might be possible.

"I can help," Emily said brightly.

***

Once they were settled in the apartment, Seward began to make telephone calls, while Tara checked the Internet for details and views of the Werner warehouse facility.

"Wow, this place is huge," Emily said. "John must be very rich," she said to Roland.

He smiled, noting her use of Seward's first name. "Yes, I've gained that impression."

Tara chuckled. "Love the Net. I've got floor plans of the warehouse and the attached offices. I also have the name and staff strength of the so called 'security consultants' that provide the heavies for Werner in

196

London and elsewhere. They're called Blue Streak Security. According to the bloggers who track these kind of things, BSS is infamous for hiring some of the most vicious mercenaries on the market, and is unofficially said to specialise in 'wetwork', a euphemism for assassinations and massacres. All in the name of freedom and democracy of course."

"Of course," Seward said sardonically. "I used to give people like that the 'honour' of leading the charge in battle. If I was lucky, most of them would be heroes and get themselves killed in glorious combat." He rubbed his chin as he studied picture after picture. "Speaking of getting killed, that's a bloody big bunch of buildings. We need to pick an entry point and an objective, and not just wander around the place like tourists."

"How do we do that? We can't just call them and ask them who's there and where they are," Tara said.

"I can," Emily said, holding up a hand.

"What?" Tara said.

"I escaped from the lab complex and I'm looking for my boss Mr Rometty. We got separated during the escape and I want to know what to do with the box of funny looking things I took from Professor Maeda's laboratory before climbing out the window using a rope I found in the lab."

"There wasn't any rope in the laboratory. I would have seen it when I searched," Roland said.

"Rometty never steps foot in the labs and the Auditors just arrived from the US. They won't know that."

"How did you get away from the werewolves?" Seward asked, looking for holes in her story.

"Dennel and Sam bravely fought them and last I saw they were being chased upstairs by the werewolves."

Her incongruously girlish voice lent an air of innocence and veracity to her account and Seward nodded. "It's worth a try. They won't turn her away if they think she has some of the alien devices whether or not Rometty is there."

"Should I call them now?"

"No. Tara and I will drive down there first and when we're in position I'll call you. That way we should hopefully catch them unawares once we know where they are." He looked at Tara. "Unless you have any objections or better ideas."

"We're going to need weapons. These guys are going to be heavily armed and well trained. Claws, fangs, and speed might not be enough," Tara said thoughtfully.

"Body armour might be a good idea. Super healing is all good and well, but not having to heal at all might be better," Roland said.

Seward grinned. "I've spent half of my long life in armour and with a sword in my hand. We were caught with our trousers down around our knees at the laboratories, and once is enough, as so eloquently stated by ex-President Bush."

"Ooh, I'd love to see you in armour. Armour is sooo sexy," Emily said.

Tara shook her head in bemusement. She was unable to tell whether the woman was putting on an act or actually managed to combine the mind and discipline of a scientist with the attitude of a heavy metal rock groupie who also happened to be a cosplay fanatic.

Seward got up from his well-padded recliner chair where he had been sipping a pack of the artificial blood. "Come with me," he said to Tara, but nodding to the others to include them.

The apartment was huge and the luxurious appointments brought home to Tara just how rich Seward had to be. "Do you have properties and businesses overseas?"

"Oh yes, I have interests just about all over the

world. The US of course, France, Germany, Russia, Singapore, Hong Kong, Shanghai, Sydney, and lots of smaller operations in the Middle East and Africa, not counting the oil companies, of course."

"You own oil companies?" Roland asked.

"Not own, but I'm a significant investor in several. I also exercise control through influence and allies. Once a politician, always a politician," he said with a disarming smile.

"It must be a great difference from being practically a King," Tara said. This was the first time in a while that she had been close to him in a non-threatening situation. She felt her heart jump when he put his hand on the small of her back, which made her bite her lip. Seward had not given any indications of romantic interest, and there was Emily, and … and she didn't know what she felt about him. He was still Vlad Tepes, Dracula, the man who had had thousands impaled, and was the template for most of the modern vampire legends. But he was also undeniably good looking, charming, insanely rich, and possessed a charisma like no other man she had ever met. She was amazed that he didn't have a retinue of screaming girls following him around. And he made her feel like a silly schoolgirl with a crush. She swore silently. This was not the time for soap opera antics. His hand guided her to the second bedroom door, and in her preoccupation she almost walked into the polished wood.

Apparently unaware of Tara's emotional conflict, Seward opened the door. On the bed lay half a dozen more of the high-tech ski suits that she wore in various muted patterns and colours, as well as selections of lingerie, and accessories. On the floor next to the bed was a selection of foot ware, ranging from boots like the pair she wore to jewelled slippers. "I thought you might need a new wardrobe." Turning to Emily he said, "I haven't had time to make arrangements for you, but if you go to the next room down the hall, you'll find a closet with a selection of female clothing that should fit you until we can do better."

Eyeing the lingerie Emily said, "I wouldn't mind just wearing Victoria's Secrets while these are being washed if you don't." From the way she smiled at Seward it was clear that her offer was quite sincere.

Roland tugged at his collar. "Ahem. I'm not sure my heart could stand the strain," he said, eyeing Emily's figure admiringly.

"I know how to do CPR. My trainer said my mouth to mouth technique was excellent," Emily offered helpfully.

Seward chuckled and pointed at the doors leading to a walk-in closet. "In here we have the other things we were discussing earlier. He opened the ordinary looking closet door to reveal the smooth steel of a second armoured door with both the dial of a combination lock and retinal scanner.

The door clicked open under Seward's touch and Tara gasped when she caught sight of the contents that filled the space behind it. Rows and rows of weapons gleamed under display lighting. Everything from swords and daggers to heavy machine guns, and grenade and rocket launchers. There was also suits of armour, again ranging from chain-mail to modern Kevlar and ceramic models. "Wow. This stuff can't be legal."

"Actually most of it is. I have licenses for a lot of it, and others are product samples. I told you I have a wide ranging investment portfolio, and I'm an official sales representative for several arms and military supplies companies." He entered the closet and selected what looked like an unusually high collared sweat shirt. "Here. Try this on. It's made of new slash resistant fabric. It will stop cuts from daggers and razors, as well as claws. It won't stop a direct stab with something sharp though." Then he selected a more conventional looking bullet resistant vest. "The vest itself only weighs 2.5 kg with two ultra-lightweight trauma plates weighing 1.25 kg each. Together it will stop bullets from most modern assault rifles." He looked around. "I also have some Kevlar knee protectors somewhere and a helmet that should fit you if you want one."

"Will you be wearing all this stuff too?"

"Something similar. I have a custom built suit for this kind of situation. If we were only dealing with werewolves, I'd prefer chain-mail." He rubbed his hands. "Now for weapons. Ever use a sword before? A real one, not those fencing toys."

Tara shook her head, holding the sweatshirt and vest in her arms and looking like an army recruit on her first day.

"Then you'd better stick with a knife. Hmm, yes, this one. It's high carbon steel plated in silver." He dumped the dagger and sheath on top of the garments in her arms. "Now the guns. We'll be fighting indoors if at all, so I think we go with shotguns. Here. This is an AA-12 automatic shotgun with a 20 round drum magazine. The recoil on this one is really light. With your new strength you'll be able to fire it single handed like a pistol. Very rugged and simple to use."

Tara raised an eyebrow when this too was dumped on top of the pile in her arms.

"Last of all, your side-arm. A 1911 .45 colt. What can I say, I'm old fashioned." Going down on one knee, he extended his arms and fastened the gun belt around her waist.

When his hands lingered just a fraction of a second longer than necessary on her buttocks she started to say something, but then closed her mouth again and smiled at him when he stood up to look into her eyes.

"Why don't you go and take a shower before putting everything on, and I'll do the same."

Shaking his head at the display of firepower,

Roland said, "In that case I'll borrow your computer and do some work."

Emily pointed at Roland's back. "I'll see if he needs help … with anything."

Tara stared suspiciously at the woman's retreating derrière. She wasn't sure if she found Emily's apparent liking for her father or her fan worship of Seward more disturbing. The thought of having Emily as a stepmother made her shudder, although she had to admit that the girl seemed nice enough.

She jumped when Seward leaned over her shoulder and whispered, "Need help soaping your back?"

"I'm too tense right now. Rain check?"

"Of course," Seward said with a nod and wave as he headed for the master bedroom.

Tara covered her face. "Rain check? Oh my god, why on Earth did I say that?" she groaned to herself. Now Seward would assume … assume what, she asked herself. And would he be wrong? She picked up the AA-12 and stroked the smooth stainless steel. Machines she understood. Her own feelings were uncharted territory. "Here be monsters" she said out loud and chuckled as she undressed and headed for the shower.

Chapter Ten

"All I know is that I was in my office while Dennel and that other person..."

"Sam. His name is Sam," Garcia snapped.

"– Dennel and that Sam person were snooping around, when all hell broke loose. Perhaps they stuck their nose where they shouldn't have, I don't know. Suddenly I see a werewolf running loose in the building and heading in the direction of my office. I decided to investigate and see if I could help the others contain the specimen. For her safety I brought my secretary along with me. I couldn't find Dennel or … Sam, but I discovered the bodies of most of the guards and many others. Deciding that the situation was out of control, I decided to salvage as many of the alien devices as I could carry and escape. That's where I found the test subject. From appearances she had already been exposed to the alien virus or nanites or whatever they are, so I decided to bring her along." Rometty nodded at the confused and frightened girl who was handcuffed to a steel framed chair, one pair of handcuffs per wrist.

"What about the lockdown protocols? And what happened to your secretary?" Turner said suspiciously.

"Those protocols are designed for a viral, bacteriological, or chemical hazard and to contain contamination. This was one or more human sized creatures. So long as I was able to exit the building without setting them free there was no risk to anyone except myself. As for my secretary, we became separated when she panicked and ran away, so she must still be in the building."

After asking a few more questions, Turner nodded. "All right. I think I have a clear picture of what happened and what we need to do to normalise the situation at the labs. Let me report to Mr Werner and get his approval regarding how we should proceed. We'll be back in just a moment. Don't go anywhere in case Mr Werner wants to talk to you." He looked at Garcia and they both exited the large, high ceilinged room which served as a general purpose hall for the security company, and which adjoined the main warehouse complex. There was a large roller shutter door that opened into the warehouse which allowed direct delivery of heavy items including weapons, explosives and body armour, and even specially armoured and armed vehicles. Next to it was a more normal human sized door. Both could only be opened from this side by entering a security code and thumbprint scanner.

Rometty paced around impatiently as he considered his situation. He touched the scanner with his thumb and smiled when the light turned green. At least he had not been shut out of the security system. He was tapping thoughtfully at the numerical keypad when the girl spoke. "Did you say something? I'm so sorry, I was preoccupied."

"I said, am I going to turn into one of those things?"

He strolled over and rested his hand on the back of the chair which imprisoned her. "To be quite honest my dear, I have no idea. The good doctor Maeda was apparently caught completely by surprise when one of your compatriots unexpectedly took a funny turn."

The girl shuddered. "It tore him to pieces and … and *ate* him."

Rometty's fingers rhythmically tapped the chair. Talking to himself he said, "On that subject, I wonder what happened to Viktor. There's been nothing on the news of werewolf attacks. Of course there wouldn't be, would there. They'd never publicly admit there was such a thing as a werewolf or that one was running loose in the countryside gobbling up the voters."

"What are you talking about?"

Rometty patted her bare shoulder absently.

"Nothing, my dear. Nothing to worry your head about. Just let me know if you start feeling um … furry."

The girl shuddered.

***

Viktor had learned caution, even in his werewolf form. He had followed the Auditors to the warehouse complex, and then prowled around the perimeter warily until he had decided that he would not be able to get in past the double wire fence and guard patrols without some very special equipment or the use of a Challenger Main Battle tank – at least not in human form. After making sure he was alone, he extracted a stolen pocket knife from his pocket and put it on the roof of his car. Then he undressed and put his clothes and shoes inside the car. He had discovered that it was surprisingly hard to steal a pair of shoes that fit comfortably, even when you were willing to slaughter entire families at a time. From the back seat he lifted out a hunk of roast beef wrapped in aluminium foil, which he set down on the bonnet of the car. The sun was setting and he shivered as he locked the car and hid the key chain.

Finally, he recovered the knife from the roof of the car, unfolded the blade, and held it in a reverse grip, blade extending from the bottom of his fist. He focused his eyes upon the exterior fire escape ladder that led to the roof of the warehouse complex and concentrated upon his desire to go there. Then he gritted his teeth and drove the ten centimetre blade into his belly and pulled it out again. The pain was nauseating, and he tasted blood from where he had bitten the inside of his cheek. But even as a groan forced itself from between his lips, it merged into a low, rumbling growl. Once more the transformation racked him, bones and joints cracking and twisting as the e-nanites efficiently re-formed his body. The change grew faster each time, the alien medical system gaining an increasingly deeper knowledge of his human body. In a matter of minutes, it was complete and the werewolf sniffed the air around it and its ear twitched as it listened to the sounds of the city all around it. Its paw darted out and snatched up the large roast, and it growled impatiently while it clumsily ripped off the foil covering. It gulped down the juicy pink tinged meat, feeling strength flow into its limbs as the e-nanites accelerated the digestion and absorption of the meal and utilised it to strengthen and power the body. It licked its paws clean of the juices, and then turned its muzzle towards the building in the distance. It vaulted over the car in a single bound leaving claw marks in the paint, and on all fours galloped towards its objective.

****

Still standing behind the girl in the chair, Rometty watched as the two Auditors returned. "It's about time. It certainly took you long enough. Well? Has the boss given the green light to proceed with a clean up?"

Turner nodded as he continued to advance. "He did. He wanted me to pass this message to you." His hand reached under his coat and whipped out with his pistol. Beside him Garcia did the same.

But Rometty, not the most trusting of souls and particularly suspicious of Auditors, already had his revolver in his hand and hidden behind Subject Five's body. As soon as he saw Turner move he had ducked down, using the girl as cover and fired at Turner over her shoulder.

The girl screamed in shock and pain, first from the ear bursting explosion going off next to her head, and second from the impact of Turner's bullet slamming into her shoulder.

Turner dived to the side and rolled, blood dripping from his ear, torn by Rometty's bullet.

Rometty grunted in agony when Garcia's bullet hit his side just above his hip and missing his lung. He fired back at the same time as Garcia's second shot, which also hit the helpless girl, this time in the belly.

Garcia stumbled and fell backwards when Rometty's bullet tore through the side of his thigh, and like his partner he instinctively rolled to the side in search of cover.

"Sorry about that," Rometty said to the badly wounded girl as he spun and sprinted towards the exit leading to the warehouse, pursued by shots from both Auditors. Another bullet cut a groove in his buttock when he was forced to pause in order to open the door which he had previously unlocked. He had hoped that his employer would be reasonable, but he had made preparations just in case. Remembering to plan for contingencies was the sign of a good manager or military officer, he thought in self-congratulation. Clutching the wound in his side, he ran into the darkness of the warehouse.

***

"Fuck! The bastard's tougher than he looks," Turner said, pressing his handkerchief against his ear. Holstering his gun, he selected one of the radio transceivers charging on a table. "This is Turner. All of you get your asses down her right now. Bring some firepower for yourselves as well as me and Garcia. Rometty's gone rogue and we need to take him out." He had already spoken to all the mercenaries who happened to be in the office and impressed upon them the fact that he, and not Rometty was in ultimate charge of all Werner UK operations for the duration of the crisis.

Garcia limped over to the first aid box attached to the wall and grabbed rolls of gauze, sterile pads and antiseptic to deal with the wound in his leg. "If he had been a slightly better shot he might have got at least one of us." He grimaced in pain as he ripped the leg of his trousers open to expose the shallow through and through wound.

"Only if he went for head shots," Turner replied, tapping the armour under his shirt.

Neither of them paid any attention to the moans of the woman handcuffed to the chair or made any effort to ease her pain. They were both aware that being shot in the gut was agonisingly fatal unless she was taken to a hospital immediately, which was not going to happen. Both men were fully focused on finding and finishing Rometty. She was just collateral damage.

Four more mercenaries came into the hall in response to Turner's summons, all dressed in black and fully equipped for battle, each wearing body armour and carrying their weapons of choice. One of them set down two Tavor assault rifles and spare magazines. There were also four guards on duty, but they were uniformed and patrolling the grounds.

Turner scanned the name tags on their breasts to refresh his memory. "Capaldi, Duncan, Fraser, Dixon," he recited, nodding to each of them in turn. Duncan was female, and rather good looking, and he let his gaze linger on her for a moment longer than necessary.

Undisturbed by his scrutiny she grinned challengingly back at him. She was no slapper, but she wasn't a cloistered virgin either.

"All right. Listen up. Rometty's in there," Turner said, pointing at the door to the warehouse. "The guards will get him if he tries to leave the grounds. We're going to hunt him down. He's armed with a .357 revolver and he's wounded, but we don't know how seriously. Shoot to kill, but be careful. There may be a few night shift workers in there too. Try not to shoot any of them. There's a bonus for the one who gets Rometty. Any questions? Sam, you all right?" When Sam nodded, he said, "All right. Let's go. We'll search in pairs. Two of you take the left and right, Sam and I will go down the middle. It can be dark in there so for fuck's sake watch out for friendly fire." The facility was huge, handling shipment and distribution for clients as well as Werner owned companies and was filled with row after row of tall racks and shelves as well as automated overhead track mounted cranes and cargo movers, as well as full sized shipping containers, so it was like entering an artificial jungle.

***

Rometty ran as far and as fast as he could, dodging through the rows of shelving and around stacks of crates, until pain and weakness forced him to stop. He found a niche formed by crates of heavy machinery and ducked inside. The front of his shirt and trousers were wet and glistening with blood and he knew he was going to bleed to death before blood poisoning from the perforated bowel would kill him. But he was determined not to die and to let his former employer be shed of him so easily. He had taken the possibility of Werner's betrayal into account as soon as the Auditors had turned up, and he had prepared for it. Now he was forced to employ an extreme option that he had hoped would never be necessary. He twisted his upper body and reached into his trouser pocket, gasping and shuddering at the pain that the effort cost him. His hand came out holding one of the cross shaped alien devices. He peeked out of his hidey hole to ensure that he wasn't about to be discovered, and then pulled open his shirt and slapped the bottom of the device against his belly.

The intricate sensors built into the base of the circular unit immediately came to life and began scanning his body. The microcomputer studied the results of the scan and determined that the biological creature fell within the range of physical and mental advancement required by its makers, and noted that it was injured and near to death. This activated its emergency protocols, overriding its basic species-specific requirement and consent requirements. It molecularly bonded to the creature's skin and commenced the transfer of its load of medical nanites into the creature's body.

Mere minutes later, Rometty's body began to twist and ripple. Expensive fabric and hand stitching ripped and tore, and his skin began to darken as fur sprouted all over. The bullet wounds healed as if a time-lapse video was being run in reverse, and his jaw began to elongate and his teeth changed into long pointed fangs.

***

The girl's head slumped, her head resting against her chin as the mercenaries trooped out of the hall led by the two Auditors. Congealing blood pooled in her lap and dripped onto the sealed concrete floor in great gory dollops. The clenched fingers of her fists relaxed, and if not for the handcuffs she would have toppled out of the chair. For a moment there was complete silence in the hall, even her laboured breathing fading into inaudibility.

Then the stillness was broken by a jerk of her shoulders, as if her spine had been hit by an electric shock. Her head lifted and fell, her chin bouncing off of her chest. A single finger flexed, and the muscles of her calf flexed in a spasmodic twitch. With a violent movement that sent her hair whipping through the air her head lifted until she was looking straight up towards the ceiling, her eyes unnaturally wide and dark and her mouth opened so wide that it seemed her jaws would dislocate. Her legs kicked hard and would have toppled her over backwards if the chair hadn't been bolted to the floor. Her arms twisted and pulled against the embrace of the handcuffs in an eerily uncoordinated manner, as if responding to a remote control that was being manipulated by a child, making the stainless steel clash and rattle against the frame of the chair. She inhaled, a great whooping breath filling her lungs, the veins and tendons of her throat bulging from under pale skin.

The dribble of blood from the wounds in her abdomen and shoulder abruptly ceased, the bullet wounds closing as if they were tiny mouths. Her entire body began to twist and writhe and *change*.

High above her in the steel rafters, the werewolf crouched and watched the changes with fascinated interest. Its nose twitched and its jowls flexed, waving its whiskers in the air. Under the omnipresent odour of humans and the myriad of chemicals that they carried with them, there was a more familiar and interesting scent. And it was coming from the slight figure shackled to the chair directly beneath it. It had climbed up onto the roof and then ripped a hole through which it had entered the building. Moving along the steel rafters it had gradually been drawn towards the meeting hall by Rometty's familiar scent. It had arrived just as Rometty had staggered out into the warehouse. The werewolf had been tempted to follow, but natural cunning made it stay and watch, and to learn more about these other enemies; who might also soon be prey. More humans had come, and then they too had left in the same direction as Rometty. But one had remained. One that was covered with the scent of fresh blood and raw flesh. For a moment it had been tempted to feast, but then the new but also old scent had sprung into existence. It was like him, but different. It was … a female. Driven by a new instinctual prerogative, the werewolf slowly climbed down a steel pillar, all the while searching with its keen senses for enemies, all the while acutely conscious that the human woman was becoming more and more like him. By the time he came to stand warily in front of her, she was fully transformed, and he leaned forward to sniff at her.

The female werewolf opened its eyes. Some of the memories of Jenny Smith, who had been Subject Five, remained, and she remembered being shot and knowing that she was dying. But now the pain was gone, and she felt … strong. The shape of the werewolf standing in front of her was familiar. She remembered being tied down and helpless and seeing them, werewolves prowling around her naked body. But the bowel loosening fear that she had felt then was gone. She was still tied down, but something was different. Her vision was in some ways keener, shadows were less murky and the slightest movement was sharp and clear. Some colours were brighter, while others were muted into faded pastels. Sounds were louder, and she could tell more precisely the direction from which they came. But most amazing of all were the smells. It was as if she had gone all her life without a nose, and suddenly some magic had given her one. She could detect the scents of different kinds of woods, plastics, metals, oils, and more distantly, natural scents of plants, grass, and trees, and many, many, people. Each scent was overlaid upon the other like the instruments of an orchestra, but if she concentrated, she could isolate each one. But strongest of all were the scents of the creature that stood before her, and of herself. Then she understood. She was a werewolf too. Instead of panic and terror, she felt a strange acceptance and kinship. And she could smell his maleness and something inside of her responded. She looked up at his face, and despite the fur and fangs and dark glistening nose, she could tell that he was smiling. She tried to lift her arms, and realised that they were held by steel chains. She looked at the male again, and saw him make a ripping, jerking motion with his powerful, muscular arms. She looked down at her own arms and saw that they too were large, and rippling with muscle. She pulled against the chains and saw him nod. She growled softly and pulled harder. Metal squealed and groaned, and then with a rapid-fire rattle, the catch on each bracelet failed under the pressure and her hands sprang free. The steel had cut and torn her skin and fur, but the wounds were already healing. She stood up, and her paws reached out to meet his. Her jaws opened wide in a smile.

In his werewolf form, Viktor had been robbed of human speech, as well as that of the alien werewolf form that had been grafted upon him. But even more than Earthly wolves and dogs, the alien species had been highly social even before it had developed speech, just as the great primates of Earth were. He sensed her intense hunger and he nodded towards the warehouse door, his body signalling that prey was to be found in that direction.

The prospect of a hunt and a fresh kill made the female quiver with eagerness and she followed the male as he headed for the door, instinctively adopting the bounding, alternating movement of a hunting pair of her species.

***

Capaldi and Duncan advanced slowly down the left side of the huge warehouse building, their eyes and the muzzles of their weapons constantly moving in a pattern that covered all approaches including from above. Capaldi had point, while Duncan spun to check their rear every few paces.

Capaldi came up to the next junction of the huge looming storage shelves and held up his fist to signal a halt. He listened for sounds of movement or breathing, then rapidly snatched a peek into the intersecting aisle. When he didn't see anything he stepped into the open, slightly crouched and rifle pressed tightly to his

213

shoulder, searching for the slightest flicker of movement with his peripheral vision.

Duncan stood back to back with him, swapping from side to side of the aisle they were following. Something caught her eye and she thought she heard the faintest of sounds. "Twelve o'clock," she hissed and glided forward, relying on Capaldi to cover her rear and the connecting aisle as they advanced. She saw another flicker of movement and reached up to touch the switch on her throat microphone. "Duncan. Movement spotted directly ahead. Advancing to investigate," she said softly, alerting the other two teams and preparing them to move in her direction if Rometty got spooked and headed away from her. She reached a large metal cabinet attached to the wall, took cover, and signalled for Capaldi to advance.

Leap frogging with his partner, Capaldi advanced down the huge length of the warehouse, both of them now focused upon the spot where they had seen the movement.

***

The werewolf that was Rometty crouched frog-like, belly down on top of a stack of large packing cases. In the mixture of deep shadow and islands of bright light, he could see much better than the two humans who were advancing towards him. He had deliberately waited until one of them was looking in his direction before allowing his arm to flicker across a beam of light, knowing that the movement of the shadows would attract their attention. When he was sure that he had been seen, he faded back into the shadow and sprang up on top of the packing cases three metres away and to the side of the spot where the hunters had seen his shadow. There were two of them, and his human knowledge told him that their weapons could hurt him, but he was a predator and he was not going to run. He caught their scent floating through the air and silently bared his teeth as he prepared to spring.

***

Turner advanced confidently down one side of the central and widest warehouse aisle, with Garcia moving parallel to him across the aisle. He had seen how badly Rometty had been wounded and knew that he only had an eight shot revolver. By now the Managing Director had to be near dead from blood loss and was unlikely to be much of an active threat. However he had not survived this long by being stupidly rash and he flitted smoothly from cover to cover, taking advantage of every shadow and avoiding the well-lit areas wherever possible.

***

Across the width of the warehouse, Fraser and Dixon moved in parallel to the other teams, taking the same care not to get shot by Rometty.

Dixon paused in mid-stride. "Did you hear something?"

"Where?" Fraser asked, dropping in to a crouch and scanning the aisle in front of him over the top of his rifle.

"Behind us. I thought I heard something."

"Probably Turner or Garcia. Don't get distracted. Rometty managed to put bullets in both of them … Dixon?" He glanced over his shoulder when there was no reply. "What the fuck..."

Dixon stared in disbelief at the creature that was slowly advancing upon him. The mercenaries had not been briefed about the alien discoveries or about werewolves, and probably would not have believed it without concrete proof. Common sense told him that it had to be a man in a costume or some kind of escaped animal, and he was reluctant to fire both because it would expose their position to Rometty, and because the 5.56 x 45mm ammunition in his military rifle lacked the stopping power required for big game and he was likely to get ripped up by the creature's nasty looking claws and teeth before he could bring it down. Instead, he slowly moved backwards towards his partner, hoping that the animal would just go away.

Fraser frowned. He was a hunter and the animal's behaviour was unusual, neither stalking nor making a threat display. Then the realisation struck him. "It's a decoy! Watch out for..." A tiny sound made him spin around and up. He yelled in shock and fired a three round burst at the dark shadow dropping down on him from the top of the storage rack. The glare of the muzzle flash lit the falling werewolf like a strobe light, the deadly looking creature getting closer with each flash. Something struck the barrel of his rifle hard enough to send him spinning to the ground and a terrifying roar made his bowels vibrate even as he desperately rolled away from the nightmare creature.

His partner's shout and the gunfire so close behind him made Dixon twist and lift his rifle's muzzle towards the new threat. Then he realised his mistake and started to turn back to face the creature in front of him. His face twisted in horror when he realised that the *thing* had managed to close the distance between them in that fraction of a second that his attention had wavered. A paw bristling with claws slashed at his face and he raised his rifle horizontally in a block. Fire blazed across his belly when the werewolf's other paw slashed across his body in a disembowelling blow. His body armour absorbed some of the impact, but it had been designed to be bullet resistant and not slash resistant. The werewolf's impossibly sharp and hard claws ripped the Kevlar to shreds and tore into his flesh. Dixon screamed in shock and pain and staggered backwards, desperately trying to bring his rifle's muzzle to bear.

***

The screams and crackle of gunfire made Duncan spin and raise her rifle. "They've found him! Come on!" she shouted, starting back towards the aisle junction they had passed.

"Duncan wait, what about – aaagh!"

The moment his prey had turned the werewolf that was Rometty had leapt off the top of the crates to land right in front of Capaldi. It snapped its jaws around the mercenary's left wrist and with a grinding crunch it bit through flesh and bones severing Capaldi's hand from his arm.

Despite the agony, Capaldi managed to bring his rifle around one handed when the werewolf paused to chew on his amputated hand and he fired a burst right into the centre of the thing's chest.

The alien werewolf form was extremely tough and naturally able to heal at an incredible rate, and with the aid of the military nanites in its bloodstream it was able to shrug off the small calibre bullet wounds. However, it still hurt, and the werewolf ducked and dodged when Capaldi continued to fire.

"Duncan, run!" Capaldi shouted when he saw how little effect his bullets were having. He dropped the rifle when the firing pin fell on an empty chamber and drew his pistol. Blood was pumping out of the stump of his torn left arm and he leaned back against the shelving when his vision blurred. Pulling the trigger as fast as he could and still keep his aim, he emptied the pistol at the monster, only hitting it twice. The thing seemed to grin at him when it realised that his gun was empty. With only one hand he knew he could never reload in time so

217

he threw the pistol at it and ripped the fighting knife from his harness. "Die you fucker!" he screamed and charged.

The female mercenary watched in horror as the monster ripped Capaldi's right arm off at the shoulder and buried its fangs in his throat, and then she turned and sprinted down the perpendicular aisle, thinking that if she joined up with Turner and Garcia they might stand a chance of stopping the … whatever it was.

With all the injuries the werewolf had taken, first as Rometty and then in its own form, it needed food to fuel its healing, so instead of going after Duncan it stopped to tear at the downed prey, ripping open its belly with its claws and fangs to get at the rich liver.

***

"We seem to have arrived at an opportune moment," Seward said, peering down through a hole in the roof of the warehouse that he had just made.

"What the hell is going on in there?" Tara said, trying to sort out the mess of movement below her.

"I hear werewolf. More than one of them."

"It's a good thing we came prepared then." She dropped the drum magazine from her AA-12 and swapped it for one from her backpack loaded with shells filled with silver pellets alternating with silver tipped lead slugs.

Seward did the same, and then nodded at the hole. "Shall we join the party?" Strapped across his back was a silver inlaid shortsword and he reached back to check that the handle was in position for a quick draw before climbing down onto the rafters below. Crouching on the rafter he had a panoramic view of the warehouse floor, and with his enhanced vision and sonar he was able to see each of the humans and werewolves as if looking at the screen of a tactical computer game. In seconds he

218

zoomed in on each of them and then pointed at the pair moving down the central aisle. "Those are the two Auditors we saw leaving the lab facility and the ones who killed my people."

"Let's take them then," Tara said. She felt a momentary flash of unease at her willingness to kill, but given the things the Werner people had down to her family and friends she decided that it was entirely logical to feel that way about these particular people. As for the werewolves, the tang of fresh human blood in the air was all the justification she needed. She and Seward might drink blood, but they were not conscienceless killers like the werewolves appeared to be.

Seward extended his arm across her chest. "No. Those two are mine. Wait here, and when I'm done we can take the werewolves together."

Tara reluctantly nodded and watched as Seward leapt off the rafter, throwing himself in a shallow dive that was almost flight, only to miraculously land running along the top of a row of steel shelving. Suddenly fresh movement to her right caught her attention. Two warehouse employees, a man and a woman, were running towards an exit on the right side of the building and their path was taking them directly towards the pair of werewolves who were standing over a body, one of them ravenously tearing at the corpse. She glanced back at Seward, but he was too far away for her to call him back. She told herself that she didn't have to take on the werewolves, but just warn the innocent employees and guide them to safety. Lacking Seward's confidence in her own abilities and skill, she ran along the rafters like a gymnast on a balance beam to the pillar closest to the fleeing employees. With her claws digging into the steel and paint, she slid half-way down before springing onto the top of the shelving. She landed on a cardboard box that collapsed under her weight, and had to perform a forward flip onto her hands and then back onto her feet, narrowly missing an embarrassing fall onto the concrete floor below. Since she had never done gymnastics, she was nonetheless impressed with her own agility and grinned to herself even as she readied her AA-12 in case the werewolves came her way.

The pair of Werner warehouse employees skidded to a halt when Tara leapt off the top of the shelving to land in front of them. "Wh-who are you?" the man asked, eyeing her warlike appearance suspiciously.

Tara had fabricated a believable story on the way. "There's been a problem with a shipment of dangerous animals, hyenas, on the way to a research facility. They're loose in the warehouse. I'm one of the handlers hired to round them up. The animals are frightened and hungry, and very dangerous. Follow me, and I'll show you the way out and protect you if we bump into them.

Relieved to have an explanation for the terrifying sounds they had been hearing, the two workers were not inclined to question her story, despite the rather large holes in it, and eagerly fell in behind her. She tried to pick a route through the maze of aisles that would go around the spot where she had last seen the pair of werewolves, and she strode steadily along, her sonar relieving her of the need to constantly glance behind or above her. Then suddenly everything went to hell.

"Why are we going down here? The nearest exit is that way," the woman employee said loudly.

Tara winced and made hushing motions.

"Don't you hush me. I work here and I'm telling you that you're going the wrong way!" the woman snapped angrily.

Softly Tara said, "Look, trust me. You don't want to attract attention or go..."

"Hello! Who's that? Identify yourselves. Say something, or I'll shoot."

Tara rolled her eyes in disgust. "Stop shouting you idiot," she said, realising that it had to be the surviving member of the mercenary team that had been attacked by the pair of werewolves, who had probably been drawn towards them by all the racket.

A moment later the mercenary jumped out from around the corner, and from his wide eyes and the trembling of his hands and rifle it was obvious that he had been badly shaken by his recent experiences. "Whoever you are, you've all got to get out of here. There's some kind of monsters running around in here. They killed my partner and … and they're *eating* him." His rifle itself had a series of deep scratches on it that even cut into the hard metal.

"They're not monsters, silly. They're just animals. Hyenas. Just ask her," the woman said, pointing at Tara, glad to be able to make someone else look foolish.

Noticing Tara's weapons and armour, the mercenary said, "Who the hell are you? You're not one of our people."

But Tara's super sensitive hearing had detected the clicking of claws on concrete and she knew it was too late. Instead of answering him, she pointed. "They're coming."

The mercenary's face turned pale when he realised what she had said and he started to run.

Tara crouched and leaped upwards with the full strength of her legs, literally soaring into the air and landing back on top of the shelving. She had picked the row on the left of the aisle and away from the direction the werewolves were approaching from, because there was a draft coming from the direction of the exit and that left her downwind of the werewolves.

The two workers stared in shock at Fraser's running figure, then realised that Tara had seemingly disappeared and after a second took off in pursuit of the mercenary.

A Hollywood hero would have stayed to block the aisle so that the civilians would have a chance of escape, but Tara was not in the self-sacrificing mood. She intended to do her best to kill the werewolves, and the fleeing trio could provide both bait and a distraction that might let her go undetected long enough for her to cause some real damage.

***

Werewolf Viktor had been annoyed that one of the mercenaries had escaped his claws, but he had been content to stop so that the female could eat and regain her strength, so he had stood guard while she had gorged herself. However the loud voices had drawn the female's attention from the food and they had mutually agreed to continue the hunt.

When they rounded the corner and spotted the fleeing humans, two of whom were unarmed and helpless, the female had roared in excitement and rushed in pursuit.

As time had gone by, the werewolf who was Viktor found that it had increasingly greater access to the human Viktor's memories and knowledge. Just as he was about the join the female in pursuit of the prey, a familiar scent reached his nose, a scent that indicated danger. The image of a human female formed in its mind. Tara! The werewolf remembered their last encounter and its head snapped up just in time to see her take aim at him from the top of the shelving.

Up to that moment, Tara had just seen two werewolves, one slightly larger than the other. But when the larger one looked up at her as she took aim, its posture, body language, and the look in its eyes told her that it was Viktor. She fired, but the microsecond of hesitation that recognition had cost her gave the werewolf the time it needed to dive aside. She saw several pellets strike, but not enough to do significant damage. She continued to fire, tracking the rapidly

222

moving creature with her sight, but she was not expert with firearms, especially long guns like the AA-12 and she failed to hit it. She was caught by surprise when the werewolf snatched up some kind of metal spare part and threw it at her. Her accelerated reactions were faster and she dived and rolled before the missile reached her, but it gave Viktor time to leap up onto the side of the shelving and clamber up onto the top beside her just as she was rolling to her feet. She saw the claw shooting towards her face and she raised the AA-12 to block, but because she wasn't braced for the impact, the force of the blow sent her tumbling backwards and she lost the shotgun over the side of the shelf, although it wasn't a great loss because the werewolf's blow had bent it into a shallow "V".

The werewolf charged at her, but the silver pellets embedded in its right thigh were a searing fire and slowed him down, even though the damage wasn't sufficient to shock its system back into human form.

Tara didn't have time to draw, aim, and fire her pistol, so she grabbed her combat knife instead. It was longer and heavier than any knife she had used before, but felt right and balanced in her hand as she ducked, rolled and slashed at Viktor's already wounded thigh.

The werewolf roared in pain when the silver impregnated blade bit into the back of its leg, narrowly missing its hamstring. Spinning around on its good leg it lashed out backhanded with his left hand, his claws catching Tara across the shoulders just as she stood up from the roll.

She felt the back piece of her body armour tear free from one shoulder and the claws dig into her back. The slash resistant shirt she was wearing underneath prevented the claws from ripping the flesh from her body, but nonetheless the points of the claws cut across her skin like razors and the impact of the blow felt like being hit by a sledge hammer and would probably have shattered bone if she had been still completely human. The force of the blow threw her forwards and to the side, and the momentum kept her moving as she slid off the top of the shelving. She lost her armour vest entirely on the way, and only just managed to stop from falling to the floor by digging her claws into the edge of the shelf and gripping the metal frame. She had hung on to her knife, but even with only the strength of one arm she managed to throw herself back up onto the top of the shelving and scramble to her feet moments before Viktor reached her. But Viktor had not been the only one who had been adapting to changed conditions, and when the werewolf pounced, claws outstretched and jaws wide, she threw herself forwards in a flat dive, her HUD marking the path going under the werewolf's body with a visual trail of green brackets. She flew forward like an airborne torpedo, spinning on her body's lengthwise axis so that she passed under the creature face up. She raised her knife as she passed under the werewolf's body and slashed it along its chest and belly. But Viktor managed to retaliate, and she hissed when she felt his claws rake her unprotected thigh as they flew past each other. She skidded to a halt on her back and with a convulsive effort of back and legs, sprang forward and up onto her feet in a single motion. She felt blood run down her leg as she crouched, knife and claws extended, to face the werewolf which had landed on all fours and then spun around like a top to face her before rising onto its hind legs.

A dark torrent of blood ran down the werewolf's front from a long gory diagonal slash, and because of the silver in Tara's blade, it was healing far more slowly than normal. Driven to berserk rage, the werewolf's basest instincts came to the fore and Viktor's logic and cunning faded. It waved its arms in the air, threw back its head and roared a challenge at its tormentor.

Blood red memories of the terror, the agony of the

bullet slamming into her body, and the sense of absolute betrayal when Viktor had tried to kill her and hijack her plane hit her like a hurricane, and Tara uttered her own scream of rage and hate and she charged her former friend and co-pilot. She collided with the werewolf in a mad tangle of claws, fangs, and her silver inlaid blade. The werewolf was stronger, but she was faster and neither of them was able to inflict a telling blow, until the werewolf managed to throw its arms around her in a crushing hug and lowered its muzzle, twisting its head sideways in order to sink its teeth in Tara's throat. But instead of struggling to escape, Tara braced herself against its grip and her jaws opened and stretched like a moray eel, while her teeth extended into needle pointed spikes. Her head darted forwards and jaws snapped shut around the werewolf's black, dog-like nose, ripping it off of the creature's face.

The werewolf uttered a high pitched howl of agony and its grip loosened, allowing Tara to drop back onto the roof of the industrial shelving.

Tara's claw tipped fingers shot out to grip the silver inflicted wound in the werewolf's thigh, forcing another agonised howl from its blood filled jaws. Using the grip for leverage, she thrust the knife and the silver that covered it at an upward angle into its belly and twisted.

The searing agony of the blade and the silver was too much for the werewolf and it lashed out with a kick, lost its balance, and toppled over the side, ripping the blade from its body as it fell.

The kick hit Tara like a hydraulic battering ram and she felt a steel hard rib crack as she was thrown backwards and off the opposite side of the shelving. Even then, the vampiric alien's amazing sense of spatial location and balance allowed her to flip and land on her feet before she sank to the floor clutching her chest in agony, red critical damage warnings flashing all over her

HUD.

***

The mercenary's bullets had hurt her before she had gutted him with a swipe of her claws and ripped out his throat with her fangs, so the werewolf that was Jenny Smith paused to feed again in order to assuage the ravenous hunger created by the alien nanites in her body working overtime to repair the accumulated damage her body had suffered. Then the crash of a falling body behind her and the smell of werewolf blood made her lift her muzzle in alarm and spin around. Twenty metres down the aisle lay the limp form of her hunting mate, and she growled and whined in alarm as she abandoned her meal and bounded towards him. Seeing his injuries she growled in rage, but since no enemy was in sight, she decided that tending to her fallen companion was more important than vengeance, and she dragged him over to the prey that she had killed. She ripped a leg off of the female corpse, and gripping that in her jaws, she lifted her partner's bleeding form in her arms and headed in the direction that her sense of smell told her lead to the outside. She could see his torn muzzle slowly reforming even as she walked, and whined in relief. She would search out a safe hiding place where they both could fully heal, and then they would hunt again.

Chapter Eleven

Despite his reputation for cruelty and harshness, Vlad Dracula was a great believer in the law, and in justice, which were not always the same thing. In fact, the original laws of Wallachia had not provided for impalement as a punishment. He believed in the law so much that whenever he punished foreigners, he would apply the laws of their individual homeland, which coincidentally were usually much harsher than his own. Strangely enough, the foreigners did not often seem to appreciate this courtesy. Over the centuries, he had increasingly allowed the courts and police forces of his current host country to deal with those who offended against him, rather than seeking his own justice. However, when those under his protection were injured or killed by others, he would not be satisfied until he had rendered justice upon the offenders with his own hands, no matter how long it took or how great the risk or cost to himself. If the so called "Auditors" had contented themselves with burning down his home, he might have allowed British justice to take care of them. But by cruelly and needlessly killing men and women who had looked to him for protection, Rometty and the surviving Auditors, would face the justice of Dracula. Although he knew that all of them ultimately served the one called Werner, he would be satisfied with punishing the ones who were directly involved in the crime, unless he were later to discover that Werner had personally ordered the killings, or if he and his people attempted retaliation. He had understood the fine art of Vendetta long before the Italians had invented the word, and he had all the time in the world.

He glided soundlessly along the top of the shelving, easily keeping track of the Auditors by their sounds, even though they fondly imagined that they were being extremely stealthy. He could have killed them before they even realised that they faced a threat other than Rometty or the werewolves, but justice demanded that they be made aware of the reason that they were going to die.

***

"Capaldi's dead! Some kind of sodding monster just tore him to pieces. What the fuck is going on? I'm headed your way." Turner winced at the shouting and crackling of radio static that suddenly burst out from his earpiece. He turned to look at Garcia and silently mouthed, "Werewolf?".

Garcia muted his throat microphone with a tap of his finger. "Where the fuck did it come from? We locked up the stuff that Rometty brought with him … shit, he must have pocketed one of them! It has to be Rometty who just killed Capaldi," he said, swearing under his breath.

Turner looked up at the aisle navigation signs. "Duncan, come to us, and we'll ambush it if it follows you," he said over the radio, and gave her the aisle junction numbers at their location. Then he turned off his microphone. "Take up a position over that side of the cross aisle and I'll stay on this side so we'll catch it in a cross-fire when Duncan leads it here. I'll aim for centre mass and slow it down and you go for head shots. It's not going to heal or regenerate if we blow the fucker's head off."

"Works for zombies," Garcia said giving his partner a thumbs up. Both of them had been in the same unit of the US special forces in Iraq and they were a smoothly oiled combat machine. With the advantage of surprise, not even a werewolf stood a chance against their assault rifles and combat experience. He found a suitable stack of boxes bearing the logo of a British brand of canned soup to use as cover and went down on

228

one knee behind it with his rifle peeking around the side, his elbow resting on his raised knee. He checked his visibility and aim through the MARS red-dot sight, and then settled down to wait, working to steady his breathing.

On the other side, Turner found a cased generator to serve as cover and a support for his rifle, which he laid over the top of the packing crate. He couldn't see Garcia, but he was confident that his partner would be in position and ready when the time came. He activated his microphone. "Duncan, what's your status?"

***

In her panic, Duncan had run into the next aisle and then turned and headed deeper into the warehouse by mistake, thinking she was heading towards the centre aisle and Turner and Garcia. Now she had to make her way back, but she had lost track of the werewolf, which could be anywhere in front or to either side of her. This uncertainty prevented her from simply running madly towards the protective guns of the two Auditors, and instead she had to creep along, her heart jumping into her throat at every creak or click of sound in the vast building. She felt like a rat in a giant maze which also contained a hungry cat. Or two hungry cats. Rometty could still be around and a bullet from his pistol could kill her just as effectively as the werewolf's claws or fangs. Memories of the werewolf tearing Capaldi apart played over and over in her mind like a looped soundtrack and she wanted to scream in terror. She had to constantly force her finger away from the trigger and to resist blasting away at every suspicious shadow like some stupid space marine in a cheap sci-fi film. Only this monster was real, her ammunition limited, and firing would only draw the murderous thing towards her. Worst of all, she suspected that the Auditors knew what the

229

creature was and were using her as bait. She held her rifle tighter to her body and clenched her teeth in determination. She was no female Rambo, but she wasn't going to go down easily either.

The intersecting aisles were not aligned in straight lines across the warehouse due to the different lengths and sizes of the items being stored, which ranged from litre sized cartons to odd shaped industrial machinery and bundles of rebar, which made the warehouse floor more of a maze than a grid layout. Duncan was moving down a particularly long stretch of aisle with no junctions and had just moved behind a rack of vertically stored PVC piping when she spotted movement ahead of her. A moment later a brighter patch of light confirmed that it was the werewolf. Heart pounding, she glanced behind her. If she tried to retreat, she would be in full view of the creature for at least fifty metres before she would reach a junction. Another peek revealed the werewolf standing still at the far junction and sniffing the air. The thought of standing her ground when the werewolf seemed to be largely immune to bullets didn't appeal at all, so what could . she suddenly realised that the wooden frame holding the column of PVC pipes that she was pressed up against formed an excellent makeshift ladder. She immediately began to climb, moving upwards like a paranoid spider, painfully aware of making the slightest sound. Unable to see the werewolf, she had horrid visions of claws closing around her ankle and hauling her down to be painfully ripped apart, and she could feel sweat streaming down her face and neck and soaking into her clothes and armour vest. The pipes extended past the top of the shelving, but the frame stopped just short of it. Unable to bear the suspense, she peeked around the pipes when she reached the top and almost wet herself when she saw that the werewolf was slowly making its way in her direction.

Unlike some of the other shelves, this one even

had the occasional crate sitting on the top, and from the thick coat of dust on them, they had been there for some time. One of the crates sat just a metre to the left of the pipes, preventing her from swinging her leg over the top and rolling onto the shelf. Instead, she had to push herself up and onto the top with her arms; all in total silence and without kicking the pipe rack over. The sharp pressure of the edge of the shelf rack against her belly didn't help her already urgent need to pee either, and Duncan wanted to cry in frustration and bowel loosening terror. Straining against her own weight and that of her equipment, she pushed herself up and then face down onto the dust and spider web covered surface of the shelf, leaving her legs dangling over the edge. A soft growl gave her the strength to pull herself all the way up, and she collapsed, trembling from the effort and with the side of her face pressed into the accumulated dust and dirt. The next growl was even closer and she scurried into the middle of the rack on all fours like a giant lizard, not even feeling the strain on her arms. In slow motion she unslung the rifle from her back and returned to the edge. Tilting her head, she strained to hear footsteps, breathing, any fucking thing that might tell her where the werewolf was.

What she heard was the sound of claws clicking and scratching on PVC as the werewolf stealthily attempted to duplicate her climb. In an adrenaline fuelled rush she sprang up onto her knees and poked her muzzle over the edge. Looking over the top of the rifle barrel she saw the werewolf looking back up at her from a metre away. Without a conscious decision she flicked the fire-selector to "auto" and squeezed hard on the trigger. Pointing almost straight down, the rifle hammered painfully against her shoulder as she emptied the magazine right into the surprised werewolf's face and chest, the glare of the muzzle blast spoiling her night vision and creating a pattern of spots that danced in front of her eyes. With her left hand she shoved the pipes, all need for silence gone, and they toppled with a deafening hollow clatter and smashing of timber.

Fortunately for her, the twenty round burst knocked the surprised werewolf off of the rack to crash onto the floor on its shoulders. Not so fortunate was the fact that its incredible toughness allowed it to be back on its feet and climbing up the side of the shelf moments later, even though parts of its face were still hanging off in shreds.

Realising that she couldn't eject the empty magazine, pull another from the pouch attached to her harness, and reload before it got to her, Duncan let the rifle drop to hang from its sling and shuffled over on her knees to put her shoulder against the rotting cardboard box, which was labelled "Silver nitrate powder: For electroplating use only", hoping to knock it down again long enough for her to reload. The box fell apart just as it went over the edge, and the heavy plastic pails of powder tumbled down upon the climbing creature.

One pail fell directly towards its head and the werewolf lashed out angrily with a paw to swat it aside. The plastic of the pail was old and deteriorating, and the impact shattered it, causing a shower of silver nitrate to pour directly into its face, entering its eyes, nose, mouth, and the various half healed wounds that Duncan's bullets had caused. The intense allergic reaction it had with the werewolf's metabolism had the same effect as pouring a bucket of pepper spray solution onto a human's face. With a howl of agony, the werewolf tumbled backwards, frantically spitting and rubbing at its eyes.

Without waiting to see any more, Duncan jumped to her feet and sprinted madly along the top of the shelf, all the while fumbling for a spare magazine, her eyes searching the suspended metal signs for the shortest direction towards Turner and Garcia.

***

The burst of gunfire in the distance behind him followed by the enraged roaring of two werewolves made Garcia jump. "Shit! There's more of those things. Where the fuck did they come from? This situation is going from bad to worse."

"Never mind that. Sounds like Frazer and Dixon are taking care of business over there. Keep your eyes peeled for..." Turner was interrupted by another crash of full automatic fire and the loud pounding of booted feet running on what sounded like the top of the shelves, as well as the roaring of a severely pissed-off werewolf, but coming from the opposite direction to the first noises. "Sounds like Duncan's still alive and headed our way. Get ready!" He braced his rifle's butt against his shoulder and moulded his cheek against it, preparing to blast whatever came through the opening.

***

Like the experienced sniper that he was, Garcia was already in position and ready to fire, his attention totally focused on the target zone. If anything, the sounds and his partner's warning made his focus even more intent, although a slight uneasiness remained over what was happening on the other side of the warehouse. But the first sign he had that something was very wrong was when an impossibly strong and long fingered hand came from behind and closed around his throat. Before he could react, another hand gripped his right wrist and squeezed so hard that he lost all feeling in his hand and the end of his rifle fell onto his lap. A voice that was as cold as death hissed in his ear.

"Struggle or make a sound and I will tear out your throat." The threat was reinforced by the pricking of claws that delicately pierced the skin of his neck,

233

drawing shining beads of blood.

Garcia's right hand was held completely immobile, as if his arm was set in concrete, and a martial arts break move backed up with all of his considerable strength achieved nothing except a grinding pain that told him that the bones of his wrist had fractured. For the first time since he was a very small child, he felt utterly helpless in the grip of a force totally beyond his ability to resist.

"You murdered helpless men and women, you dared to violate my home, and you hurt someone I call friend."

"Fuck you. You have no idea who you're dealing with. Hurt me and my people will kill you and all those you love," Garcia whispered, barely managing to force the words out of his throat. The voice in is ear chuckled.

"I have been threatened by kings, popes, entire armies, and monsters more terrible than you could imagine. The one thing that all of them ultimately learned is that you do not threaten Dracula without paying the price." His hand that held the mercenary's wrist twisted and pulled with terrible and irresistible force.

"Drac..." Garcia's puzzled whisper was choked off by a silent scream when his right arm was snapped at the elbow as casually as someone might break a twig. His left hand dropped the rifle and clawed frantically at the arm holding his throat, but it was like beating at a shaft of steel, and just as effective. He tried every move he knew to break free, but slowly and inexorably he was forced to his feet and made to turn around until he stared into the red, maddened eyes of a monster. His left hand shot out in a palm strike at his attacker's nose, a blow that would have been fatal if it had landed. But his entire body was jerked to the side by the grip on his throat and his blow shot over the shoulder of the man whom he now recognised as John Seward. Searing, unbearable pain exploded in his belly. Then the grip on his throat was gone. Garcia looked down and he whined in horror when he realised that Seward's hand was buried inside his abdomen.

***

Turner frowned when he heard the faint clatter of metal and plastic falling against concrete. "Garcia? What was that sound? Are you all right?" His eyes narrowed in puzzlement when Garcia stepped into the open, his eyes wide and shocked and his right arm dangling limp at his side. "Garcia! What the fuck happened to..." Then he saw the obscene glistening mass of intestines that dangled from the gaping hole in his partner's belly all the way down to his feet. "Shit!" Assuming that the werewolf had somehow managed to circle around and attack his partner, Turner sprang to his feet, the muzzle of his bullpup rifle pointed at the space behind his friend. "Where is it? Garcia, where's Rometty, where's the werewolf?"

"Not .... " Garcia croaked, and then fell to his knees and then onto his face.

"Not what?" Turner shouted, spinning about and trying to watch all directions at once. He spotted a movement and fired, shifted his aim and fired again, his bullets smashing into crates and ricocheting from metal. A sound behind him made him spin again. The barrel of his rifle seemed to slam into something solid, and he gasped when the figure of a tall man seemingly materialised in front of him like magic. "You!" he cried, recognising Seward from the video and photographs he had seen. Before he could pull back or attack, the TAR-21 was ripped from his hands, tearing skin and breaking one of his fingers as it went, and he watched in open mouthed shock when Seward swung the rifle against the metal frame of the shelf, shattering the synthetic stock

235

and smashing the receiver, parts zipping through the air like hornets. In what seemed like the same moment, his pistol was ripped from its holster and flew upwards to punch a hole in the roof. An iron hard hand slammed against the middle of his chest, sending him staggering backwards, arms flailing as he fought for balance. His face flushed with rage, Turner drew his combat knife. "Bastard! I'm going to gut you just like you did to poor Garcia."

"Poor Garcia? You mean the coward who murders women with fire?" Seward said, his face inhumanly stretched and gaunt. "It's a pity I didn't have the time to properly impale him."

"Who are you? What are you?" Turner asked as he slowly advanced, hoping to distract his opponent. "You're not a werewolf like the others."

"If you believe in werewolves, why don't you tell me what I am?" Seward said, his eyes growing even redder and his canine teeth extending into long points.

"You're shitting me! You're a fucking vampire?"

Seward bowed, never taking his eyes from the mercenary. "Not just a vampire. In fact, I'll wager you know my name, or one of them at least." He held up a hand and let Turner see his fingers turn into long tapering claws. He smiled when he saw Turner's lips silently mouth the word *Dracula,* as if afraid that speaking it out loud would make it real.

Turner shook his head. "No. You can't be. You're just playing with my head. I don't care what you are, I'm going to smash you and your fucking tricks like a bug." He shouted wordlessly and darted forward, his hand and the blade of his knife weaving an intricate pattern in front of him.

Seward met his attack head-on, blocking and defeating Turner's strikes with sheer skill and experience alone, even though the keen edge of the blade cut through cloth and occasionally skin and flesh. His hands and entire body moved in a dazzling dance of violence, slapping, dodging, and blocking as if they were engaged in a martial arts demonstration instead of life-and-death combat, until Turner began to gasp and pant from exhaustion and he could see the desperation and uncertainty grow in the professional killer's eyes. At last, Seward struck back, another pushing palm to the mercenary's chest, shoving the man backwards. "Never let it be said that Vlad Dracula did not give his opponent a fair chance. But now..." He crooked his finger at Turner, daring him to try again.

Catching his breath, Turner advanced again, more cautiously this time, watching for the opening that would let him get in a fatal or incapacitating strike. The man was undoubtedly skilled, very skilled, but he had killed skilled fighters before, and he had a knife. He eyed the slashes in Seward's sleeves and the front of his coat, and told himself that his opponent was not invincible. He feinted high, then low, always watching for the chance to cut Seward's hands and forearms. Then he saw the tiny opening and his blade darted forward, fast like a striking rattlesnake. But his point met only air, and then he hissed in pain when something sharp sliced across the back of his hand.

Dracula licked the blood off the tip of his claw and smiled. "Killing your enemy is nothing. Any peasant with a club can do that. Even defeating a skilled opponent in a duel is just play. No, the art and the joy of combat is in seeing the hope die in your opponent's eyes to be replaced by absolute terror and the knowledge that he is doomed." He moved and struck, darting in and back out again before Turner could even begin to move his blade or block with his other hand.

A line of fire burned across Turner's cheek. He raised his hand to touch it and felt a flap of skin and flesh hanging and blood flowing down along his jaw and side of his neck. With a roar of anger and hate, he charged forward, slashing wildly at the unarmed man in front of him. But this time was different. Each of his strikes and lunges was punished by a slash of claws or a precisely aimed blow until at last he realised that he was hesitating. Both of his forearms and hands were slashed and bleeding, one of his earlobes had been torn off and he leaned to one side, favouring a cracked rib.

The vampire's smile widened, but it was utterly cold, as cold as a crypt. "I was relatively merciful with your partner because I know that you were the leader. You were the one who decided to lock my servants in the room, and you listened to them scream as the flames ate at their flesh."

Turner spat blood in front of the monster in human form. "Kill me then. Get it over with. Or are you going to suck my blood?"

"Perhaps I should geld you and cut out your tongue, and allow you to live out your life as half a man, a thing to be pitied and despised," Dracula said musingly.

Pushed beyond his limits, Turner lifted his chin and brought his knife up to his throat. "Fuck you!" he screamed and cut his throat. Or tried to. A blow that was too fast to see struck his arm just above the elbow, snapping the bone and leaving his arm dangling uselessly. The knife fell from nerveless fingers, but was snatched out of the air before it touched the ground. A rush of wind was followed by a crushing blow across his chest that sent him sliding across the floor to crash into a pyramid stack of black and blood red painted steel rebar that was bound in tight bundles with wire. Stunned and unable to move, Turner watched as Dracula walked up to him. He watched as the vampire gripped one of the rusty steel rods and with inhuman strength, bent a 1.2 metre-long section to form the vertical arm of a capital "L". And when the vampire's arms lifted him up like a child and held him above the tip of the vertical rod, he began to scream.

***

Amazed that she was still alive, Duncan turned the last corner into the aisle that Turner had specified. She stepped into the open just as the screaming began. She froze, paralysed with shock and horror at the scene in front of her. Garcia lay on the floor, broken and gutted. But her eyes rested only briefly on the grisly corpse, drawn by the shrieking of a man in unbearable agony and terror. Turner stood immobile, and for a moment she didn't understand … and then she saw the metal shaft that rose up from the floor and up into his body, glistening with thick, pulsing rivulets of blood. She realised that the Auditor had been skewered like a roast pig, but the skewer didn't go all the way through his body and so left him alive. The rifle fell from her hands and she doubled over, vomiting as if she was going to throw up everything she had ever eaten in her life.

"Where is the werewolf?"

Duncan sprang upright only to look straight into the eyes of a nightmare. She glanced down at her rifle and saw him watching her. With the examples of Turner and Garcia right in front of her, she was not tempted to do anything foolish. "I-I don't know. It was chasing me, then I managed to hurt it and then I just ran … and then I got here …. "

Dracula glided closer. "These men chose to be my enemy. Are you my enemy?"

Duncan didn't have to think about her answer. "Fuck no. I mean, no. I just work here. And after today, I think I'm going to find another employer. That is if..."

"If I don't kill you?"

She nodded.

"Aren't you going to beg for your life?"

Duncan nodded at Turner. "I bet they begged, and

239

a fat lot of good it did them. I'd offer sex, but I'm afraid I might offend you."

He tilted his head and then smiled. "You have courage, and good judgement. I like that."

"Like as in dinner, or as in 'lets go to the pub for a drink' ?" She winced at her own words. "Perhaps I shouldn't have mentioned drinking. Um, is it too late to offer sex?"

He laughed. "Perhaps we can discuss sex some other time."

It took a moment for her to realise what he had said. "You're l-letting me go?"

"Because of your courage, I am giving you this one chance. Abuse my generosity at your peril."

She glanced at her rifle and decided not to press her luck. She stammered her thanks and backed away into the adjoining aisle from which she had come, fading quickly into the shadows.

Seward had been so preoccupied with his vengeance that he had completely forgotten about Tara. But now, as he looked at the frightened mercenary, he remembered the sounds of the werewolves on the far side of the warehouse and the sounds that could only have been someone fighting with them, someone who had survived more than a few seconds and had managed to hurt at least one of them. "Tara!" he said aloud. The werewolf chasing this woman must have heard, and perhaps scented the others of its kind too. He began to run.

Duncan had not gone far when she realised that she had no idea how many werewolves were stalking the warehouse and the surrounding grounds. Having seen a werewolf in action, her pistol felt incredibly inadequate, and she felt soul chillingly alone. She slowed and came to a halt, looking around at the vast roof of the building and shivering at the eerie hollow sounds that echoed through the cavern-like space. Then she did an abrupt about-face and retraced her steps. Turning her eyes from Garcia's corpse and Turner's horribly twitching form, she set off in the direction that the vampire had taken. Monster or not, he had been the only one to show any concern for her wellbeing so far in this nightmare.

***

Tara sat with her back propped against a crate covered with stencilled warnings and skull-and-crossbones labels. The cuts and bruises she had received during the battle with Viktor were quickly healing, even the claw slashes that were bone deep. But she guessed that the final hammer blow she had taken to the chest had done significant internal damage. If she had been fully human it was probable that she would have died from internal bleeding by now, but even those traumatic injuries were also gradually healing, and it had stopped feeling like her chest was filled with razor blades whenever she took a breath. On the other hand she was ravenously hungry, her fangs insisted on popping out and her jaws ached and flexed uncomfortably. The scent of raw meat and blood from the three dead bodies further along the aisle didn't help, although she couldn't bring herself to go over and drink or eat from the corpses. Biting into a warm smooth neck, male or female, or even a furry bovine one, was one thing, but feasting on carrion was too zombie-like for her to stomach. "Braaiins," she croaked and chuckled to herself. She had listened anxiously as the sounds of the two werewolves had slowly faded into the distance, and when she heard the thudding and crashing of a door being broken open, she had finally allowed herself to relax. Without blood or food she wouldn't recover her full strength, but she would heal and survive until she could get to the Rover where Seward had stowed an aluminium briefcase filled with packs of his synthetic blood substitute.

241

She clutched her ribs in pain when she suddenly sat up and tensed, hearing the soft clicking of claws and the panting breath of a werewolf, but this time coming from the left side of the warehouse. Climbing to her feet with a stifled hiss of pain, she made her way as quickly as she could manage towards the trio of torn up corpses. She wasn't going to eat their flesh, but she could use the dead mercenary's rifle, provided there was any ammunition left. She heard the thing getting closer as she knelt down beside the broken pieces of flesh and bone that used to be the mercenary. His rifle was intact, but there was only the single magazine which contained five rounds. She checked that the rifle's action was still working, firmly seated the magazine, and clicked the selector to full auto fire. She would only get one chance to hit the approaching werewolf, and she wanted to do as much damage as she could before resorting to hand-to-hand combat using her knife.

The tall shelves and massively varied composition of the items stored on them made her sonar pretty much useless so far as precisely locating the werewolf, and there were too many lights for her to shoot them out to give her the advantage of total darkness. Her HUD displayed an incoming missile indicator, but the icon flickered and wavered from side to side which was of little help. However, the afterburner indicator unexpectedly came to life, and she felt a surge of energy and the pain in her chest eased. The alien combat AI built into the e-nanite system understood that she was about to enter a fight and it was preparing her body as best it could. She hoped that she wouldn't kill herself through overexertion even if she survived the werewolf.

A loud roar of challenge made her start, and she realised that the werewolf had caught her scent. A moment later it stalked around the corner, its inhumanly jointed legs giving it an odd bouncy stride. It stopped in the middle of the aisle, and its back and shoulders hunched. Its lips curled back in a snarl as it sniffed the air, scenting the blood of another werewolf.

The rifle snapped to Tara's shoulder and as soon as it came to a momentary standstill she took aim at its head and fired. Five shots rang out with a jack-hammer rattle, pounding her eardrums in an extended explosion of sound. Three shots hit the werewolf, two in the upper chest and one glancing off of its sloping brow, making it stagger. Throwing the rifle aside, she drew her blade and sprinted towards the stunned creature, ignoring the dull pain and tearing sensations in her chest and ribs. As a test pilot she had learned not to think about the possibility of death, otherwise she would never have climbed into the cockpit at all. The only thing that mattered was doing the job perfectly. Perfect focus, perfect determination. If anything could ensure survival, it was that.

Two metres in front of the werewolf, who was still shaking its head and recovering from the hammer blow to its skull, Tara sprang into the air and somersaulted over the angrily growling creature. She lashed out with her sliver coated blade as she passed over its head, cutting open its scalp and the back of its neck. Landing in a crouch she spun around in a blur of motion and cut across the back of the werewolf's calves but failed to cleanly hamstring it.

The werewolf that was Rometty roared in anger and pain. It dropped onto all fours and scampered forwards and clear of Tara's blade before turning around to face her. It shook its head violently to remove the blood from its eyes and gathered its hind legs in preparation for a charge.

Tara's vision blurred and she staggered, the extreme exertion taking its toll on her battered body. The tiny hesitation was nearly fatal. The werewolf crashed into her before she could dodge, knocking her onto her back. She attempted to stab at its face, and then screamed in pain when its jaws closed around her hand, forcing her to drop her knife. The werewolf's right paw drove towards her throat but she managed to grab its wrist with her left hand, barely managing to hold it off. However this left her defenceless against the other paw and she ducked her head when the claws slashed at her eyes, taking the blow on the top of her head, the claws raking across her scalp, tearing out tufts of hair and ripping skin and flesh. Twisting her neck she clamped her teeth on its forearm, ignoring the torrents of her own blood streaming down into her eyes. There was a momentary stalemate, but she knew that even uninjured she was not as strong as the werewolf and this time there was no escape, and she could see the same knowledge in the creature's vicious gaze.

Suddenly the werewolf yowled in pain and broke free from its death grip on Tara. It sprang forwards and crashed into the side of the giant shelving rack, sending boxes and items spilling onto the floor. It dodged just in time to avoid the point of Seward's sword, which punched a hole in a crate, sending polystyrene packing peanuts flying like snow when the blade ripped free and slashed sideways to cut off the tip of its ear.

Seaward had fought many werewolves during his long life, and he knew the secret to victory was speed and constant, unrelenting attack, never giving the creature a chance to brace itself and to employ its greater strength. He grunted when its claws ripped across his shoulder, but retaliated by backhanding a cut at its throat and following up with a slash of his own claws across the werewolf's belly. He dropped into a deep squat, avoiding a two handed or pawed blow to his head that would have crushed a human's skull like a melon. Although he couldn't be certain, he guessed that this werewolf was Rometty, the man in charge of Werner's UK operations and the attack on Tara. Even though the Auditors were sent from the USA, he held Rometty responsible for their actions while in his territory as well, and was therefore determined to kill this man who had deliberately chosen to become a monster and a cannibal. He cut across the front of its thighs and then rolled to the side when the werewolf pounced, dropping down on all fours.

The werewolf lashed out with a hind leg, its foot catching Seward in the side and sending him skidding across the floor, only stopping when he hit the towering shelf wall. The metal mass of a portable generator fell from the racks and crashed down between his shoulders, flattening him momentarily against the floor. Growling in pain, Seward rolled aside just as a claw tipped paw slammed into the concrete where he had been a microsecond ago, cracking and chipping the stone hard surface. Rather than rolling clear, Seward immediately reversed the direction of his roll with a twist of his body and a kick of his leg against the shelf, his sword slicing across in a whistling arc to slam down upon the werewolf's extended right arm, cleanly cutting its paw off in a spray of blood.

Because of the silver in Seward's sword blade, the werewolf's stump continued to bleed copiously as it sprang upright, clutching its wounded arm against its chest and roaring in agonised rage.

Despite the searing pain in his back and shoulders from the crushing blow delivered by the generator, Seward sprang to his feet and attacked, hacking and thrusting at the wounded creature, fiercely pressing his advantage. "Die, hellspawn! Vlad Dracula shall never be defeated by the likes of you," he cried, not noticing or caring how his speech reverted to an older form under the pressure of combat. He didn't stop even when his point sank into the werewolf's shoulder and the blade snapped off near to the hilt when the werewolf's jaws snapped shut upon the blade. With both of its arms at least partially incapacitated, Seward flung himself at the monster, pounding at its face with the stump of his broken weapon. When the creature drew back its head to avoid the painful blows from the silver treated blade, Seward dropped it and both clawed hands reached out to clamp around the werewolf's jaws, holding them shut as his claws dug deep. Still holding onto its head, Seward sprang into the air, vaulting over the werewolf, his body twisting and spinning.

The werewolf's neck snapped with a loud sickening crack. But although it was temporarily paralysed, it still refused to die and the e-nanites immediately began repairing its broken spinal cord.

However, Seward wasn't done yet. With his hands locked in a death grip upon the werewolf's jaws, his own head darted forward and his long pointed vampire teeth sank deep into the creature's neck. His jaws crunched down hard and with a twist of his head he ripped out the werewolf's throat.

The werewolf collapsed, and lacking the use of its arms, it fell forward onto its chest with a deep hollow thud, driven by Seward's weight on its back.

Seward's knees slammed into the werewolf's shoulders, pinning it to the ground, his hands closing around its head once more. The muscles of his back rippled and bunched, tearing open the half healed wounds caused by the falling generator. Blood ran down his back and around his ribs, soaking his shirt and dripping onto the werewolf's body as Seward strained, his lips pulling back in an inhuman snarl. Dark hairs formed on his forearms and his eyes widened and turned a dark red, glistening like rubies. His entire body began to shake, while joints and tendons popped and cracked under the strain.

The werewolf began to kick and struggle, ineffectually because of its broken neck, whining and panting through torn and bloodied lips.

Tears of blood ran from Seward's eyes as he

pushed his body to the very limits of its superhuman abilities. Suddenly there was a horrid wet ripping sound, and the werewolf's head tore free from its body, trailing part of its spinal cord like an obscene glistening tail. He tossed it as far away as he could, the head bouncing from side to side off the shelves to finally roll off into the shadows. Seward fell sideways and collapsed onto his back, gasping and panting, his body rocked with shuddering tremors as it struggled to recover from the damage and overexertion. But Vlad Dracula was not one to lie helpless on the battlefield when there might still be enemies around. A tiny sound made his head jerk around and he flowed up onto one knee, preparing to resume battle, even though his original mortal form would have been at death's door from the damage done to his body. His eyes locked onto those of the female mercenary Duncan. "What are you doing here? I told you to run."

She glanced in shocked amazement at the headless body of the werewolf, which was slowly reverting to Rometty's human form. "Wow. You did that? I'm glad I didn't piss you off earlier." Moving very slowly, she lifted her pistol out of the holster with thumb and forefinger, bent over to place it upon the floor, and slid it over to the … whatever he was. "I decided that I was safer if I stuck with you. It looks like I was right." She took a step forwards holding out her hands, palms facing him to show that she was unarmed. "It looks like you could use a hand," she said, taking another step. She took his silence for agreement and went over to put his arm over her shoulder. She grunted in strain when he put his weight upon her. He was a lot heavier than he looked.

"What about your duty to your employer?"

She pointed at Rometty's corpse. "My bosses sent me into combat without telling me that things like that existed, let alone that the warehouse was full of them. Besides, the man who hired me, his superiors from the US, and all my colleagues appear to be dead. I think it's an opportune time to look for a new job. Would you happen to know anyone who needs a good merc who looks pretty good in a swimsuit – or nothing at all?" She didn't believe in underselling herself.

Seward chuckled. "Aren't you afraid I'll suck your blood?"

She turned her head to look at him and shrugged. "I don't mind making a donation if it won't kill me and it looks good in my resume."

"I like you. We'll talk about your employment prospects after we get out of here alive."

"Sounds good to me."

Seward nodded in the direction of Tara, who had managed to sit up and had recovered her combat knife, and was studying the werewolf's corpse with evident satisfaction. He walked slowly towards her, his hand holding on to Duncan's shoulder.

"Making new friends? You seem to have a knack for picking up stray women," Tara said eyeing Duncan curiously. "No offence," she said to the woman.

"None taken," Duncan said, noticing the way Tara's obviously werewolf inflicted wounds were visibly healing and all the blood that spattered her face and hands. It didn't seem wise to upset someone who could survive hand to hand combat with werewolves. She grinned ruefully. "I'm pretty much a stray at the moment anyway."

Although Seward was tempted, they made it all the way out of the building without tapping any of Duncan's blood.

Duncan was dismayed to find more bodies outside that unmistakably bore the marks of a werewolf encounter.

"Damn. It looks like Viktor not only survived but was strong enough to do all this," Tara said.

Seward examined the ground. "I see two sets of werewolf tracks. He had company."

Tara scanned their surroundings with both vision and sonar, as well as checking her HUD for any proximity warnings. They were in no condition at the moment to take on two more werewolves. There was no sign of enemies of any kind, and she sighed with relief when Seward tore a hole through the fencing and they reached the Rover.

Duncan watched in amazement as the pair of them guzzled down packs of reddish liquid that didn't look quite like blood, and the way that their healing accelerated to the point of magic. "Could I get some of that?" she asked, watching enviously as a scar that crossed Tara's cheek faded disappeared.

"It's possible, but it's kind of like in the films. One of us has to bite you, then let you drink some of our blood and then you have to die – or very close to it at least," Seward said.

"Hmm, I'd have to think about that," Duncan said.

"We have to go back in to recover any of the nanite dispensers that might be lying around," Seward said. "You can go your own way if you prefer," he said to Duncan.

She shook her head. "No, I'll stay if you want me, but you'll have to trust me with a weapon."

Seward considered her for a moment and then held out his hand. "You're hired. You can call me Boss." He opened a locked compartment in the Rover and produced another pair of AA-12s with magazines and shells, as well as an HK MP5 sub-machine gun with collapsible stock with silver tipped ammunition. "My motto was 'Be Prepared' long before Robert Baden Powell was a gleam in his father's eye." He also had a variety of silver inlaid blades. When they all had some warm coffee from a Thermos, they set off to retrace their steps, except that they headed for the door that led to the security service side of the complex.

"Looks like everyone's out or er, gone," Tara said,

raising an eyebrow in emphasis.

Duncan nodded. "A team went out to Hemel Hempstead to contain the situation at the Labs. I hope they didn't underestimate the werewolves that Turner and Garcia saw. With those two out of contact as well as Rometty, someone might have had a rush of initiative to the brain and opened a door."

Seward winced. "We'll have to head there after we're done here, but I suspect we're in for an outbreak of lycanthropy in England. He sighed. I wonder what ridiculous explanation the authorities will come up with this time. Rabies again? LSD? Ergot poisoning?"

Tara broke open a locker with a crowbar. "Hey, look! This bag is full of the medikits. It must be Rometty's." She continued to another larger steel locker. The crowbar quickly took care of all the padlocks and she gasped with excitement when she saw the contents. "It's the parts from the DNIA, my aircraft that they tried to hijack, or some of them anyway. I can't tell if its all here until we do an inventory and compare it to what's left in Romania."

"There's a trolley over there that we can use," Duncan said and brought it over. With Seward and Tara's speed and strength, they quickly had everything loaded.

Tara noticed a notebook computer. "Who's notebook is this?" she asked Duncan.

The mercenary frowned. "The operation used the desktops in the office upstairs, and all of us have tablets, so that must have belonged to Rometty, Turner, or Garcia. I can't be sure. We weren't called in until they tried to kill Rometty and the test subject, and everything went to hell."

Tara added it to the pile of stuff on the trolley. "Maybe we can learn something from it."

"Pull the battery first. It might have a GPS tracker or some other kind of location system built in," Seward said. "Duncan, you push the trolley while Tara and I watch our backs.”

Nothing jumped out at them from the darkness, and they were soon driving away in the Rover. “What now?” Duncan asked.

“First we drop this stuff off, and make sure that Emily and Tara's father are safe, then we're off to Hemel Hempstead,” Seward replied.

“To the Werner laboratories?” Duncan asked.

“Yes. And more werewolves – if they haven't already gone,” Tara said with mixed emotions. The werewolves at the Werner labs were no direct threat to her or her father, but it seemed foolish not to at least try to find out what happened there before the authorities began to “manage” the information. In addition there might still be items there that could lead back to Harker Industries. On the other hand, she didn't exactly look forward to another encounter with those vicious monsters. And then there was John ….

***

Viktor had gorged himself on the guards and even his silver inflicted wounds were beginning to heal. Both he and Jenny had returned to their human form while sitting behind a hedgerow and waiting for Viktor to recover his strength. Sitting in his stolen car, he watched as Tara and her companions loaded up their car and drove away. “It looks like that other werewolf – I'm guessing it was Rometty – isn't coming. Tara and that man with her are a lot more dangerous than I had ever expected.”

“What about us? What are we going to do?” Jenny asked.

“Us? You want to stay with me? But you don't know anything about me,” Viktor said.

They were both still naked and she hesitantly reached out to touch his arm. “I know that you're the

251

only other person I know who's … like me, and you cared enough to help. I can be useful and … if you like what you see, you can have me. I know the filth will lock me up like some kind of a freak, and the Werner people will probably want me back for their experiments too. I … I don't have anywhere else to go."

Viktor nodded. "You stayed by me when you could have run, and probably saved my life." He put his hand on her naked thigh, and when she put her hand on top of his in welcome he smiled. "I could use the company."

Relieved, she leaned across and kissed him, welcoming his caress. "So where do we go next?"

"Back to Hemel Hempstead."

"That laboratory place?" Jenny asked apprehensively.

Viktor grinned and shook his head. "Not inside, but nearby. I have a little experiment of my own going on back there."

Chapter Twelve

"Oh shit," Duncan said, her breath fogging the car window as she looked out at the scene of carnage in front of the laboratory building. The lockdown light was off and the main doors gaped open. Bodies, or at least parts of bodies lay strewn all over the tarmac and concrete in front of the door, mixed with the sheen of the steel and plastic of various firearms. On closer examination, the façade of the building was dotted and pitted with bullet holes and the heavy bullet resistant glass was frosted and spider webbed where it had been hit. More ominous were the deep claw marks and tears in aluminium cladding and the steel panels of the vehicles in the driveway.

Shotgun in hand, Seward got out of the car and went over to examine the ground. Because of all the blood and other bodily fluids spilled there was a profusion of footprints. "From the spoor, it looks like there were two of them." He looked around at the scene of slaughter and shook his head. "I can't believe it. They were trying to capture them," he said. "Those are tranquilliser guns and that's what's left of a shock noose. Poor sods, they never stood a chance."

Tara nodded at the laboratory building. "We need to make sure the werewolves are all gone before we call in the police and emergency services or they'll be massacred as well. And there might be injured survivors." She looked at the green faced Duncan. "Are you all right?"

Duncan nodded. "It's just that … I knew these people. Worked with them. No one should have to die like … like that. Someone has to pay. And we have to stop these things – if we can."

Tara was surprised by the passion and determination in the female mercenary's voice and body language, and she felt her reservations about the woman's sincerity fading. "All right then. Let's take a look inside." They were wearing surgical gloves and masks just in case the camera system was still functional.

"Hey, some of their guns are missing. All of us wore side arms, but the gunbelts are missing from two of the … bodies. There aren't any rifles or magazines either. They wouldn't have gone in with just dart guns. I know I wouldn't have." Duncan pointed at the torso parts of the dead mercenaries.

"Damn. That means we have to watch out for gunfire as well as claws and teeth. Watch out. They may have reverted to human form. Don't turn your back on anyone we meet inside." Seward missed his sword as he led the party into the huge building. In the close quarters of the corridors and offices, a fast moving werewolf could be very hard to hit with a gun, especially when he had friendly-fire to worry about. It would be all too easy to shoot one of his companions or vice-versa in the excitement of combat. After some discussion the agreed to do a top down search of the building, so they climbed the first emergency stairs that they came across. Dead bodies were everywhere they went, and the stairs were slippery with blood. The entire stairwell stank like an abattoir, and there was the slow, sticky, ominous drip, drip, drip, of congealing blood running off the sides of the stairs. The sound of their footsteps echoing along the length of the tall vertical concrete tunnel of the stairwell was reminiscent of any number of horror films or survival games.

Tara suspected that the medical AI was suppressing her emotions and shock reactions. Under normal circumstances, she knew she would have been hysterical by now. She would have had to be truly inhuman not to be. The medical indicators on her HUD only covered basic biological functions, temperature, pulse rate, blood pressure, and the like. Emotional state was not one of them. She snapped out of her introspection when they arrived at the sixth floor landing. This was not the same one they had entered the building from the first time.

Seward opened the heavy fire door just a crack and peeked out. "Same as before. Let me take out the cameras before you come out, unless I get jumped by a werewolf, in which case feel free to lend a hand."

Her cracked rib still ached even though it was fully healed and she slipped her hand under her new armour vest and rubbed it. "Do I have to?"

Seward grinned and slipped out into the corridor like a moving shadow.

"He can be quite nice for um …" Tara looked over her shoulder with a raised eyebrow. "A monster?"

Duncan looked taken aback. "I didn't mean to … well, yes."

Tara smiled. "Yes he can be – nice and a monster, both."

"Are you um, like him?"

This made Tara chuckle. "I'm a member of the RSPCA and I'm good to my father. Does that help you?"

Duncan blushed. "I'm being too nosy, aren't I?"

"Stay with us a while, and when we know each other better, maybe I'll tell you more. For now, you just need to know that Viktor, who was my co-pilot, shot me from behind and tried to hijack an aircraft that my father's company is building, and he was working for Werner, who in turn kidnapped my father and want to turn me into a lab specimen."

"Those seem like really good reasons to be pissed-off with my ex-employers. Are those wolf things really werewolves, like the ones from the legends?"

Tara nodded. "They're not supernatural, but it looks like they're the same as the creatures that must have given birth to the ancient legends." She saw Seward beckon. "Time to go. We can chat later."

The entire sixth floor, which consisted of support services and storage was a charnel house. The employees had been told to stay put in any emergency other than a fire and to wait for help. This allowed the werewolves to go from room to room and to slaughter the trapped employees. Even when the survivors realised what was happening, they were still trapped in the building and were individually hunted down. Makeshift barricades and improvised weapons showed where some had tried to make a stand, but always with the same ultimate result. Duncan grew more and more angry as they swept the floor looking for survivors. "Bastards! How could they let this happen? Why didn't they take more precautions?"

Seward sighed. "Unless you've personally seen a werewolf in action, it's almost impossible to believe how fast and dangerous they are. And the ones that retain a greater degree of human intelligence and memory are even more dangerous because they have the mental framework to understand this environment. Scientists can be the worst when it comes to dealing with such things. All too often I've seen them mentally refuse to accept the existence of such 'superstitious nonsense' such as werewolves, and insisting on treating them as simply some new or mutated species of animal."

The female mercenary's anger and disgust seemed genuine, and Tara silently patted her on the shoulder as they completed their search of the level and started down to the fifth floor via the doorway that they had used in their first sally into this building. The fifth floor was the same, though with less victims, until they were half way along the building. She held out her arm to stop the others. "I saw movement."

Seward moved forward and to the other side of the wide corridor, leaving Duncan in the middle and slightly behind, forming a shallow "V" before nodding to Tara. His eyes searched every nook and cranny of the area in front of them and then he caught sight of the motion. It was a hand, palm up and lying on the carpeted floor, protruding from a doorway and half hidden by a stand holding a potted plant. Suddenly accelerating to his fastest speed, he darted past the doorway, keeping the muzzle of his AA-12 pointing towards the room. From his new position, he could see the rest of the person lying on the ground. It was a woman, naked except for a pair of thong panties. Her entire body was splashed with bloodstains, but his heart sank when he saw that the most serious of her wounds, including what must have been a huge jagged tear in her belly, were healing at a miraculous rate. He waited until Tara and Duncan were close enough to see what he was looking at. "She's turning."

Duncan frowned. "Turning? I don't … oh. You mean people who have been bitten really do change into werewolves as well?"

Seward gestured towards the twitching woman. "Sometimes. The werewolves salivate heavily, and their saliva seems to carry a lot of the alien nanites. Normally they self-destruct as soon as the saliva leaves the body, but if enough of it gets directly into a wound and the victim doesn't die too quickly, then yes they can be infected. It doesn't happen all that often or we would be hip deep in werewolves, but every once in a while..." He nodded at the woman.

"So what do we do?" Tara asked, ever practical.

"Wait a minute. You're thinking of killing her?" Duncan said.

"What would you suggest?" Seward said patiently, understanding her shock and reluctance.

"Can't we take her to a hospital? They can give her a blood transfusion, or antibiotics, or something."

"And what happens when all the treatments fail and the alien medical AI changes her completely in order to complete her healing? Do you want to be responsible for the deaths of all the nurses and doctors and the other patients in the hospital?" Seward asked grimly. "And no, there is no cure. I've been trying for … a very long time."

"Damn. This is completely fucked up," Duncan swore, punching the wall.

Tara looked at Seward. "We can't just shoot her in the head, can we?"

Seward shook his head. "The gunfire would alert everyone and everything in the building that we're here. We have to cut off her head. You two go on ahead and check the rest of the floor. I'll take care of this."

Duncan slung her MP5 and drew her knife. "No. You need to know I'm completely in with you. I'll do it."

"You sure?" Tara said softly. "You don't have to do this."

Duncan looked at Seward, who nodded at her. "I really do. Don't worry. I'm up to it."

"You scout forward. I'll help Duncan," Seward said, aiming his shotgun at the infected woman's heart. "Just in case."

Duncan knelt and rolled the woman over so that she was face down. With one knee planted between her shoulder blades, she cupped the woman's forehead and tilted her head up to expose her throat. "I'm sorry," she said softly, and then drew the razor sharp edge of her knife across, pressing hard. Blood spurted in huge jets, soaking the carpet beneath them.

The woman's body began to violently shudder. "All the way," Seward said, preparing to fire.

Duncan tangled her fingers in the woman's hair and sawed with the blade, searching for a gap between the vertebrae.

The body bucked harder and Seward planted his foot on the base of the woman's spine to hold her down. "Hurry!" Hairs were beginning to sprout in patches across the woman's naked back.

Duncan sawed desperately, and gasped in relief when the blade finally went through the spine and severed the final muscles in the back of the neck. The body fell with a thud, and Duncan almost fell over backwards when the head came free.

"Throw it across the room. Don't just drop it next to the body."

Duncan looked up at Seward in horror. "You mean they can..." With a convulsive jerk of her arm she flung the head away from her and sprang to her feet.

Seward nodded. "I've seen it happen." He didn't mention that he had once done it himself. All it required was the tiniest contact between the two stumps for the nanites to maintain coordination, even a trail of fresh blood could potentially lead to a regeneration.

***

Nothing else noteworthy happened, and they reached the familiar third floor without incident. Tara pointed. "This lab is probably where the outbreak started. We found the alien nanite dispensers here and signs that they had been testing them on live humans; and I doubt they were volunteers."

Seward held up a hand. "Wait. Listen."

Tara strained her ears and nodded towards the adjoining laboratory.

Duncan looked puzzled, not hearing anything with her ordinary hearing, but prepared for trouble based on the reactions of her companions. "Next door?" She silently jogged over to the next lab entrance and pressed her back against the wall beside the door, her weapon at her shoulder, then nodded back at the others.

"Tara, you take the other side, and remember to watch your back. I'll go in first," Seward said, checking that his AA-12 was ready to fire and the drum magazine was firmly seated. The sliding doors were locked in the open position, and when Tara had dashed across the open doorway to take up her position for the entry, he plunged into the room, moving so fast that Duncan blinked in surprise and shock. His eyes and sonar swept the large open space of the laboratory, and isolated the point that was the source of the faint sounds. "Tara, you and Duncan can come in," he said, using an ultrasonic frequency that only Tara could hear. He had discovered that the werewolves, unlike Earth canines, couldn't hear ultrasonic sounds well. He pointed at the heavy steel store room door, which was open just enough to show that it wasn't locked, and then at Duncan. He made an opening gesture. The door opened outward, which would put her behind it if something nasty came bursting out. When she was in position and Tara also had her weapon pointed at the doorway, he held up three fingers and silently counted down, 1, 2, 3.

Duncan snatched the door open, leaning back and heaving with both hands.

Tara was almost disappointed when nothing horrible was revealed. Instead there was just the body of another man lying on the floor. Then his foot twitched and would have hit the door if it had been closed. "He's still alive!"

"Another infected?" Duncan said apprehensively.

"I don't see any bites, just that wound in his belly. If I didn't know better, I'd say he had been shot," Duncan said, peering around the edge of the door.

Seward cautiously moved closer. "It certainly looks that way. Hmm, that's funny. There's a pressure bandage on the wound."

"I recognise him! He's the guy who was being chased by a werewolf while we were searching the other lab, just before we were attacked by two of them," Tara said.

"That's Sam, one of the Auditors. I remember his picture in the email from Head Office notifying us that a team of Auditors was coming."

Seward knelt down and checked the man's pulse. "He's alive. Barely. Get him some water." When Duncan returned with a beaker of water, he gently lifted the man's head and shoulders. "Can you hear me?

Sam groaned and sipped a little of the water. "The bastard tricked me," he murmured painfully.

"Who did?" Seward asked.

"That fucker … Viktor," Sam replied, his voice barely audible.

"Viktor was here?" Tara exclaimed, swivelling around as if expecting the co-pilot to appear behind them.

"I … I hid in here … jammed the door … werewolf went away when it couldn't break in. Wait … waited for help." He paused to cough up bright red blood.

Seward gave him more water and said, "What about Viktor?"

"Knocked … knocked on the door. Said it was safe. Re-recognised his face from videos. Went for my gun … he was ready … too slow. Shot me … then patched me up."

"Why would he do that?" Tara asked.

"Gave me m … message for you."

"Me?"

"Tara H-harker. Said you … were coming."

"The message?" Seward prompted, sensing how little time Sam had left.

"Tell her … I don't need the alien things. I can make … my own. I'll be seeing you."

"Damn! He's discovered that he's infectious," Seward said grimly.

Sam's head slumped back and his eyes rolled up in his head.

"I think he's dying," Seward said, feeling Sam's neck for a pulse. "No, correction, he's dead." He didn't say it out loud but Sam's death had saved him the trouble of deciding whether or not to kill him or just to leave him to die. The Auditor certainly had been complicit in the massacre of Seward's household staff, and nothing he had done or said provided any reason to show him mercy. He saw from Tara's guarded expression that she was thinking along the same lines. "All right. Let's finish up the sweep of the building and be gone before anyone else turns up – or just turns, period."

***

They made no further significant discoveries, other than the security centre where Seward removed all the hard disks holding the security video of the past several days. They were hot swappable units, so he just checked the date labels, pulled the relevant ones out of the bank of drives and replaced them with blanks waiting to be recycled. This wouldn't fool the subsequent investigation, but it would help to confuse matters. He led the way through the lobby and out of the main doors to the scene of utter carnage that lay in front of the building, with Tara and Duncan following behind.

Shading her eyes from the sunlight as they headed for the car, Tara said, "After seeing all this, are you sure you want to stay with us? No one would blame you if you decided to head off to somewhere safer, like Somalia."

Shaking her head, Duncan said, "Maybe the police or MI5 or someone can stop this, but I fear the situation is too far gone. Werner's people are not going to give up, and it looks like this Viktor person has ideas of his own." She twisted her body to look back at the entire scene. "I'm afraid that this is just the start, and it seems like only you and Mr Seward have any idea what's really going on. " Her eyes caught a movement in the distance, outside of the perimeter fencing. "Hey, that looks like –

262

sniper!" Training and instinct took over and she threw herself in a tackle against Tara. Then a giant hit her just below her shoulder with his hammer, a really strong, angry giant, sending her twisting and staggering to the ground.

Once Tara recovered from the surprise and realised what was happening, she whipped around in a blur of speed to grab Duncan under her arms and dragged her behind the large van that had belonged to the Werner response team.

Although his shotgun was largely ineffective at that range, Seward also took cover behind the front of the van and fired over the bonnet at the sniper. The huge slugs that were alternately fired by the automatic shotgun could still do considerable damage if he was lucky, and being peppered with silver shot would distract the sniper even if it didn't hurt him – or her. One of the radio transceivers lying on the ground beside the van crackled. Seward picked it up. "Hello?"

"Now that I have your attention, may I speak to Tara please? Tell her it's an old friend."

Seward held it out to Tara. "It's for you."

Tara took the transceiver and pressed the send button. "That you, Viktor? What do you want – aside from seeing me dead, of course."

The radio crackled again. "It was never personal, Tara. I want you to know that. In fact, I'm rather fond of you; even after you shot me in the face with that silver chain. I wish to propose a truce. You and your capable friend don't come after me, and in return I and my new family won't come after you. Plus, as an added bonus I will throw in some information that I guarantee you will want to hear."

"Do you trust him?" Seward asked.

"Not as far as Duncan could throw him," she replied, conscious of her new found strength.

"I doubt he trusts us either, but it appears that a

truce would be beneficial to both sides — for now," Seward said.

Tara nodded in agreement. She pressed the transmit button. "All right, I'm willing to deal. What's this important information?"

"I want your friend's word as well," Viktor replied.

Seward leaned towards the transceiver. "I agree to a truce for the next 24 hours. But if you break your word..."

Viktor laughed. "Your threats are unnecessary. My word is good too. Very well. We have a truce."

"The information?" Tara said impatiently.

"Before I and the Werner Corporation had our little falling out, I heard some interesting things because they were unaware that my hearing is now much keener, even in human form. One of the things I heard was that in addition to going to London to commit murder and arson, the pair of Auditors had also arranged to send a crate of the alien medical dispensers to their headquarters in the USA. So I'm afraid your attempts to police up all the alien devices have not been completely successful. I suspect that ultimately this is going to prove to be a threat to both you and me. So we might yet be allies, dear Tara. Until that time, la revedere."

Tara put the radio down and stepped out from behind the van. When she wasn't met with a bullet she nodded to Seward. "He's right. If he wasn't lying and Werner has his hands on more of the medikits, the e-nanite dispensers, he's going to find a way to use them. And he'll want the ones that he knows we have too."

Seward nodded. "Viktor was also right that Werner will not want someone like Viktor spoiling his little monopoly on the werewolf market either. That's why Viktor was willing to call a truce."

Tara sighed and knelt down beside Duncan. The mercenary was conscious and clutching her shoulder.

"How are you feeling?" she asked, examining the point in the back of Duncan's vest where the bullet had struck. "Luckily the bullet didn't penetrate, but it missed the trauma plate."

Duncan winced and nodded. "I know. I think my shoulder's broken or at least fractured. But it could have been worse. A few inches higher and it might have gone through my neck."

Tara touched the woman gently. "I know you tried to protect me. I'm grateful."

Duncan chuckled softly and winced again. "If I had been thinking more clearly I would have dodged behind you for cover. You're the one with the super healing thingy."

Seward rapped the side of the biohazard response van. "They might have some medical supplies in this thing. Let me take a look. It would be better if we could immobilise her shoulder and give her some pain killers before we drive back to London and get her some proper medical attention." He looked around. "Don't put down your gun. Viktor may have been lying or might have changed his mind. And there may still be stray werewolves running around."

"Strays?" Tara grinned, imagining a mangy, flea-bitten werewolf rummaging in dustbins.

***

Viktor studied the small group around him, his hands on his hips. "So, are you all decided?"

Jenny glanced to either side of her and then nodded. "I'm with you. You know that. And the others are too. They know they don't have anywhere else to go."

One of the other former test subjects said, "I can't go home to my ma and dad and sisters. I might murder them the first time I change."

The others nodded and murmured in agreement.

Viktor clapped his hands together and rubbed them briskly. "Excellent. We have weapons, drugs we can sell, supplies, and the money we took from the labs. All we need to do is find a home for our new family, and then we can make plans."

"What sort of plans?" Jenny asked.

"We need more people on our side, so we need to look at a careful programme of um, recruitment. And with our new abilities, I'm sure we can find ourselves some generous sponsors or clients."

The others realised what he was saying and began to grin at each other. The London underworld had just gained a new, and very significant player.

Epilogue

"Really?" Roland Harker said excitedly.

Seward nodded. "I'll finance and support the development of your aircraft and the nano-interface system, as well as set up a research facility to study the alien technology. We're going to need all the advantages we can get in order to face up to whatever Werner and Viktor have up their sleeves."

"We're also going to need people specially trained and equipped to face werewolves," Tara said. "You're not going to need a full time test pilot for a while, so I'll head that project up, aided by Duncan."

"In the meantime, I'll be engaged in keeping an eye on how the government responds in my capacity as a prominent industrialist and military technologist, rubbing shoulders with the people involved. They may not know everything, but they're not fools. There's bound to be an investigation, both overt and covert, arising from the massacre at Werner Biotechnologies and the random killings in the surrounding countryside. That could be both good and bad for us, depending on how it works out."

Seward smiled at Emily, who was staying close to Roland. "You two seem to be getting along well."

Emily smiled. "Roland's work is fascinating, and I've always had a thing for smart men," she said, leaning against Roland's shoulder. Emily wasn't sure what was happening between Seward and Tara, but she was wise enough not to get between two vampires, even though she was still open to approaches – from either of them. Vampires were just so hot.

Tara raised an eyebrow. "No wonder you've been looking insufferably smug of late, father." She had no objections to her father having fun, so long as she didn't have to call Emily 'mother'.

Roland's neck reddened. "Emily is most … um,

enthusiastic and flexible." He realised how that sounded and hastened to add, "In terms of her work, of course."

"Of course," Seward said straight faced, and then spoiled it by winking broadly at Emily, who just giggled.

***

"Let me get this straight. Rometty and the entire Internal Audit team are dead. Our UK facility is a disaster zone and is being investigated by the authorities, and I'll have to use my influence to pressure them not to get too nosy. The clowns you sent there also failed to eliminate or capture Tara Harker and her father, plus they lost the technology from the aircraft. Do you have any good news for me at all?"

Everyone who worked for him knew that Werner's icy calm was worse than his rage, and the head of the Internal Audit division, Dan Jackson, had to force himself not to back away from the huge screen. "My men shipped a load of the alien devices back to us, so we didn't lose them all. There were three hundred pieces in the crate."

"So they weren't complete morons. Guard that shipment with your life until I can set up a research unit to handle them. Tell me that you have more people on the ground in the UK?"

"Yes sir. A new team of Auditors were flown out in a chartered jet as soon as we lost contact with the first team."

"Have them find Viktor Tiranul and the Harkers, and discover what they are all up to. I also want a full and detailed report on whoever it was who helped them. Make the necessary arrangements for extraordinary rendition once we have our hands on Tiranul and the Harkers."

"Understood sir. And what about whoever helped them?"

"I trust that you'll take the appropriate measures with regard to these people. That's what you're paid for, isn't it?"

"Of course sir. I'll personally ensure that they're appropriately handled, sir." The screen went black and Dan wiped his brow with the back of his hand. He had just been given an order to kill anyone and everyone involved in helping the Harkers and Viktor Tiranul. But he knew that if the shit hit the fan, he would be portrayed by the Corporation as a maniacal rogue killer who chose to misinterpret his orders. If he was lucky he would end up with a life sentence, but it was more likely that he would suffer some kind of unfortunate and very fatal accident. He knew this because he had arranged more than a few of them himself. For a moment he felt a tinge of pity for those Brits. Unknown to them, the full might and fury of the Werner empire was about to come thundering down upon their heads. Then he straightened his tie, picked up his phone, and dialled the first of many numbers. "It's me. Pack your bags. You're going on a trip."

The End